THE JOURNEYS TO

NEW HOME

TO THE READER

Please bear in mind this is a work of complete fiction. There is no scientific or other information to support any of the events presented in the text. I made it all up. Those of you familiar with my family will notice I have included many family names. Ego?

Perhaps just a wish to see the names perpetuated. You will see more names mentioned in a following volume so don't feel slighted if you were omitted in this one. This is an amateur undertaking with no intent on my part to submit it for publication. Since my typing skills would be rated at least a minus eight I have written it all in longhand. A wonderful lady here in the park, heard of my efforts and volunteered to type it for me.

Her name is Linda Keltz. I will never be able to thank her enough but once again THANK YOU, Linda. Then there is Carol Ann. She has encouraged me to do this and she keeps the Atta Boys coming in a steady stream. Thank you beyond words my Love. Without a doubt you will notice that the chapters do not appear in chronological order for the years 2106 through 2113. This is because those chapters were taken from the journals Chris had compiled over the years. Starting in 2114 the narrative unfolds in real time so to speak.

You will notice I have used a pseudonym for the author's name. I'm not sure why except a friend of ours named Penny Hepworth insisted on it and I had to agree just to get her off the telephone.

Elliott Combs   9-25-12

P.S. I was convinced to change my mind about seeking a publisher. You are about to read the results

PROLOGUE

The people of earth are about to undergo a cataclysmic event such as has never been experienced since man began walking upright. This is the story of how a very small number of them survived and began the long, slow process of building their civilization anew.

Chapter 1 — 2113

Chris finally admitted to himself that he was in trouble. It had been dark for over an hour and the snow seemed to be picking up in intensity. It had become noticeably colder and the wind had increased in velocity until the snow was coming almost horizontally. He was a good 40 miles from home and on a road he had never before traveled. Chris checked to make sure all three dogs were still with him and trudged on.

Fortunately the wind was at his back and with the occasional lull he was able to see little glimpses of his surroundings. He became aware that the dark on the right side of the road had become a little deeper. He stopped and tried to peer into the darkness. During another lull in the wind he saw that the darkness was actually a building of some sort. He also discovered a driveway leaving the road and leading alongside the building.

Fighting his way through a snowdrift which had begun to build up across the driveway, he slogged down the driveway until he was at the front of the building which he could now see was some type of metal quonset hut style. The front of the hut contained a large rolling door and set into the big door was a small hinged one. The small door was held closed by a hasp which had a small T-shaped bar holding it in place. Removing the bar he pulled on the hasp and the door opened on rusty complaining hinges which was no surprise since the door most likely had not been opened in more than seven years.

As he opened the door he recognized the musty odor of old hay. He reached back to a side pocket of his back pack and extracted his perpetual lamp. Shining the lamp around the inside of the building he could see nothing except an old tractor with tires long since gone flat and neatly stacked bales of hay. There were a few broken bales but for the most part the barn appeared much as it had when the long gone farmer had last closed and latched the door. He and the dogs stepped inside and he closed and hooked the door shut with the rusty hook which was still attached to the door frame.

Taking off his back pack and removing the small packs carried by each of the three dogs, Chris decided he would eat a couple of his travel bars rather than heating something. Besides, if he wanted something hot he would have to go back outside to get snow to melt and he had spent enough time in the snow for one day. He wasn't concerned for the dogs as they had caught and consumed two jackrabbits late in the afternoon.

It had been a long tiring day. Chris had intended to continue walking until midnight then get a short night's sleep and try to make it home in two days. The sudden onset of snow had foiled that plan and now all he wanted to do was get a good night's sleep and see what the weather was doing the next morning.

Unrolling his bed roll he then broke open a couple of hay bales. He spread the hay for a bed then laid out his sleeping roll. Spreading more hay for the dogs to sleep on and indicating to them what it was for he then dug out two travel bars and his canteen. As he slowly chewed the bars and sipped some water he used the lamp and took a closer look at his shelter. On the far side of the building was a door he had missed on his first inspection. It was standing half open so he got to his feet and went to see where it led. It opened into a small room of perhaps eight by ten feet. The room contained a work bench with a few rusty tools on top plus some shelves build into the end wall. He notice a small hole, low in one corner, and could see that a small amount of snow had blown in. Moving a wooden crate from under the work bench he place it in front of the hole.

Returning to the main room Chris removed his boots and prepared to get into his bed. Deciding that he needed more padding he opened another bale and put it in his sleeping spot. Before turning the lantern off, he looked at his watch. It was one of the new models which had promised accuracy within 5 seconds over 200 years with a battery life of 100 years. The digital display indicated that it was 8:47 P.M. CST on October 13, 2113.

After dousing the lamp Chris nestled into his sleeping bag but did not immediately go to sleep. He was thinking of what he needed to get done after he arrived home to get prepared for what was surely going to be another early winter. He became aware of a rustling chittering noise which seemed to be coming from overhead. It had not aroused the dogs so he wasn't overly concerned about any sort of threat. He did turn the lamp on and began to shine it around the room. He eventually saw a flash of eye reflection and then the shape of 3 raccoons peering out from the top of the stack of hay bales. Chris didn't think the raccoons would come down from the hay with the dogs present but he went into the side room and moved the crate as he was sure that was where the coons were going in and out.

Chris soon went to sleep and didn't rouse until 7:30 the next morning. The dogs were up and pacing with the need to go out. Putting on his boots and letting the dogs out he stepped out into bright sunshine and much warmer temperature than the previous evening.

The snow was already starting to melt and it was obvious that it was going to be a glorious autumn day. He decided that he would stay where he was for the day and another night, then make a hard push on the road to insure that he would arrive home early on the second travel day. He also realized that he was ravenously hungry. He still had sufficient dried travel food but today he wanted fresh meat. Walking down the side of the building he spotted what appeared to be reasonably fresh tracks in the snow and surmised that sometime in the night the raccoons had risked rousing the dogs and made their way outside. Returning inside he replaced the crate in from of the hole. He didn't want pesky critters tearing up his pack to get at the dried food inside.

He went to his pack and un-strapped the rifle which he always carried. It was an old Marlin lever action carbine firing the even older 30-.30 caliber cartridge. The gun was truly an antique. It had belonged to his grandfather and had been in the family for more than 50 years. Going back outside, he whistled for the dogs. They soon appeared and he set off across what appeared to be pasture but which was probably abandoned crop land. Deer and turkey were plentiful but he had decided if there were any cattle in the area that today he wanted beef. Beef had become somewhat tough and stringy since the cattle had reverted to a semi-wild state but he wanted a change from the gamy taste of the deer, elk and wild birds he had been subsisting on. After walking no more than 200 yards he crossed a small brushy creek bed. As he stepped out of the brush, there, not more than 30 yards away stood a group of 25 to 30 cattle. The cattle had spotted the dogs and appeared ready for flight. They were a mixture of breeds with a preponderance of Hereford blood with a scattering of Holstein and perhaps Brown Swiss. Quickly raising the rifle Chris picked out what appeared to be a yearling Hereford heifer. When she moved to the edge of the little herd he fired and she went down instantly with first shot. The rest of the herd stampeded away at the sound of the shot and Chris quickly cut the throat of the downed animal. He sat down for a few minutes to wait for her to bleed out. He didn't bother with proper field dressing her but simply skinned out a hind quarter and after cutting it loose from the body, tied it to his pack frame. The rest of the body he left where it fell. He knew the coyotes, vultures and perhaps timber wolves would soon dispose of the carcass. The hindquarter on his pack frame would be more than adequate to feed he and the dogs for the rest of the trip home. Back at the barn he made his breakfast from the last of his raisins and a slab of precooked oatmeal. He had cut off three big chunks of meat for the dogs and they were eating at the same time as he. Knowing the dogs would want to sleep after gorging on the meat he slipped back in to his own bed and was soon fast asleep. Chris awoke in mid-afternoon feeling more refreshed and well rested that he had for ten days or so. Finding a stack of lumber beside the barn he soon had a fire going. Cutting three big steaks from the beef quarter and using a grating he found hanging in the tool shed he broiled the steaks over the embers of the fire. He put two of them aside to cool and promptly devoured the other. The dogs which had been out hunting or exploring returned at dusk. As soon as it was dark Chris closed and latched the door and all of them found their beds. By 5:00 AM Chris had eaten more cold oatmeal, put his and the dogs' packs in order and was ready for the road. He knew he was only 2 or 3 miles north of Carroll and wanted to reach Grand Junction before stopping for the night. Carroll, like every other community he had been through was a ghost town. The streets were empty except for a few rusting cars. Weeds and grass filled cracks in the sidewalks and streets and it was apparent that there had been many fires, caused, he supposed, by left on stoves, wind-blown wires and lightning strikes. The dogs were eager as if sensing that they were nearing home. They maintained a steady pace all morning, stopping only once when a magnificent bull elk crossed the road in front of them, seemingly unconcerned by their presence. In early afternoon they stopped in Jefferson where Chris ate one of his steaks, fed the dogs some of the meat he had carried for them and all of them rested tired feet. He carried the meat wrapped in the ever present plastic cling wrap which he always carried in his pack. It helped to insure that the inside of the pack stayed a little bit cleaner. Reaching Grand Junction he walked to a small house which was only a block from the highway and in which he had stayed on two previous occasions. Standing on the front porch he removed the packs from the dogs and with a sigh of relief took off his own and leaned it against the porch railing. Removing the .22 caliber Colt pistol, which he always carried, from it's holster he pushed open the from door and stepped inside. It appeared that no one had been in the house since his last visit, however he checked all five rooms. Except for a sagging ceiling in one bedroom everything appeared the same. He assumed the roof was leaking and in a few years the house would be in ruins like so many others.

Calling up the dogs he went, as he liked to call it, shopping. He remembered a small market out on the highway and went there first. This time he was in luck. The building was intact and the front door was unlocked. Going inside he soon found the canned food section. Here he was disappointed. The labels were still legible, but most of the cans were swollen and many had burst open. Winter freezing and summer heat he supposed. Turning to leave he noticed a door back in a corner. Opening the door he discovered a set of stairs with another door at the bottom. Using his lantern he descended the stairs and upon opening the door and flashing his light around he felt as if he had discovered a gold mine. Lining the walls and filling the center of the room were shelves holding hundreds of cans and boxes of food waiting to be moved upstairs. There were also bags of rice, dried beans of several varieties plus flour and cornmeal. The first items to go into his back pack were a two pound boxes of salt and a one pound can of coffee. He had used the last of his salt when he cooked the steaks two days ago and had not had coffee in over a month. He didn't carry a coffee pot when he was on the road as it was too bulky for the use he got from it. Taking only what he and the dogs would consume that night and the next morning, he took his loaded knap sack and making sure the door was closed and securely latched, he walked back to the house. He had already decided that if the food was good he would return with his cart and stock up for the winter. He, and a few others whom he had never seen but had seen sign of, had depleted most of the food sources close to his home. He made his supper that night from canned peaches and a small canned ham. All of the food tasted of age, however, it was still delicious after a diet of travel bars and cold oatmeal. Even the dogs seemed to relish the seven year old bag of dried dog food.

Going to bed early Chris was up and dressed before dawn the next morning. Breakfast was another can of peaches while the dogs were out doing their morning business. They were on the road just as the sun began to rise in the east. It was chilly but promised to be a good day to travel. He saw numerous deer and in mid-morning while stopped to rest a bit he spotted a small herd of elk feeding beside a wooded creek bottom. He wondered where they had come from and how they had re-populated so much of the country in the seven years since humans had virtually disappeared. By late morning Chris and the dogs were passing through what had once been the little town of Rippey. Buildings had fallen in, others had burned and except for a group of feral hogs rooting under a huge old oak tree there was no sign of life. He had not expected any and so was not disappointed. Maintaining a brisk pace they soon left the ghost of Rippey behind and by late afternoon they were approaching the bridge spanning the Raccoon River just a half mile north of Dawson. Chris could see that the bridge deck was in bad shape and the bridge itself was twisted out of line. Part of the south approach had washed away and another spring flood or two might dump the entire bridge into the river. They crossed the bridge safely, skirted the washed out approach and were soon in the middle of what had once been a town. With the exception of the community hall which had some roof damage there was not a building left standing in the entire town. It was apparent that a powerful tornado had hit the area and left a path of total destruction. Hurrying through the rubble he was soon on the road leading east out of what had once been a town. He was now only two miles from home and was anxious to get there to see if it had survived the destruction. He was soon standing at the end of his half mile long driveway but from that point could not see his house. The driveway made a sharp turn where it entered the timber so the house was not visible from the road. When he finally turned the corner he let out a huge sigh of relief. It appeared the house was untouched and in fact he could see the red warning light of the electric fence glowing in the shadows. Reaching the gate he touched the key pad to unlock the gate and turn off the power to the fence. He entered the yard and looked around. Nothing seemed amiss except some of the shrubbery looked a little droopy as if needing water. Stepping up on the low porch he opened the front door which was never locked. In the ten years he had lived in the house there had only been one break in. That event had cost him a shattered door and a broken window. Since then he had never locked either the front or back doors. Tongue in cheek he had installed a small sign by each door which read, "Caution, this door is not locked but is wired to an explosive charge which will detonate if entry is attempted." There was no demolition charge and he suspected the previous break in had been by a sixteen year old neighbor boy, who had later been convicted of a similar crime and sent to a youth detention center. Turning on a light switch he was pleased by the light from the big wagon wheel chandelier hanging overhead. It proved that the solar system was working and that the electrical grid was charged. He then checked the water heater drain and flipped the breaker for the well pump. When water began flowing from the hot water tap he hit the water heater breaker then turned to other chores. He went to the walk-in freezer at the back of the house where he took out one of the frozen meals he had prepared back in the early spring and set it out to thaw. Remembering the dogs he filled food and water dishes on the back porch where they customarily ate. He flipped the switch unlocking the dog houses he had built on the east and south sides of the house The kennels were both heated and cooled insuring year round comfort. The dogs were seldom in the main house and when that happened it was usually on winter evenings when Chris felt the need for company. Chris put his frozen meal in the micro wave oven to finish thawing and heat, then sat down to eat his first meal at home in more than six months. While the meal had been heating, he had inserted two discs into the player and ate his meal to music recorded more than one hundred fifty years before. Bands led by men named Glenn Miller and Tommy Dorsey played music which was both soothing and nostalgic. It made him think of the past and he decided that as soon as he had the house and property prepared for winter he must read his journals again. He had purposely not done so the previous winter and he felt the need to review the past. Finishing his meal of peas, mashed potatoes, and roast pork, he sat in his favorite chair. Not intending to do so he soon fell asleep. Waking after 12:00 AM with a stiff neck he decided that rather than get in bed without having a bath he would sleep on the floor for the rest of the night. Tossing down a rubber mat and putting his sleeping roll on top he was soon asleep again.

Chapter 2

Chris was awakened the next morning by the sound of the dogs barking. He walked out onto the front porch to see a dozen or so feral hogs milling about in the driveway near the front gate. Returning inside he put on a pair of leather work boots. It was the first time in months he had worn anything on his feet other that athletic shoes and the boots felt stiff and awkward on his feet. Going outside again, he opened the yard gate so the dogs could get out, then watched as they put the hogs to flight. Fortunately, the hogs ran straight up the driveway and were soon out of sight around the corner. He whistled for the dogs which soon came loping around the corner and into the yard with what almost seemed to be smug looks on their faces. Knowing the dogs would not go far if they left the yard, Chris left the gate open in the event that the hogs might return. After feeding the dogs he got a loaf of bread and a can of powdered eggs from the walk in freezer and put together a quick breakfast. He then went to the upstairs bathroom and with the water as hot as he could tolerate, spent a long time in the shower. Refreshed and wearing his first set of really clean clothing in weeks, he felt ready to face the day.

Getting a new legal pad and pencils he sat at his desk to make a list of what he needed to get done to prepare the place for winter. Before starting that list he wanted to list what he had and how he came to possess it. This was routine he had first initiated after his return home after the day of the great catastrophe as he referred to it. He repeated the routine every year and each year he seemed to remember some detail which he had overlooked in previous years. First his name, his middle name Elliott had been used by the family for seven generations. Not every generation of his direct ancestors had carried the name, but in those generations a brother or cousin had been so named. Some had used a spelling variation but the basic name carried on.

His father, named Daniel Elliott Weddle had died on the day of the catastrophe. At the time he was 41 years old and was president of the family business which he had been preparing to expand once again. His grandfather John E. who as president of the company had been murdered by a disgruntled former employee who had been fired for trying to steal and sell manufacturing secrets. So revered by his employees was John that a group of them captured the killer the next day and promptly hanged him from a lamp post in front of the Dallas Center city hall. It was John who had encouraged Chris to start flying lessons at age 15 and had given him the 80 acre farm, plus building the house for his 18th birthday. Chris had logged over 1000 flying hours by the time he turned 20, 200 of those hours being multi engine time. His grandfather had purchased an old twin engine, jet powered aircraft as a company plane. He then had the jet engines removed and replaced with a pair of engines replicated from a design popular in the mid 1900's and used to power several war birds during WWII. Chris became the chief pilot for the company's one plane air fleet. He was kept busy flying company executives, customers plus parts and machinery around the U.S. and Canada.

Great grandfather Dallon James was the genius founder of the company. Dal, as he was called by friends and family was a chemical engineer by education and training. Working for a company near his home in Washington State he was restless and seeking to strike out on his own.

Seeing the possibilities for a new composite plastic which had been developed by a young independent chemist, Dal had borrowed heavily and purchased all the patents pertaining to the new material. The plastic turned out to be a wonder material. It could be formed, machined and heat treated until it had comparable strength and wear characteristics to most metals. Searching all over the country, he found a small manufacturing company near Dallas Center, Iowa which had gone into bankruptcy and whose property was up for tax sale. Borrowing again, he purchased the entire concern. Pleased to discover that much of the existing machinery could be used to process the plastic, he immediately opened production. The product turned out to be a best seller. In three years, the company was out of debt and in less than ten years was a billion dollar a year concern. Facility expansion was a continuous operation with no end in sight. Dal had hired the young chemist who had invented the process and who over the years became a millionaire many times over.

Dal knew from old family correspondence that his great grandfather had been born and grew up in the little village of Dawson, which was only about 20 miles from Dallas Center. He visited Dawson several times and met a number of distant cousins who still lived in the general area. He bought property on what had once been the main business street and hired a contractor to build a community center which he then endowed with funds to operate and maintain it for the next century. He also erected a column inscribed with the name of his great grandfather and all eleven of his siblings plus their parents. It was grandfather John who when he presented Chris with the 80 acre farm insisted that Chris lay out the general size and form all of the buildings. Those sketches were turned over to an architectural firm which then turned out finished drawings of the final product. John had insisted on the installation of the solar array which had made it possible to be independent of the local utility company and in fact often sold power back to the utility. He had also insisted on building the root cellar, smoke house and green house. At the time Chris thought these were frivolous additions but since grandpa was footing the bill he made no serious objections. In retrospect, it appeared as if the old man had a vision of the future. The house was an A-frame in shape and 2200 square feet in size. The main floor had a large combined living dining area with the kitchen open to the main room and separated by a long, wide counter. Also on the main floor were a large bedroom and adjoining bathroom, plus a walk in freezer, pantry and utility room. Overhead was a 700 square foot loft. The loft was divided into two sleeping areas with a bathroom between them and separated by a privacy curtain. Outside a wide deck wrapped around three sides of the house. The house sat on the brow of the hill above the Raccoon River bottom. This north view was the favorite one for Chris. He could see the river which came from the west, made a little turn north then ran east again.

Hidden from view of the house by trees was a small barn plus swine and poultry houses. All of the buildings had lifetime roofs and none of them had ever held a single head of livestock. The shop building which sat apart from the outbuildings contained 4000 square feet and was equipped to support a small town if needed. Finishing his third cup of coffee Chris decided to make a list of his chores. He wanted to hike down to the river but knew that should wait until he had completed other higher priority tasks. First on his to do list was the garden. He had planted potatoes and set out tomato and green pepper plants before leaving in the spring. He had also put out some onions started in the greenhouse. Going into the shop and turning on lights he first checked the panel to determine that the charging grid was on and operating. He then checked all of the individual battery indicators and was assured all of the batteries were fully charged and ready to be used. Every piece of equipment on the farm was battery powered and those with wheels were equipped with the relatively new airless tires which not only provided a ride comparable to tires filled with air but were long wearing as well. With the new battery technology each of his machines had a minimum operating time of at least 12 hours when used at maximum power. The big 4WD ATV had a battery life of 18 hours at 40 MPH. Removing the tiller head from the tractor, he bolted on a set of digging forks then drove it out to the 1 acre garden plot. To keep deer and other critters out of the garden it had been surrounded by an 8 foot high electric fence. The voltage was very low but it was enough to keep curious animals from trying to climb or go under it.

Looking over the garden he could see that the peppers were a total loss, however, there were a few green tomatoes which could be picked and allowed to ripen in the greenhouse. Turning the tractor down an onion row, he was soon at the other end and turning around he quickly plowed the second row. Looking back he was surprised to see the number of onions lying out on the ground. One row was a white onions while the second was a yellow variety. He alit from the tractor and walked down the row inspecting his crop. He was pleased at both the quantity and quality of his efforts. Turning to the potatoes he soon had those out of the ground as well. He now began to understand the excitement displayed by his mother when she harvested produce from her tiny garden in Dallas Center.

He returned the tractor to the shop after stopping to hose dirt off the tires. Watching the water flow he was thankful for the foresight of his grandfather for insisting the well be drilled deep enough to reach the level of the river. It insured he would never have to worry about drought and running out of water.

Chris pulled the ATV out of the shop and hooked it to a large trailer. Going back to the garden he began to pick up onions and potatoes. By the time he finished, it was after noon so he parked the ATV and went back to the house to have lunch. Lunch was another frozen meal. This time it was stew and it reminded him he needed to lay in a new meat supply while the animals were still carrying their summer fat. Returning to the cart he began unloading the produce onto a plastic tarp on the shop floor. He would let it dry for a day or two then brush off the loose dirt and store it in the root cellar in ventilated crates. He estimated that he had at least 300 pounds of potatoes and 50 or so pounds of onions.

It was now mid-afternoon and taking a .22 rifle, he slipped quietly into the hickory grove a short way east of his house. In a matter of 30 minutes, he had bagged two young squirrels and was on his way home. After cleaning and quartering the squirrels, he dredged them in flour with salt and pepper. Placing the meat in a large cast iron skillet he then sliced a new potato and some onion in another. Soon the house was filled with the aroma of frying squirrel, potatoes and onion. Putting out a container of apple juice which he had frozen three years earlier he soon sat down to what he considered a sumptuous feast. He was home and eating at his own table. After cleaning the kitchen, feeding the dogs and making a quick check around the immediate property, Chris took a shower and was in bed shortly after dark. Next morning he was up before the sun and decided he would go back to Grand Junction and salvage what looked usable from the storeroom of the market. After tending to the dogs he went out to the shop. He checked to insure that the ATV battery was fully charged and hooked it to the large trailer. The weather looked threatening so he stopped at the house and picked up a foul weather suit. On a whim he picked up the old Marlin in its' scabbard and strapped it to the brackets he had welded onto the ATV. Chris considered whether to go back through Dawson, which was the shorter route, or go through Perry and check the river bridge there. He thought he could get the trailer past the washed out approach at Dawson so he decided to go that way. He was soon in Dawson and stopped to check the Community building. A quick inspection indicated that some of the roof panels were loose but not seriously damaged. Finding the door unlocked he went inside and could see no water damage from leaks. Making a mental note to return and try to get the roof panels securely fastened down he was soon on the road. After working his way around the washed out bridge approach he was on his way again. Driving at a moderate speed he passed through Rippey and again saw the herd of hogs searching for acorns. It reminded him of the need to replenish his meat supply. Arriving in Grand Junction at about 10:00 AM he set about moving the groceries out of the store basement. He found a hand cart which didn't help on the stairs but saved many steps from there to the trailer. The trailer was soon loaded and he could see there were enough goods left to warrant another trip if the weather permitted. Heading home again he looked back at the trailer and was pleased with the results of his labor.

Noting the many young willows and cottonwoods growing in the ditches and fields, he could see it would not be many years before they became forest again, As he drove over a little rise he was surprised to see several hundred Canada geese beside the road. They appeared curious but unafraid. Pulling out the little .22 Colt, he took careful aim and with two shots hit what appeared to be an immature goose through the neck.

The rest of the flock moved off no more than two hundred yards and settled again. Chris cut the head off the goose and hung it on the outside of the trailer so it wouldn't make a bloody mess on his cargo. He arrive home in late afternoon and pulled the ATV into the shop. He would unload it in the morning. He had forgotten to take water so he went to the house for a drink. The dogs had been cooped in the yard all day so he let them out to run off their excess energy. Almost as soon as they had disappeared the corner of the driveway he could hear them barking. He wondered if the hog herd was back. Chris plucked and dressed the goose putting the feathers and entrails in a plastic bucket to be emptied into his garbage trailer. The trailer had not been emptied the previous spring so he knew he would have to make a trip to the old coal mine shaft soon or else he would not have room for the refuse he would accumulate over the coming winter. He took the goose to the house where he salted it inside and out. He then went to the outside grill, put the goose on the spit and turned the heat on low, set the timer for eight hours and knew that in the morning he would have a perfectly roasted goose which had cooled enough to handle. In the house he took an elk steak out of the freezer along with some mushrooms and wild carrots. The mushrooms had come from the timber and he had found the carrots growing in the long abandoned garden of a former neighbor. The carrots were small and somewhat stringy but they still tasted like carrots. He only wished he had some green peas to go with them. While he was eating his supper he heard the dogs return. Turning on the deck lights he could see them at their food dishes. After eating and cleaning up he went outside to close the gate then spent some time petting and talking to the dogs. Talking to the dogs was as close as he had come to having conversation in more than seven years. In the back of his mind was the fear that he would lose the ability to converse if he ever met another human. Luxuriating in another long, hot shower, he was in bed early again. Tired from a long day of labor and travel he slept unusually late the next morning. His breakfast was left over elk steak between slices of very old tasting bread from the freezer.

After letting the dogs out for a run, Chris hitched the ATV to his junk trailer and drove the mile or so to the overgrown driveway leading to the abandoned coal mine. The top of the shaft had been fenced to keep out curious pets and children. While building his house and other buildings the construction people had built a cover over the top of the shaft. The shaft itself was eighteen feet square and more than one hundred fifty feet deep. He opened the cover then backed the trailer up to the stop blocks. Pulling the pins which allowed the trailer to tilt he watched as a year's worth of trash and garbage slid out of the trailer and into the hole. He closed the cover and after driving out, closed and latched the gate. He estimated the old mine shaft would hold all the trash from his lifetime and more. Beyond that it would be the responsibility of someone else, if in fact there was anyone else. He had just about given up hope of that possibility.

Returning home Chris hooked up to the trailer holding the goods he had brought from Grand Junction. Unloading bags of flour, cornmeal, rice, dried beans plus a variety of canned goods he soon had the pantry filled to the point of being crammed and cramped. Looking at what was still on the trailer he was at a loss as to where he was going to store all of it. He finally remembered that in the unused barn there was a tack/feed room which had been built to be rodent proof. In addition it could be heated or cooled as the season required. He soon had the trailer unloaded, returned to the shop and had the ATV plugged in to the charging grid.

It was no mid-afternoon. Rather than start a major project or chore, Chris obtained a bowl and scissors from the kitchen. Walking out the driveway and into the adjacent field he soon located a patch of thistles. Then using his knife, cut the tops from several small dandelions. He noticed several areas where the hogs had been rooting and it appeared to be an area they visited on a regular basis. It was close to and had a good line of sight from the blind he had put in a tree several years before. It should enable him to harvest his winter supply of pork with little effort.

Returning to the house he washed the greens, cut a drumstick and thigh from the goose, and left them out to warm to room temperature. He put more of the old, old music on the player and turning on the outside speakers, he went out to the deck and spent two hours listening to the mellow music and talking to the dogs. For his supper he opened small cans of peas and corn and adding vinegar and olive oil, he made a salad from the thistles and dandelions. The goose was moist and delicious as were the vegetables even though they and the olive oil tasted of age.

After his meal Chris decided it was past time to update his journal. Checking the calendar he was surprised to see seven days had passed since his walk in the snow. Using his version of shorthand he reconstructed the seven days. He had been using school tablets to keep his diary and often wondered if he should look for some hardbound books to keep his records. Transcribing all his notes would be a major undertaking and he put the decision off for a later date. He went to the library shelves to find material for his winter reading. He had become a fan of the late 20th early 21st century author Jean Auel. He had the complete collection of her works on audio discs but tonight he wanted the feel of an actual volume in his hands. Pulling out the first volume of her "Earth's Children" series he retired to his favorite chair. He was soon engrossed in the travels of Ayla, the protagonist of the series. By 10:00PM, he found himself dozing so he put the book down and went to bed.

Next morning his breakfast was toast from frozen bread and two glasses of reconstituted dried milk. Of all the frozen and dried products milk seemed to be one of the longer lasting ones. Getting out a ladder Chris cleaned all the leaves and accumulated litter from the rain gutters of the house and made sure the down spouts were clear. He then loaded the ladder and an assortment of hand tools into the trailer and drove the two miles to what was left of Dawson. He climbed onto the roof of the community hall where he discovered the damage was less than he had expected to find. It was not a big job to bend and hammer the roof panels back into place. After putting in a few well-placed screws he was satisfied that, barring another tornado, the roof was good for many more years. Driving around the town was difficult but by carefully choosing his route he was able to see all of it. He became aware that many of the houses had been built in the recent past and that much of the construction material was of the composite plastic from his grandfather's mill. Much of it could be salvaged and used by anyone determined to rebuild in the ruined town.

Returning home he stopped only long enough to turn the dogs out, then took the tractor and drove out to the hickory grove. In the spring he had felled six tall trees and after trimming and topping them he had left them where they lay. By dragging them two at a time, in less than two hours he had them at the shop to be bucked into firebox length for the smokehouse.

He showered, had supper, spent time with the dogs and was in bed early. Next morning Chris noted that it was October 21 and decided it would be a good day for what he referred to as a "shopping trip" to Perry. It was really a scavenging trip but he refused to think of it in those terms. He decided to make a written list rather than trying to remember everything. First on the list was clothing. He needed everything, especially underwear plus winter boots and socks. He added dry yeast and salt, always salt. Various spices were always a bonus but it seemed to him they were beginning to lose their potency. He needed fresh bedding for the dogs and decided to visit some local farms to look for usable baled straw. Realizing the list could become endless he hitched the ATV to the large trailer and set out.   Taking the "old" north road towards Perry, he was soon at the bridge only to find it completely blocked by a half dozen fallen trees right at the bridge. He dismounted from the ATV and climbed through the tangle of downed limbs to inspect the bridge which appeared to be sound and undamaged. He estimated that the trees could be cleared by a couple of men with chain saws in three and four hours but that would have to wait for another day. Reversing his route he drove back west almost to his own driveway then turned south and in less than a mile was on highway 141. This road had been widened and repaved twenty years before. In only a matter of minutes he was in Perry where he stopped in front of a clothing store he had visited on previous shopping excursions. He was pleased to find an ample supply of underwear and tee shirts in his size. Cotton and wool socks followed into the shopping cart whose wheels squeaked but still turned. He found a half dozen cotton flannel shirts plus several heavy wool ones.

All this was followed by six pairs of cotton like synthetic material work pants and four sets of long winter underwear. On a whim he picked up an insulated one-piece snow suit. It was labeled, "April Sale. 50%off". Good price he thought, as it went into the cart. On the south side of town he located a warehouse for a local grocery chain. The door was locked but he had discovered that a three pound hammer opened most doors with a minimum of effort. Just inside the door was a faded but still legible layout of the building's contents. Going to the area containing baking goods he located a shelf holding cartons of dry yeast. Opening a carton he found the yeast packed in glass bottles. Opening a bottle he smelled and tasted the contents. Based on his limited experience it looked and tasted as he thought dry yeast should. He took three cartons of yeast thinking that amount should provide a ten year supply, assuming it was still effective. He also carried out a carton of baking powder and one of baking soda. He carefully wired the door closed knowing he would return at some time. A half block from the warehouse stood a Farm Supply store. Since he wasn't farming he had never felt the need to investigate this store. Finding the door not locked he went inside then stopped to get his bearings. Except for the layer of dust which was to be found in any store, this place looked as if it was ready for business. There was a huge footwear department which would save him a stop at a shoe store. Into the ever present cart he put five pairs of athletic shoes, two pairs of leather boots and a pair of insulated snow boots. Taking time to look around he was impressed with the quantity and variety of merchandise. With the exception of furniture and groceries you could just about equip an entire home from this one store. There were at least a dozen saddles plus the additional tack needed for riding horses. In addition there were several sets of harness for work horses. Looking into a side room he discovered the prize of the trip, curing salt. There was at least a ton of the material in fifty pound bags. Further checking the area he discovered several books on curing meat. He carried out five hundred pounds of the salt, several of the books plus a dozen syringes for injecting the brine solution into the meat.

Heading home with the loaded trailer he was there in less than a half hour. He carried the clothing, books and baking items into the house and unloaded the salt in the shop. It was early afternoon so Chris got his chain saw and proceeded to cut the hickory trees in firebox length. The wood was damp from being on the ground all summer but would burn slowly and produce more smoke.

While eating his supper of cold goose and leftover vegetables, Chris made the decision to make his annual trip to Dallas Center the next day. It was a trip he looked forward to but at the same time dreaded making it. He wanted to look through some of the manufacturing facility of what had once been the family business and visit the home of his parents where he had buried them on his return after the day the world, at least as he knew it, ended.

The next morning Chris was on the road by 7:00 AM. He was pulling the small trailer with nothing in it except for a light weight sleeping bag. He planned to spend the night at the home of his parents as he wanted to look at old papers and photos to see if there were any he wanted to take home and preserve. By mid-morning Chris was in Dallas Center. He went directly to the plant, where using the palm print scanner, which surprisingly was still working, he entered the building. Everything was covered in a thick layer of dust but appeared to be untouched since his last visit. He walked through several of the buildings and finally admitted to himself that he was stalling. It was extremely difficult for him to visit the home of his parents but it was time. Driving the mile and a half west of town, he turned up the long driveway leading to the modest house where his parents had lived. The driveway was becoming overgrown with brush along the side and his mother's treasured front garden was a disaster. Walking to the backyard he could see the grass had finally covered the graves completely and the roses he had planted in place of the headstones were thriving. The roses were in need of pruning which was something he would do before leaving in the morning. Entering the house Chris could see that the electrical system was working and checked to see that there was pressure in the water lines. This house had been built only four years before his own. The solar array and electrical grid had been copied in the construction of his own home.

Carrying his sleeping bag into the house, Chris after shaking the dust from the bed cover, tossed it onto the bed where he had slept for four years. Going to the freezer he found a carton of his mother's stew and put it out to thaw. For some reason this freezer seemed to keep food tasting fresher than the one at home and Chris was anticipating the stew. After he had eaten and cleaned up, he didn't dare leave a mess in his mother's kitchen; he selected some discs, put them in the player and turned the music on low. The system, as was his at home, was really an antique. He and his father had preferred it to the new so-called stick systems. The music he was playing was also old, in fact, it was from the middle years of the twentieth century. He played it because it was the favorite of his grandfather. As Elvis Presley and Buddy Holly bopped and rocked, Chris found himself in tears. He sobbed long and loudly. When the tears finally stopped, Chris sat and pondered the reason for them. He had cried for his parents whose lives had been cut so short, for his grandfather whose life had been stolen from him, for the hundreds of millions, perhaps billions of people who had perished and not least of all, for himself and the terrible, terrible loneliness he had endured for more than seven years. All he could do was ask himself why and again there was no answer.

Chris spent a restless night, tossing and turning, and was happy when the east facing windows began to lighten with the dawn. He took time to prune the roses marking the graves and was soon on his way home. He was not sure he ever wanted to return to Dallas Center, but time would tell.

He was home by mid-morning and set about cutting up the rest of the hickory for the smokehouse burner. Digging a large piece of camouflage netting out of a crate in the shop he hiked out the driveway and draped it over the simple blind he had put up in a large maple tree. Most of the leaves had fallen so he had a clear view of the area where the hogs had been rooting in an old clover patch. The next day he planned to take a large thermos of coffee, the Auel book and spend three or four hours in the blind.

He would continue this routine until the hogs returned or he became bored and moved on to a new spot.

He returned to the house then took the dogs and walked down to the river bottom. The sandy bottom covered perhaps two hundred yards from the bottom of the hill to the river itself. He could see large areas which had been cleared of the young willows by the beavers to stock their winter larders. He considered digging out a book dealing with tanning animal pelts and then harvesting a half dozen of the big rodents and tanning the hides. He also considered that perhaps that was more primitive than he was prepared to turn just yet. He looked at the river and picked out a spot where he could put his two fish traps. Fresh fish would be a nice change from the game and wild birds he had been eating since early spring.

Back at the house he ate more cold goose and some dried apples he had been soaking. He set his alarm and was up in his blind before dawn. By nine o'clock his coffee was gone and he was thoroughly chilled so he decided to call it quits for the day. As he was preparing to climb down he became aware of the snuffling of hogs. As he looked down they were directly under the blind heading for the open field. He carefully took his seat and waited until the pigs were out in the open. He slowly raised the Marlin and through the scope, identified two females which did not appear to have been nursing young ones. With two quick shots the animals were on the ground and the rest of the herd scattered and disappeared into the timber. He hurried into the field and cut the throats of the two downed pigs. While the hogs were bleeding out, he drove the ATV and trailer into the field. Field dressing the animals where they were, he left the offal where it lay except for the livers which he would use as bait in his fish traps. Using the ATV winch he quickly loaded the animals on the trailer. Pulling the trailer under a beam he had put up just behind the shop for this purpose he hoisted the animals and prepared to complete the butchering. He didn't have a pot big enough for the scalding the pigs to remove the hair, so he resorted to a heavy pair of clippers and shaved the hams, shoulders and flanks over what would become bacon slabs. It was a crude and messy process and when he finished he spent considerable time with a stiff brush scrubbing the carcasses. He removed the head, feet and what hide wasn't going into the smoker. With an axe and saw he split each pig in half and hoisted the pieces high enough that they couldn't be reached by animals. A quick trip to the mine shaft and all the refuse was taken care of. The bodies would be left hanging until noon the next day to completely cool.

Gong to the storeroom in the shop, he took down the two homemade chicken wire fish traps and tossed them in the trailer along with the can holding the two hog livers. Following a circuitous route, he made his way to the river where it made a turn south. Along this stretch there was a low bank with deep water facing it. Putting the liver into wire baskets which were fastened inside the traps he secured the traps with long pieces of nylon line and tossed them into the river. After driving back up the hill and putting the ATV away re realized that he was very tired and very hungry.

Chris took a long hot shower to rid himself of the wild pig smell. He put on a complete set of his new clothes and thought in the morning he would go through his closet and dresser and put all of his old clothing in the incinerator. That way he wouldn't be tempted to wear them, "just one more time". They were worn, torn, stained and never seemed to come completely clean when they came out of the laundry. Chris went to the freezer and picked out a steak plus a large roast. It reminded him that his supply of beef was very low and was another task he needed to take care of before the hard winter set in. He put the steak on the outdoor grill and a potato in the microwave. What he really craved was something green. If he stayed home another summer he vowed to search the stores for lettuce, cabbage, kale and spinach seeds and hope they would still germinate. Then a light bulb moment struck him. He had a greenhouse sitting empty except for a few tomatoes ripening under a sum lamp. He told himself, he was slow, but he wasn't very sure. He added a small can of peaches to his steak and potato supper and when finished put more 1950's music on the player and then went out to spend some time with the dogs. As he sat, he pondered his breakdown at his parent's house two nights ago. He wondered if he was destined to spend the rest of his life with no contact with another human He couldn't imagine becoming old, frail and unable to care for himself. If he were to become seriously ill or incapacitated it would be the end but then he had always known that. He was careful on ladders and when he was driving, but beyond that took no special precautions. He had decided if something happened it was just part of life and he didn't want to waste time or energy worrying about it.

Chris took his book to bed, read until ten o'clock, then slept a full eight hours. Next morning after tending to the dogs and eating his own breakfast, once again leftover steak, he went out to check on the hog carcasses. They were hanging high and untouched, but both trees supporting the beam held deep scratches indicating some animal had tried to climb them. Puzzled, he thought it would be a good idea to get the meat cut up soon. He walked out to the field to see if anything had begun scavenging the remains he had left there. As he stepped out into the field something caught the edge of his field of vision. Looking around he could see nothing out of place or moving. Then, looking up, he could not believe what his eyes were telling him. There was a long silver white streak stretching across the sky in an east to west direction. It could only be from one thing, an aircraft flying at thirty to forty thousand feet. He had heard nothing but it could have passed over while he was still in the house. He ran to the shop and turned on the radio. It was the same model used in his company airplane. He spent the better part of an hour switching between channels commonly used by aircraft, but heard nothing. Deeply disappointed but at the same time highly elated, he turned to the task of getting the meat ready for the smoking process. He started the fire in the smokehouse and began cutting. Using a handsaw, an axe and old woodworking band saw, he soon had hams, shoulders and bacon slabs lined up on the meat cutting table. He cut the backs and ribs into slabs and decided to smoke the entire amount. Before injecting the brine solution he trimmed off as much fat as possible to be rendered down for lard. While doing all this his mind was thinking ahead and he came to the decision to harvest two more hogs. One of them, except for the hams, he would grind up for sausage, freeze it and in the winter when he was essentially housebound he would try smoking it.

Next morning as he was feeding the dogs Chris heard the distinctive sound of coyotes yipping. Thinking they were probably arguing over the hog remains, he walked out to investigate. As he walked out of the trees he became aware the coyotes were not alone. There were six or eight of them circling and darting at a very large bear. In his travels he had seen a number of bears but never one of this size. The bear turned so it was in profile and Chris could see the distinctive dish face and the obvious shoulder hump. His reaction on recognizing what was in front of him was to blurt out, "My God it's a grizzly." On hearing his voice, the bear immediately turned and charged. Chris knew he had no hope of outrunning the bear, but he was no more than ten feet from his tree blind. He dashed for the tree and scrambled up into the blind. The limbs which provided Chris with easy access also enabled the bear to climb with little effort. Chris pulled out the little .22 pistol and when the bear pushed his head over the floor of the blind, he fired three rapid shots into the head of the beast. He was hoping to blind or at least distract the bear until he could bail off the blind to reach the shop and the always loaded 12 gauge shotgun he kept there. Before he could move the bear toppled out of the tree. Chris emptied the rest of the magazine into the bears head then began to tremble and had to sit down before he fell down. He sat in the blind for an hour waiting for the shakes to stop, never taking his eyes off of the bear. He finally felt composed enough to climb down and in passing nudged the giant beast with his toe. He stooped to examine the head and concluded that one of those first three shots had penetrated the top of the skull killing the bear instantly. This didn't mean he wanted to face another bear armed with only a .22 pistol. He could hear the dogs raging and assumed they had smelled the bear. Chris returned to the house and opened the gate so the dogs could get out. He watched them race down the driveway then into the trees where he could hear them growling and probably chewing on the bear carcass.

Earlier he had been hungry, but the rush of adrenaline seemed to have quieted his hunger pangs.

The fish traps had been in the river for two days so he drove the tractor down the hill. Driving along the edge of the water he saw tracks which must have been made by the bear and wondered whether he had overlooked them two days before. He pulled the first trap from the water and was rewarded with eight small catfish. The second trap yielded only three small carp which he tossed up in the weeds for the animals to find. He cleaned the fish there on the riverbank, tossing the heads, fins and entrails into the water. The turtles would find those tasty, he thought. Driving home he immediately put two of the fish in a fry pan and the rest in the freezer. He nuked a potato and had a nice mid-day meal. After eating, he took the tractor and with a length of chain dragged the bear a mile and a half east and into the edge of the timber. He thought it would keep the coyotes and vultures content for a few days. He, himself, was not yet ready to start eating bear meat.

Taking the ATV, Chris began driving the roads south and west of Dawson looking for cattle. He wanted two of them as that was about the capacity of his freezer space. Two miles south and a mile west of town he came upon a large herd of them. He estimated that there were at least two hundred of them. They didn't seem apprehensive about the appearance of the vehicle and the many, which were lying down chewing their cud didn't bother to get up. There seemed to be a preponderance of Hereford blood in the group, although there was a variety of colors. Several seemed to have strong genetic ties to the old Texas longhorns. There had been a few farmers in the area who had been breeding longhorns just for the uniqueness. Chris decided he needed to look no further and headed for home. As he neared home he could see the ever present vultures gathering and circling. He assumed they had spotted the body of the grizzly. Having had a substantial mid-day meal, he was not particularly hungry so he made his supper of canned beans and apricots. While eating his mind settled on the subject of the names given to meals. In much of the country the noon meal was lunch and in the evening one ate dinner. In the lexicon of the mid-west however, at noon you ate dinner and in the evening you ate supper. That was how he grew up thinking of meals and no amount of other usage was going to change him at this point in his life.

The next morning which Chris noted was October 27, he decided that laying in a beef supply should take precedence over more pork. He also decided since his experience with the grizzly that perhaps he should be more heavily armed. Returning the old Marlin to the gun safe, he selected a .300 magnum and ammunition for it. Driving back to where he had seen the cattle the previous day he was relieved to see they were in the same general area. Driving as close as he dared without spooking them he dispatched two of them with head shots to preserve as much meat as possible. Driving closer, he dismounted and cut the throats of both. By this time he became aware of one of the bulls which had not fled with the herd. Every time he moved into the open, the bull would start to charge, forcing him to take cover behind the ATV. After several attempts the bull showed no sign of relenting and Chris didn't have time to spare so he took out the rifle again and shot the animal through the head. Using the winch he dragged the first two into position and soon removed the heads, hooves and entrails. Winching them into the trailer, he set out for home. On arriving home he hoisted the two carcasses up on the beam and removed the hides. Using the axe and saw he split each animal in half and then hoisted them all the way to the beam. As long as the weather remained cool, he planned to let them hang and age for four or five days. After another trip to the mine shaft to dispose of the hides he was ready to call it a day.

After feeding the animals and himself, he sat down and brought his journal up to date. Finishing his journal he turned on the music and found his book. He was intrigued by the ingenuity of Ayla who was now in her valley and coping very well. At least she had the hope of one day finding her own kind. That was the hope he had about given up on until seeing the contrail two days earlier.

The next morning he loaded a number of boxes and crates in the trailer and drove south of Perry where in the old days a family had maintained an orchard and roadside fruit stand. Most of the apples were gone but there were several trees of late bearing varieties, which though heavily worm infested, still had fruit which was salvageable. He filled all his boxes and decided that if the weather held he would come back in a few days for more apples. His plan was to dry some of the apples, freeze some fresh and make applesauce with the remainder. Arriving home he was soon busy peeling and slicing apples. Eating a slice now and then he skipped supper and was reminded how much he missed fresh produce of all kinds. The peelings and discards he was saving to use as hog bait.

In the morning he made a run to the river to check the fish traps. They were heavy with fish. He counted over thirty catfish plus a few carp and even one bass of about two pounds. He cleaned the fish there on the river bank and again tossed the remains into the river for turtle food. He went back to the house where he wrapped the fish for the freezer except for the bass which he kept out for his supper. He finished cutting up the apples, then carried the waste out to the field where he noticed the coyotes had already cleaned up the remains of the two hogs. For his supper he baked the bass on the outdoor grill and baked a potato which he seasoned with bacon grease from the freezer.

The next morning, Chris was up in the blind before first light. He had looked at the magnum and concluded it was more gun than he needed for a one hundred seventy five pound pig. Putting the magnum back in the gun safe he picked up the reliable old Marlin and carried it out to the blind. He concluded the odds of another grizzly being in the area were very slight. At a half hour after sunrise he heard the pigs passing under the blind. Later, he planned to backtrack them to determine their path through the timber. Waiting until there was enough light to make the right choice, he quickly dispatched two of the herd. The herd scattered to the timber and he began the task of butchering and hanging the meat. The beam holding the animals was bending under the weight but he wanted the beef to age for one more day. This time he saved the small intestines from the hogs and wished he had done so with the first two. He could always shoot another hog or two, but he had an adequate amount of meat and didn't relish the idea of killing an animal just for the intestines. He spent the better part of the afternoon stripping and washing the intestines then put them in the cooler until he was ready to fill them with sausage.

Chris was in bed early that night anticipating the next day to be a long and tiring one. He was up with the sun and started the day by filling the large slow cooker with apples to make apple-sauce. Lowering two of the beef halves into the trailer he hauled them to the stainless steel table which he used for meat process-ing. He had fashioned a wooden chopping block by bolting two by eights together on edge. It wouldn't last like a real end grain oak block but it served his purpose adequately. Wrestling a beef half up on the table, he cut it in half again and proceeded to carve out steaks and roasts. He was aware that his cuts of meat would make a real butcher cringe but he did the best he could. Looking at his progress when he stopped for lunch he thought he could finish half of the second beef that day. He was becoming more adept at using the saw and knives and by working until nine that night he managed to process all the beef. It was wrapped and bagged and ready for the freezer. The slabs of ribs had been a problem to wrap so he put them in the freezer bare to be used later as dog treats.

He was too tired to bother with cooking so he sliced some of the roast in the refrigerator and had some of the fresh applesauce. He had a quick shower and was in bed by eleven. During the night he was awakened by a noise he could not, at first, identify. As he lay in bed listening he realized it was a wolf howling. He was accustomed to hear coyotes crying in the night and he had seen single wolves on two occasions. This was the first time he had heard the big predators and it sounded as if there were sever-al of them up and down the ridge above the river. He supposed it was a natural sequence of events. Man was essentially gone and there certainly was an ample supply of prey animals.

Eventually he slept again and was up at first light to resume his meat cutting tasks. Before going outside to work he ladled the apple sauce into pint containers and put them in the freezer.

After stoking the smokehouse fire he turned to the hogs and soon had them on the cutting table. By noon he had one hog cut up and the hams removed from the other. Injecting the curing solution and getting the meat hung in the smokehouse took another two hours at which point Chris decided he was finished working for the day. He felt the remainder of the pork would not spoil with the temperature hovering just above freezing.

Calling the dogs he hiked down the path to the river. As he was crossing the willow covered sandbar, the dogs took off, barking loudly. They refused to stop at his whistle which was unusual behavior for them. He followed to see what had set them off. At the base of the hill they were dancing around a small oak tree baying as if they were hounds. Sitting in a fork about twelve or fifteen feet up the tree was an extremely angry bobcat. The cat's ears were back flat against its head and it was snarling back at the dogs. Grasping the collar of the female, he had given her the name Lady but seldom used it, he led her away from the tree knowing the other two would soon follow. Following the river upstream he came to a pond which had no inlet or outlet. It was filled by seepage from the river. Three beaver lodges stood with their tops out of the water and he thought they would flood in the spring when the river rose with the spring rains. Hiking to the top of the bluff he walked home through the timber. Passing under a number of oak and hickory trees, it was obvious that the feral hogs were competing with the squirrels for the nut harvest. Pulling a small mesh bag from his fanny pack he filled it with walnuts and a few hickory nuts the pigs and squirrels had missed. Nearing home he came across a trail, actually a rut, being used by the pigs. Apparently they spent nights down on the river bottom and climbed the hill in the morning to access the nuts and whatever they were rooting for in the fields.

That night Chris heard the wolves again. They were close enough that the dogs came out of their shelters and were behind the house barking back at their wild cousins. He awoke in the morning to find a thin dusting of new snow covering the ground

After breakfast Chris took the industrial sized food grinder out of the carton where it had sat unused for over ten years. It had been a gift from his mother not long after he moved into his house. At the time he couldn't imagine ever having a need for it. He cleaned it, changed the cutter head and turned it on to insure that it worked. He went out to the hog carcass and began cutting the meat from the bone. He didn't try to be neat about it, just slashed the meat off and tossed it in a pile. When he finished he tossed the bones in the trailer to be taken out and dumped for the coyotes to fight over. He sprinkled a liberal amount of salt and seasonings over the meat then pushed the hog intestine up over the spout attached to the machine. Turning the machine on he began feeding meat into the grinding hopper, He soon had both intestines full and then ground the rest of the pork and divided it into approximately one half pound portions. These he bagged and took to the freezer. It just about filled the freezer to capacity and from the stand point of meat he judged that he was ready for the winter.

For supper that evening he ate some of the fresh ground sausage. He added potato and the last of the frozen carrots. It was close to freezing outside but Chris sat out for an hour listening to music and talking to the dogs. When a few snowflakes began sifting down he went inside and found his book. He left the outside lights on so he could watch the snow falling. By the time he went to bed at eleven there was at least an inch of snow on the deck. It reminded him that he still needed to find fresh bedding for the dogs. When he awoke next morning he was surprised to see little more snow that when he had gone to bed. His calendar said it was November 4th so he thought it would be wise to make another trip to the farm supply store before the road became more snow covered. He needed a spool of 3/8 inch rope and wanted to spend time really looking over the store inventory. After tending to the dogs he went out to the shop. He lowered the hard top for the ATV and into place and got it securely bolted in place. He put on the doors, zipped in the rear window and considered it ready for winter. It leaked cold air, but the heater was sufficient to keep it comfortable. He had considered leaving the top on all year round as he didn't much care for getting wet from summer showers, but he did enjoy the fresh air in good weather.

The drive to Perry was uneventful as most of the snow had blown off the road. Entering the farm store he went to the gardening section where he found a small garden tiller and another chain saw. Both were battery powered and compatible with his charging system at home. Both batteries were dead but he had spares at home if these would not take a charge. In the kitchen ware area he found a large electric pot which operated from standard household current. It had a cover and a small faucet at the bottom. He had no idea of the original purpose but thought it would work well for rendering the hog fat into lard. Looking in the pet department he found a stack of heavy cloth covered dog beds which were filled with cedar shavings. There were seven of them in the bin of which he took six. As he was loading the dog beds the snow began falling again. He covered the trailer with a plastic tarp and immediately headed home. By the time he reached home the snow had become much heavier and the wind had picked up considerably. He parked the vehicles in the shop and before going to the house he went to the storeroom and picked up a pair of snowshoes. He had discovered that it was easier to use snowshoes than to be constantly shoveling paths between the various buildings. Chris went to the house where he called the dogs out of their shelters, then opened the gate so they could have a run. They didn't take off as usual but trotted out to the corner of the driveway where they took care of their business, trotted back to the yard and went directly to their kennels. He closed and locked the gate then went into the house where he was standing at the window watching the snow fall when it suddenly stopped as if someone had turned off a machine. Getting some dry beans from the pantry he washed them, then put them to soak overnight. After cutting one last slice from the roast in the refrigerator he diced up the rest to add to the dog dishes as a treat. The slice of roast and a baked potato made up his supper. He spent the evening reading and half watching a video on world history. Before going to bed he noted the temperature was 21 degrees. When he awoke the next morning he was aware of the sound of the wind in the trees. Looking out his window he could see that most of the snow was gone, and the thermometer stood at 38 degrees. A Chinook he thought, then turned to prepare his breakfast which was oatmeal and more reconstituted dried milk. After letting the dogs out he went to the smoke house and added fresh logs to the firebox. He then picked out a piece of ham shank to add to the beans. It wasn't yet completely cured but it would cook and add to the flavor of the beans.

He spent the morning cleaning the dog houses and putting in the new beds. The old bedding went into the trash trailer for later disposal. By noon the snow was gone and the ground had started to dry. The wind had abated considerably since early morning and he decided it would be a good day to visit the home of his former neighbors. Today he would investigate the house. In the seven years they had been gone he had never been inside the house. He had intended to do so the first summer but when he walked up on the porch the odor told him there were bodies inside. He put a garden fork and spade in the trailer and drive the mile to the house. He could see that falling tree limbs had broken more of the windows on the north and east sides of the house. The door was unlocked and he entered a kitchen which had been devastated. All of the lower kitchen cabinets were standing open and the floor was littered with canisters and boxes which had once contained the staples of food preparation. There was also a liberal sprinkling of animal droppings. There were two bedrooms, one of which held nothing but a rotting bed and furniture ruined by rain blown in through broken windows. In the second room was another bed holding what appeared to be two complete skeletons. These people were a middle aged couple who appeared to have died without even waking up on that terrible April morning. He left them as they were. He considered burning the house down around them but if it had been constructed of the new materials it wouldn't burn well. In the end he decided to let time and nature take its course.

Returning outside Chris drove to the week choked former garden. Going to the area where he had dug up the little carrots in previous years he began to run over the soil with the garden fork. He was pleased and surprised at the results. He was not only turning up more of the orange roots than he had found on the previous trips, they were larger as well. He could only surmise that loosening the soil when he had dug previously had allowed or encouraged the added growth. Chris cut off the dead and frost bitten tops and put the carrots in the trailer. Looking about the garden he started to dig around some other dead tops and turned up about a dozen small turnips. These would make a tasty addition the next time he made soup.

Chris returned home and after putting the ATV away, took the carrots and turnips to the house where he washed and trimmed them. The carrots were bagged for the freezer while the turnips would go into the root cellar. He had his supper early, spent time with the dogs and was in bed early. He spent some time considering the remains of his neighbors. He decided finally that if the weather held off long enough he would take the tractor with the small back hoe and put them in the ground. They had been good neighbors and deserved to have a more dignified resting place that a rotting bed in a rotting house.

Next morning it was much colder with the temperature down to sixteen degrees. To the north and west he could see massive banks of dark clouds. It even smelled like snow. By ten A.M., the snow had begun to filter down and by noon it was falling heavily. At eleven he had let the dogs out for a run but they were soon back and after going to their food dishes went quickly to their shelters. The snowfall became heavier and by six P.M, there was an accumulation of seven inches on the deck. The snow continued without abating for three full days. On the fourth morning Chris awoke to bright sunshine and snow which was lying eighteen inches deep on the deck. The temperature was steady at ten degrees and it was obvious that winter had arrived in full force. It was November 9th and after only three days Chris could sense the onset of cabin fever. Putting on his snowshoes he made the rounds of all the out buildings. As he did so he wondered again about the expense which had gone into building the barn, swine and poultry houses. His grandfather had insisted they be built and Chris thought perhaps this time the old man had misjudged the need. He stopped in the shop to check the charging grid and picked up a shovel and snow blower. He cleared the steps and part of the deck, leaving the rest for Mother Nature to deal with. He had been eating primarily ham hocks, beans and fresh corn bread for several days. He had also tried out the new yeast and found it to be effective. He now had fresh bread in the refrigerator and eight loaves in the freezer. The aroma of baking bread had left the house smelling wonderful but at the same time evoked powerful memories of his mother and her kitchen when he was a child. He cleared the snow from around the gate and let the dogs out. They seemed to enjoy the deep snow and were soon out of sight around the corner of the driveway. He had taken a steak out of the freezer but it was too early to eat supper. He went to the shop and plugged in the big electric pot he had brought home from the farm store. It started to heat up immediately so tomorrow he would start to render the hog fat. While he was out he checked the dog boxes to insure the heaters were working. He also checked the green house and found that several of the green tomatoes had ripened enough to eat. His supper was steak, canned peas and carrots, fresh tomato plus a baked potato. Before going to bed he stepped on the scale and found his weight to be at one hundred forty one which was up two pounds since he had arrived home. Chris was slight of build and only five feet ten inches tall but a one hundred thirty nine pounds he looked emaciated. He hoped to be up to one hundred fifty five pounds by spring.

Next morning which was November tenth Chris carried the chunks of hog fat to the shop and turned the big electric pot on low. The fat had been in the freezer so it was some time before the clear lard began to flow. He had a change of mind and turned the pot off. He would let the chunks of fat sit for a day to thaw and the rendering would go much more rapidly. He returned to the house, turned the dogs out and was prepared to spend the day with his book. As he sat down he looked out the window to see three brilliant red Cardinals perched in a snow covered tree with their feathers fluffed out against the cold. Remembering the bird feeder given to him by his mother and which he had never used he went to the shop and fetched it to the house. He fastened it to the deck railing and not having any kind of seeds to put in it he filled one hopper with corn meal and the other with oatmeal. He then took a beef roast from the freezer and it out to thaw. By the middle of the afternoon he was able to carve off several slabs of beef fat which he stuffed into the baskets attached to the feeder. The rest of the roast he would chop up to make stew.

Next morning Chris was out early and had the rendering process under way. While the fat was cooking he spent three hours cleaning the band saw which was a mess after being used to cut up the cattle and hogs. By noon he was finished with both tasks. The rendered lard had been put into one pound containers and was in the freezer. He heated the last of the beans for his noon meal and sat behind the kitchen counter so he could see outside. He was astounded at the number and variety of birds at his feeder. He spent the afternoon reading and before going to bed that night he went to the cabinet holding his journals and laid them out on the dining table in chronological order.

Next morning when his chores were complete Chris went out to the greenhouse. He noted that several more of the tomatoes were red enough to be edible. They would be a welcome addition to his diet. He filled several flats with potting soil then went to his seed box where he found a full range of garden vegetables. He decided to plant twice as many seeds as was indicated on the packets and hoped half of them would germinate. When he had finished planting he adjust the temperature and humidity settings and hoped for luck with his efforts. He had never used the green house before so he was not at all sure what he was doing. He then went to the shop where he gathered some boards to put together a simple platform feeder with a flat roof cover. It was crudely built and he didn't bother to paint it. After fastening the feeder to the deck railing Chris went inside and put on snow clothing. He then went to the shop and uncovered the snow machine. He normally didn't use it this early in the winter but there was too much snow on the roads to be comfortable with the ATV. He attached a small sled to the rear and taking the Marlin he set out cow hunting. He went south to old 141 then turned west. The road was snow covered and in places there were substantial drifts but he had no real trouble getting through. Less than two miles down the road he spotted a group of cattle which were using a set of derelict farm buildings as shelter. He picked out a big animal and dispatched it with a head shot. He then dragged it over to a group of trees and using the winch hoisted it off the ground. He did a quick job of butchering. First he skinned the animal then opened it up. He then proceeded to trim off all the external fat as well as what he could get from the body cavity. He piled the fat into a tub on the sled then headed for home. While driving home Chris was passing houses which had belonged to his former neighbors. He had never investigated any of these places. Every time he had considered doing so his conscience had stopped him. It had the feeling of intruding on their privacy. He now reconsidered, telling himself they had been gone for almost eight years. If there was anything in those places which could be of use to him he was foolish not to avail himself of the opportunity. Weather permitting he planned to start the next day. It was late afternoon when Chris arrived home. He parked in the shop and went to the house where he spent some time with the dogs then prepared his supper,. After eating he picked up the journal from his first year of solitude. After some time of looking at it he concluded he was not in the mood to re-visit that terrible time tonight.

Chris went to bed early and before falling asleep heard the wolves again. He wondered if the pack had staked out this area as their home territory. If so, he would have to be more alert about when and where he let the dogs run. Next morning, which was November 14, Chris took all his baking sheets plus a roll of Aluminum foil to the shop. He started the big electric pot and added some of the beef fat he had collected the day before. While the fat was heating he fetched containers of corn and oat meals. As the fat melted he drained it into a pail and added liberal amounts of the two meals. He then ladled the mixture into the foil lined baking sheets and put them outside to cool. By mid-afternoon he had a dozen slabs of the suet, meal mixture. He refilled the feeder with corn and oat meal and stuffed chunks of the suet mix into the wire baskets. Placing a slab of the suet mix on the new feeder he then covered it with small mesh poultry wire which he securely fastened in place. Chris went in the house, made a pot of coffee and sat down in from of the window. Over the next two hours, using a field guide bird book, he identified fourteen varieties of birds at the feeders. He went to bed early that night and again lay awake listening to the chorus of wolf song. He had again looked at the journals and again found himself unwilling to relive those first days of being alone.

After breakfast the Chris determined to check out the farm of Charlie Simpson. Charlie had been a semi-recluse who had never made an effort to be very neighborly. He wasn't overly rude but he also never put forth a feeling of warmth or friendship. Charlie had farmed with equipment and methods which were one hundred plus years out of date. He did his work with two old diesel tractors and had even maintained a team of Belgian work horses. He plowed his one acre garden with the horses and a walking plow which had to be two hundred years old. His set of farm buildings were well maintained but looked as if they belonged to a farm from the mid 1900's. He even had an old fashioned slatted corn crib which hadn't been see in Iowa for generations. He didn't combine his corn but picked it on the ear and dried it in the crib.

Chris decided to drive the ATV towing the large trailer and trusted that the roads would prove to be passable. The short trip was uneventful and when he parked in the driveway he was taken by neatness of the place. There were a few dead limbs which had fallen from trees in the yard and paint on the buildings showed signs of needing to be touched up but otherwise the place looked almost lived in. He went to the small barn where the door opened on protesting hinges. The barn was set up with three double horse stalls on one side and four milking stanchions on the other. There was also a small feed room and two calf stalls. He found what was left of Charlie's body just inside the door of the last horse stall. It appeared as if he might have just closed the door leading to the pasture and fallen over dead. .He had been dressed in coveralls, boots and a light cap all of which were still in place. The exposed skin on his hands and face resembled parchment and it was obvious the body had not been disturbed since falling where it lay. Chris thought he would come back and bury the body in the spring. He climbed the ladder to the hay loft and discovered several tons of what appeared to be alfalfa hay. There was also a quantity of baled straw. Back on the ground floor Chris opened a door to the pasture. The area next to the building was trampled down to bare dirt by both cattle and horse tracks. Chris was puzzled whether some of Charlie's stock had survived and stayed close to home or perhaps the tracks had been made by stray animals passing through the area. He returned to the loft and tossed down a bale of hay. He broke the bale open and spread half of it outside the barn. If possible he would return the next day and see if it had been eaten. Leaving the barn he walked to the corn crib. He was surprised to see that the back half of the crib, which wasn't visible from the front, was almost full of ear corn. There were three grain bins over the center of the crib. The bins were sealed and a panel indicated they were fitted with temperature and humidity controls. There was also a system to stir the grain, aerating and extending its storage life. A chart by the control panel indicated there was a bin each of corn, oats and soy beans. He found a step ladder plus three pails and took a small sample from each bin. Chris knew Charlie had installed a solar array smaller but similar to his own which was apparently still functioning. The shop building was smaller than his own but just about as well equipped. The biggest difference was the lack of a battery charging grid such as Chris had at home. The machine shop resembled a museum for antique farm equipment. The machinery was old but obviously maintained to be in working condition. Saving the house for last Chris found the kitchen door unlocked and walked in. Except for the ever present layer of fine dust, the house was in good order. There were three bedrooms, two baths, the living dining area and kitchen. There was also a library/media room which was well stocked with printed and electronic entertainment items. Chris found the breaker box and turned off the water heater as a precaution against a leak or a fire. Going back to the shop Chris found two baskets. With the baskets in the trailer he drove into the crib where he filled one with corn and the other with oats, then headed for home. He parked the ATV and trailer in the shop where he prepared two large flats with soil, planted corn in one and oats in the other.

The next morning Chris took the ATV and drove to Charlie's house where he parked and walked directly to the barn. When he opened the top half of the door to the pasture he was greeted by the sight of a big sorrel horse. He immediately recognized the horse as Belle, one of Charlie's prized Belgians. He identified her from the cross shaped white blaze on her forehead. Standing just behind the mare was the other half of the team, a gelding named Beau. He was unique in that he had two distinctive black streaks in his otherwise pale blond mane. There was a third horse standing further back which appeared edgy and on the verge of flight.

Belle, with any hesitation put her head through the door and whickered softly. Beau was trying to join her but there simply wasn't room. The reaction of the horses should not have been a great surprise. When Charlie was alive he treated them more as pets than draft animals. Chris tossed out the remainder of the hay bale from the previous day and all three horses began eating. He then went to the shop and hunted until he found a small tarp. Going back to the barn he slid what was left of Charlie onto the tarp, wrapped it securely around him and tied it in place with a piece of cord. Chris picked up the bundle, carried it to the other side of the barn and put it in the little feed room. He dropped several bales of hay from the loft and filled all three mangers to overflowing. He then went to the grain bins and returned with buckets of oats and corn. Putting a small amount of each in the feed troughs he then opened the lower door and wired both upper and lower doors securely open. Water would not be a problem as there was a water tank which was obviously rigged with a heater and an automatic re-fill thanks to the solar array electric system. Belle and Beau were in the barn before Chris was out and he was sure the third horse would soon follow.

As Chris was on his way home the snow began again. It snowed all night, all the next day and all the following day. The temperature dropped to eight degrees and Chris didn't venture outside except to feed the dogs and stoke the fire in the smoke house. By the end of the second day Chris was pacing the floor and was already into a case of cabin fever. By this time there was at least two feet of snow on the ground and he knew the roads would be impassable. He would not be able to check on Charlie's horses for at least two days and that was on the condition that the snow stopped falling. It was only November 18th so this much snow was unusual. He promised himself that tomorrow he would start on the journals.

After breakfast the next morning Chris made another pot of coffee and settled into his chair with the journal from 2106. It was slow reading as he mentally transcribed his coded shorthand jottings. He relived every second of those first days and months and by 4:00 P.M. he was only half way through the journal. He was both emotionally and physically drained from the experience and knew it would be days before he wanted to resume the task.

Chapter 3

JOURNAL 2106

It was 5:00 A.M. and Chris was finishing the preflight inspection of his airplane. The plane was a 40 year old model which had started life as a jet powered machine which had been refitted with piston engines. The entire plane had been rebuilt and was really a hybrid. It could carry a ton of cargo and could be reconfigured to carry ten passengers in comfort. Today he was carrying only 350 pounds of replacement parts for machinery processing Colorado oil shale. At a speed of 375 MPH, the plane had a range of 2000 miles so Chris could make the trip without refueling along the way. He planned to stop in Grand Island, Nebraska for breakfast and arrive in Fort Collins, Colorado before noon. He would be home to have supper with his parents that evening. His usual co-pilot was out with a bug so he would make this flight solo. He started the engines and while waiting for them to warm up, checked his log book. He noted that he was starting his 2000th hour of flight time. He started his take-off roll at 5:45 and was soon up to his assigned altitude of 8000 feet. He then set the auto route and landing control for the Fort Collins signal. And relaxed with a cup of coffee. He crossed the Missouri river just south of Omaha and could see old US80 stretching away to the west. He would essentially follow this route all the way into Colorado before locking on to the Fort Collins landing signal. He took manual control of the plane before landing in Grand

Island and was soon seated at the terminal café' having breakfast. After taking off from Grand Island Chris climbed to his altitude and locked in the auto system again. As he turned west he
noticed a faint red glow in the western sky. It almost looked like
a pre-dawn sky but it was in the wrong direction and several
hours late. It quickly became more pronounced in color then
turned into a fiery ball as bright as the sun. Before he could blink
or turn his eyes away he was blind. His eyes were streaming
tears and no amount of wiping or blotting improved his vision.
He hit the button for a voice check and the soothing female voice
assured him that he was on the beam for both altitude and compass bearing. Letting the aircraft fly itself he tried to rationally
assess his situation. He knew the system was capable of taking
him to Fort Collins and landing with no input from him. He had
proven it a number of times but always with his hands and feet
hovering over the controls and his eyes looking outside the cabin. He wanted time to consider his options so he throttled the
engines back until the system cabin voice advisor told him his
speed was now 160 MPH. The Fort Collins control voice also
advised him of his new speed and ETA. The breakfast coffee
began to remind him he had neglected to use the café' restroom
after breakfast. Leaving the controls was always risky but it was
something he had done several times in the past and besides he
couldn't fly the airplane anyway. Being careful not to touch the
controls he eased out of his seat. The cabin was small enough
that he had no trouble feeling his way to the little cubby which
held the chemical toilet. After he finished he groped his way
back to his seat, and buckled in. As the plane droned on Chris
resigned himself to let the system do what it was designed for.
He had scanned all the channels commonly used by aircraft and
found no activity anywhere. The voice function on his watch
told him it was just past 10:00 AM which gave him another hour
of flight time before landing. Chris closed his burning eyes and
leaned back in his seat. He would not have thought it possible
but he actually went to sleep. He dozed fitfully and was jolted
awake when the engine throttled back and the plane banked in a
course adjustment. He immediately got on the radio and called

the Fort Collins tower. There was no response even when he had called every possible channel. The auto landing system voice informed him that his heading, altitude and speed were correct. He could do nothing except wait and hope the system worked. He tensed when the landing gear and flaps were lowered and when the plane flared out over the end of the runway. The actual touchdown was as smooth as any he had ever made manually. The plane slowed and gently braked as it turned off the runway. He waited for taxi instructions from the tower and when none were received he simply braked to a stop and waited again. After perhaps ten minutes Chris locked the brakes and shut down the engines. He was sure it would not be very long before someone came out to move him out of the middle of the taxi ramp. Opening his side window Chris became aware of one thing, the silence. There was none of the noise usually associated with a busy airport. There were no vehicles moving about and no aircraft engines turning over. He resorted to shouting out of his window and got no response. Something was very wrong and he had no idea what it could be. He settled back in his seat to wait, surely someone would come to investigate the plane parked where it should not be. While waiting he remembered the first aid kit. He knew it contained a small bottle of eye drops which perhaps would provide some relief for his burning eyes. He removed the kit from the case attached to the cockpit bulkhead. He groped in the kit until he located the eye drops and put a couple of drops in each eye. They provided almost instant relief from the burning and he actually relaxed somewhat. Taking stock of his situation Chris knew he had ample food and water for at least ten days. He also had the chemical toilet and it was probably good for a month before needing to be cleaned and recharged. He didn't want to consider the consequences if he was still blind after two weeks if no help came. He also could not comprehend why the airport seemed to be empty of people. Chris dozed again and when he awoke he was cold. The breeze coming in the window was chilly so he closed the window and at the same time realized that he was hungry. He felt his way back to the tiny galley and found one of the sack lunches which were always put aboard by his ground crew. Sitting back in the passenger/cargo cabin, he discovered he had a ham sandwich, apple slices and oatmeal raisin cookies. After he finished eating he pushed the voice function on his watch and discovered it was 11:30 p.m. He made a cool compress with a washcloth from the galley, reclined his seat and was soon asleep again. He woke disoriented then realized where he was. He drank the rest of the water from yesterday's bottle and made use of the toilet. He took two high protein bars from the galley and returned to the pilot's seat. His watch kept him current with the time and by afternoon of the second day he began to feel he could sense light. On the morning of the third day he became aware of what seemed to be a bright light out the front of the plane. He continued to use the eye drops plus the cold compresses and his eyes were feeling much better. The fourth day was a milestone. He awoke to find he could see some of the plane's interior. It was dim and very blurry but he could see. Returning to his seat in the cockpit he realized that what he had thought was bright light yesterday was actual the sun reflecting off a mirrored window of the terminal. Trying to contain his excitement he put on a pair of very dark sunglasses and settled in to wait for his eyesight to improve. Chris spent the day trying not to strain his slowly improving eyesight. It was a difficult task as he was desperate to get out of the plane and explore the airport. He didn't sleep well that night but on the morning of the fifth day he was able to make out details around him. His distance vision was still blurry but he thought if he was careful of the bright light he should be able to function outside of the plane. He washed up, shaved for the first time since leaving home and put on a set of clean clothing. He started the engines and taxied to the building where his cargo was supposed to be unloaded. When he stepped down from the plane the odor hit him like a physical blow. He knew at once it was the smell of death. As he looked around he became aware of at least a half dozen bodies lying in various poses which appeared as if the people had simply died in mid-stride. He walked to the terminal building passing more bodies along the way. He opened the door to a horrific smell. He could see people slumped over desks, in chairs about the room and others who appeared to have died on their feet and lay where they fell. Chris backed out, closed the door and stood pondering what his next move should be. He finally started looking in vehicles until he found one with the keys and a full fuel tank. He would drive into town and check the situation there. When he arrived at the security gate he found a scene of destruction. Both the in and out gates were completely blocked by a mass of vehicles. Many were crumpled from collisions while others looked as if they had been parked and abandoned. He parked the truck then got out and walked through the jumble. He soon saw that even the cars which looked abandoned contained bodies. Chris returned the truck to where it had been parked and left it. He was out of food on the plane except for snacks, so he forced himself to endure the smell and entered the airport restaurant. In the kitchen cooler he found vacuum sealed packages of roast beef, turkey and ham. He took a package of each plus cheese and a loaf of bread. He also found individual packets of mayo and mustard. He knew his eyes were not yet healed enough to fly so he returned to his plane to resume waiting. On the morning of the sixth day he decided to fill his fuel tanks. He didn't really need it for the trip home but felt it couldn't hurt to have a full tanks. He found a truck carrying the correct fuel and drove it to his plane where he topped off his tanks then returned the truck to its parking spot. Chris fired up his engines and taxied to a spot far enough from the terminal to escape the smell of the bodies. He had picked up a Denver newspaper in the terminal and read it thoroughly without finding anything pointing to an impending catastrophe.

Chris ate his sandwich that evening without savoring it. It was just so much fuel to keep his body going. He made a second sandwich for his noon meal the next day as he suspected he would be in the air at that time. The next morning, which he noted as April 13, he waited until the sun was well up so it wouldn't be directly in his eyes while flying. He performed his usual thorough preflight, started the engines and took off. After he was in the air he headed due north and within twenty minutes he was circling low over Cheyenne. There were tangles of crashed cars all over the city and a number of homes and downtown businesses which had burned. He didn't see a single living person anywhere. He turned east, increased his speed and followed the highway. Here and there he saw cars in the ditch and others which were stopped on the roadway. Nowhere did he see any sign of human life. It took him over four hours to cross Nebraska rather than the usual two at cruising speed. He circled every hamlet, town, and city across the state without seeing any sign of life. When he crossed the Missouri river at Omaha he quit searching and upped his speed to 375 MPH. He was at his home field at Dallas Center in less than an hour. He landed, taxied to his hangar and using the remote open the doors, drove inside and parked the plane. From his seat in the plane Chris could see three bodies on the floor of the hangar. He suspected he would find more when he searched the office and storerooms. Chris closed the doors and went directly to his truck. His immediate goal was to get to his parents' home just west of Dallas Center. He had no real expectation of finding them alive but he would maintain the hope until he knew for certain they were not. There had been an accident at the plant exit gate and it was blocked by the wreckage. He drove over the lane divider and went out through the entrance. The small town streets were relatively clear and he made good time. He pulled into the parking area at the house and could see both of their vehicles in the garage.

As soon as Chris stepped out of the truck the now familiar smell washed over him. He entered the house and all seemed normal and neat as his mother always maintained it. Stepping to the patio door he saw their bodies sitting side by side. They were seated at the little table where they often had breakfast and their morning coffee. He stepped outside where he could better observe that their hands were almost touching. It was as if they had been holding hands when the end came. It was a habit they had continued over the years. When Chris was a teenager it had been an embarrassment to him, but as he matured it had become an endearing quality that he hoped to attain one day. Returning inside the house he went to the linen closed and picked out two of the summer weight bedspreads his mother had made and of which she was very proud. He returned to the patio and fighting to overcome the terrible odor he managed to get both bodies out of the chairs and wrapped in the bedspreads. He fastened them in place with large safety pins from a kitchen drawer. Chris returned to his truck and made the thirty minute drive to his own home. Everything was as he had left it a week ago. He had always enjoyed his home but tonight it seemed like an empty shell. He turned on all of the lights and put on the music he always played when his parents visited. He took a long shower and thought about supper but decided he just didn't feel like eating. After it was dark he went out to the deck and sat watching the stars. After some time, he found himself weeping as he thought of how much he was going to miss them. When the tears finally stopped he tried to assess his situation. He had not seen a living person in the past week but it just didn't seem possible that he was the only person left alive. He was puzzled by the way it had happened. There had been no dramatic event. It appeared as if everyone had just stopped being alive and apparently at the same time.

Chris finally went to bed and spent a very restless night. He had much to do the next day and was up with the sun. He was on the road soon after. He drove to Perry which was a mess with cars and bodies everywhere. He didn't try to drive through town but went directly to a mortuary on the west side of the business district. He picked out two caskets and using the mortuary forklift, loaded them into his truck. He started to write an IOU for the caskets but decided it would be a waste of time. Chris drove directly to the house of his parents. Using his father's tractor, which was equipped with a backhoe, and some heavy nylon straps he moved the caskets to the patio. He managed to get the bodies into the caskets and the caskets into the back yard. Using the backhoe Chris began to excavate the grave. He wanted it wide enough to hold the caskets side by side. They had never been far apart in their life together and Chris wanted them to be close in their final rest. Again using the tractor and nylon straps he lowered the caskets into the grave and immediately began filling the hole. He began crying as the first bucket of dirt fell on the caskets and continued until they were completely covered. The excess dirt he left where it was. He thought that later he might plant flowers on the little mound of soil. His mother would have liked that idea. Chris went back into the house and removed everything which might spoil from the refrigerator. He dumped it all in the compost pile and turned it into the pile with the fork which hung nearby. Chris drove back to the airstrip and opened the hangar doors and looked at the bodies lying inside. He disliked the idea of not giving them a proper burial but he also realized there were just too many bodies for one man to deal with. He finally came to a decision and walked to the construction area where the new plant addition was being built. He found a big bucket loader and drove it back to the hangar. Chris found three more bodies in the office and two in the parts room. Using pieces of rope he dragged those bodies out into the open hangar then using a shovel and a piece of lightweight plastic he managed to get all of the bodies into the bucket of the loader. He then drove the loader outside and up on a little knoll behind the hanger. Dropping the bodies from the bucket he then scooped out a shallow depression and gently as possible pushed the bodies into the grave. After covering the bodies he sat and pondered the situation. It seemed a callous way to treat the remains because he had known every one of them and yet it was about the best he could do for them.

It was now late afternoon so he got in his truck and drove home. He had taken chicken out of the freezer that morning so he turned on the outside grill and cooked it. Normally he enjoyed grilled chicken by tonight it tasted like so much blah.

The next morning which was April 15, Chris sat and wondered what his next course of action should be and came to the conclusion that he should try to find other survivors before making any plans for the future. He drove back to Dallas Center and in the hangar he removed a large US map from the wall and taped it to the drafting table. Reading the map scale he then made a compass from a strip of paper, a map tack and a pencil. Using Dallas Center as the center he then drew a circle of 800 miles diameter and divided it into eight equal segments. He then made a list of the major population centers in each segment. He was still not convinced that there were no people left besides himself and he intended to make a thorough airborne search of the area circled on his map. The 400 mile radius of each segment insured he would have ample fuel each day. His plane had less that fifteen hours of flight time since the last major inspection so he had no concerns for the reliability of the aircraft. Driving a loaded fuel truck into the hangar was absolutely forbidden but Chris did so anyway. He fueled the plane, returned the truck outside then returned to the hangar and did his preflight inspection of the plane. After finishing that task Chris drove home, prepared his supper and after eating he packed a bag of clothing and toiletries for several days. He was in bed early and up again with the sun. His breakfast was toaster waffles and eggs after which he loaded a small cooler with vacuum packed meat, cheese and bread.

He was at the airport by 6:30 AM. He put his bag in the office, made a sandwich and put the rest of the food in the office refrigerator. He opened the doors, started the engines and taxied out into the sunshine. His takeoff was uneventful and his heading was just a little east of due south. He would search what he thought of the south-southeast sector today and work his way one sector to the left each day he flew. If weather permitted he planned to fly for four days then take two days off before resuming the search. He was in the air more than seven and a half hours the first day and saw no sign of a living person. Once he saw movement on the ground and turned back for a second look. He dropped down less than two hundred feet only to find a half dozen vultures tearing at a corpse in a farm field. After landing at his home field Chris refueled the plane then parked it in the hangar. He then drove over to the manufacturing building expecting to find it a house of death. Instead he was puzzled to find very few bodies in the plant. Those he did see were dressed in coveralls of the maintenance crew or the uniform of the security staff. It was some time before the reason came to him. Last week had been spring vacation for the local schools. In the tradition started by his great-grandfather, Dallon, the plant was closed to production that week. It was a bonus paid vacation so the parents could vacation with their children. It was a tradition which went a long way in boosting employee loyalty. Chris returned to the hangar office where he made a sandwich and put a pot of coffee on to brew. While eating, he absently picked up the video remote and turned it on to a Des Moines channel. When the screen lit up blank he turned it to two other channels before remembering there was no television, perhaps forever.

Chris was up early and in the air shortly after dawn. He was discouraged by his lack of success the day before but was determined to complete his search. Just before noon he was south of Indianapolis, making a turn to the west when he saw a moving vehicle. He very nearly missed it because he was banking into the turn but just as it passed out of sight beneath his wing he caught a glint of sunlight reflecting off of the windshield. He turned sharply and lined up over the freeway behind what appeared to be a one ton truck towing what appeared to be about a twelve foot trailer. The truck had a crew cab but Chris could not see how many people were inside. He passed low over the truck and rocked his wings as he pulled away. He crossed over to the southbound lanes and flew about two miles checking for wires and overpasses. The road seemed clear so he made a sharp turn and landed on the roadway. As the truck approached he locked the brakes but left the engines turning over. The truck pulled even with the plane then stopped after which three men got out and walked across the median. Chris got out of the plane and was instantly glad he was wearing the little .22 Colt pistol. All three of the men were dirty and unshaven plus they were also quite intoxicated. One of them was carrying a liquor bottle. As the men neared where Chris was waiting he could see a strong resemblance between them as if perhaps they were brothers. The one with the bottle was the first to speak, it was a simple "howdy stranger." Chris introduced himself and for some reason told them he was from St. Paul, Minnesota. He didn't know why but he didn't want them to know where he lived. The men introduced themselves as Pete, Joe and Sandy. The one named Pete seemed to be the leader and he had been eyeing the holster holding the Colt. He finally said "I see you are packing a gun, are you law?"

Chris told him no that he was just passing through. Pete added that they also were just passing through. He then asked "where is everybody?" Chris replied that everyone he had seen for two weeks was dead. That statement seemed to strike them dumb. The story finally came out that they were Kentucky coal miners. The three of them owned their own small mine. They had been deep in the mine finishing a twelve hour shift when a cave-in had occurred between them and the mine entrance. They had ample air but no food and very little water. Fortunately they had ample calcium carbide to fuel their old fashioned miner's lamps. The only way out was to dig so they dug. It took them seventy two hours to open a space large enough to crawl through and they finally reached the surface. Sandy then added that they were mighty thirsty when they made their way to open air and that they had been drinking nonstop since then. One of them had returned to the truck for another bottle which they passed around. Chris declined, explaining that he couldn't fly after drinking. Pete winked at Chris and said, "I can't drive after drinking so I just drink while I am driving." The three of them went on to say they hadn't been just traveling but had been collecting along the way. Pete winked again and told Chris he had an honest face and even though he had a gun they could trust him. He went on to say the truck was full of money and jewelry and there was more in the trailer. They were heading for Reno and Las Vegas. If the casinos were open they were going to have the biggest party ever. If the casinos were closed they were going on down to Mexico, buy a hacienda and retire. Chris wished them a happy trip, shook hands all around then got back in the plane as they staggered back to their truck. He waited until they had driven away then turned the plane around and took off. He did no more searching that day but flew directly to Dallas Center and put the plane in the hangar. He sat in the plane and wanted to weep. The only people he had found alive were as lost as stray puppies. He counted them as already dead and they surely would not last another year. Chris slept on the cot in the office that night and was in the air again at first light on the 18th. He spent an hour circling Chicago where the downtown area looked like a war zone. He concluded that it must have been rush hour when the devastation hit. There were piles of cars and countless bodies everywhere. The next day was more of the same. There were hundreds of wrecked vehicles and thousands of bodies but no sign of life anywhere. He began to accept the hard truth that there just wasn't anyone else left alive. He flew back to Dallas Center then drove home. He spent two days doing very little except to stare out the window and try to plot his future. In reality he could see no future. He knew he could feed and shelter himself, but he continued to return to the question of "what else."

Returning to the air Chris continued his search with hope but little expectation of success. On the third day he found his "friends" from Kentucky. Their truck was on its side in the median of US 70 west of Topeka, Kansas. There were two bodies on the ground and a third one hanging halfway out the open passenger side door. Chris knew it was them from the rental company logo on the side of the truck body. The trailer had been ripped open and he could see paper money blowing away on a strong breeze. When Chris completed his search on the fourth day he parked the plane with no expectation of ever flying it again.

The next morning Chris walked around the immediate property and concluded that he needed to do a lot of trimming and pruning. The house yard looked good. It had been landscaped with a few shrubs and was covered in river rock so there was no grass to tend. He walked out to the garden plot and decided that for the first time since moving onto the place he would plant a garden. It was late to be planting but if he selected early maturing seed he should have a vegetable crop by late autumn. That afternoon he drove to the nursery on the west side of Perry and picked out far more seeds that he had room to plant. He also picked up two varieties of onion sets and a bin of seed potatoes. When he arrived home he checked the tractor battery to insure it was fully charged and attached the tiller. When that was completed he brought two pails and began cutting up the seed potatoes.

By noon the next day Chris had the garden tilled, disked and ready for planting. Using a long cord as a marker to keep his rows straight, he began by planting the onions and potatoes.

He was almost frantic with the need to finish the planting and worked until it was too dark to see the rows. The next day was a repeat of the previous one but he finished the planting by late afternoon. As he walked to the control box to turn on the sprinklers a few drops of rain began to fall. He took the rain as a good omen and hoped it didn't rain enough to wash out the seeds he had just planted. It was still raining gently when he went to bed. He awoke once in the middle of the night and was aware the rain had stopped. The next morning the rain gauge held just under a quarter of an inch which seemed to him to be about the right amount. It promised to be a warm day which would also aid in the start of the germination process.

Chris decided he would stock up immediately on canned and frozen food. By this time there was no fresh milk available so he put dried powdered milk at the top of his "shopping" list. He still harbored a pang of guilt at the thought of just taking things without payment but there was no one to pay and he had to survive. When he arrived in town he changed his mind and instead of a grocery store he drove to the largest appliance store which happened to be on the west side of town. He drove to the back of the store and found a delivery truck already backed up to the loading dock. There were two bodies lying beside the truck. Except for the odor, Chris had become immune to reacting to human bodies. He got in the truck, saw it was full of fuel and started it. He then entered through the back door and searched until he found the freezer section. He then found the two largest home freezers in the store and went searching for a fork lift with which to move them. It was an easy task to load the freezers in the truck and strap them in place. He started to return the lift to the charging grid but realized he would need it at home so he parked it in the truck with the freezers. The fork lift battery was not compatible with the charging system he had at home but the voltage was the same so he could simply change batteries. He had a small dock on the side of his shop so when he reached home he soon had the freezers placed in a corner of the shop, plugged in and running. He decided he might have later use for the fork lift and parked it where it would be easy to work on when he changed the battery. Chris drove the truck back to town, retrieved his own and drove to the grocery store. He filled three carts with an assortment of canned foods. He then loaded four more with dry foods including salt, sugar, flour and corn-meal. He found empty boxes and found the frozen foods area. First he boxed all of the frozen meat and fish products he could find then as an after- thought added several containers of various flavors of ice cream. As he was pushing the last cart to the door the lights dimmed then went out. Chris was actually surprised the power had lasted this long and was again thankful for his solar array at home. He silently thanked his grandfather again.

Chris hurried home and wasted no time getting the frozen goods into the two new freezers plus the big walk-in freezer in the house. The canned and dry foods went into the big pantry in the house and he felt rather pleased with the results of his day of labor.

After his supper that evening Chris walked out the driveway all the way to the road. He thought instead of sitting idle all summer perhaps he would plant some crops. He had no farm machines but knew he could find all of the machinery he would need at neighbors such as Charlie Simpson and the Browns who had lived in the next place west from his own. Then he asked himself what he would do with a crop if he managed to harvest one. He had no place to store grain and no livestock to feed. It didn't make sense to plant a crop and then leave it in the field to rot. His crop land had been rented by Brad Brown who had rotated alfalfa, red clover and timothy over the acreage. He con-cluded that he needed an alternate plan for how he would spend his time. He returned to the house and sat out on the deck as the evening turned to dusk and then to full dark. As he sat in the dark he listened to the night birds talking and the soft chirping of the day birds settling in for the night. He also began to hear voices. He knew the voices were only in his mind but they were very real. He could hear the gruff bark of his grandfather when events were not going exactly as he thought they should. There was also the soft murmur of his parents as they sat on their own deck, holding hands and discussing the day's happenings. Above them all there was the laughing voice of the green eyed, black haired young woman who held his heart captive. Carol Janine McGinnis was her name. Black Irish was how his grandfather had referred to her. Chris had been ready to propose marriage when she excitedly had announced that she had been offered a job and had signed a contract for a position as doctor/surgeon in a hospital in southern Mexico. The contract had been for four years and she had been gone now for two. Their relationship had suffered from the extended separation and he was no longer sure how he felt about her. In the meantime he had never dated anyone else and had no desire to do so. His life had been on hold while he tried to decide his future. Now it appeared there might not be a future and he wondered if she had survived. Probably not he decided.

Chapter 4 November 20, 2113

HOME

When Chris awoke on November 20 the sun was shining and it was obviously warmer. He could see water dripping from the eaves and the sharp edges of the snow banks were becoming softer and rounded. He decided he would take the snow machine, he never knew whether to call it a snow-mobile or snow cat so he settled for machine, and go check on Charlie's horses. As he thought about it he decided they were no longer Charlie's horses. If he was going to feed them and worry about them, and he was sure, was going to need to start shoveling their manure from the barn they were now his horses. When he arrived at the farm all three horses were outside basking in the sun. As soon as Chris entered the barn the horses crowded in and each went to its respective stall. The two older horses were whickering and nodding their heads as if in greeting. Even the third horse seemed less skittish and waited patiently while Chris added more hay and grain to the mangers and feed boxes. After tending to the horses Chris put on his snowshoes, strapped the Marlin over his shoulder and set out to see if he could locate the cattle which had left tracks in the barnyard. He headed down the lane which led from the barnyard back to the edge of the timber. Passing through a narrow belt of trees he emerged into a pasture which was composed of open areas with here and there small groves of trees. It was snow covered but he could see where the cattle had pawed down to the tall grass underneath. The pasture probably contained 80 acres and was bisected by a small creek which ran downhill towards the river. Off in one corner stood a herd of perhaps 18 or 20 cattle. They were primarily Holstein with 3 or 4 Herefords and another few which were obviously a mix of the two. As Chris approached a young bull of mixed breed moved out of the herd to challenge him. The animal began to paw the snow and make short charges. Chris stopped at a discreet distance to let the animals settle down and the bull returned to the herd, his duty completed. Chris returned to the barnyard where he closed one gate, which limited the horses to the barnyard and opened another which would allow the cattle to enter a small feed yard containing a hay bunker. He then carried out 3 bales of hay which he opened and put in the bunker. If he could re-domesticate the cattle he might have a source for milk and beef in the future. Chris told himself that he was beginning to think like a farmer and considering that thought realized there didn't appear to be any alternative if he was going to survive.

Chris returned home and while stoking the fire in the smoke-house decided to try one of the hams which had been curing. He carried the ham to the house where he sliced off a thick slab. He cooked the ham on the outside grill and pronounced it good. He decided to continue the smoking process for two more weeks to insure that it was completely cured. As long as the weather stayed cold he could leave the meat hanging there. When Chris called the dogs for their evening meal he noticed that Lady was limping badly and seemed to be in pain. When Chris sat in a deck chair she limped over and laid her great head in his lap. Her casual response to the head and neck stroking was absent. It was her habit to put forth a low growling, almost like a cat's purring, when she was petted and stroked. Chris finally got some sausage and after it was thawed he put four pain relieving tablets in it and put it in her food bowl. He had no idea if it would help but it was worth a try. He resolved that tomorrow he was going to finish the 2106 journal. Before going to bed Chris checked to see that Lady was in her kennel. She was stretched out on her bed and when he reached in to pat her head she thumped her tail weakly and licked his hand.

Next morning was another clear, sunny day. Chris checked on Lady and found she wasn't able to stand. He carried food and water to her but she only managed to drink a little water and showed no interest in the food. After spending some time just talking to her Chris returned inside and after eating his own breakfast opened the journal and began reading.

After a breakfast of dry cereal in reconstituted milk and topped with strawberries from the freezer Chris was ready for the day. He started a load of laundry then went outside to check the garden. He knew it was too soon to see new sprouts but he had to look anyway. He turned on the sprinklers and set the timer to deliver a half inch of water. He then got out the yard tools and spent the morning trimming and pruning. After lunch he hitched the ATV to a trailer and hauled all of the trimmings out to a corner of the field that he used for burning brush. He used the tiller to maintain a ring of bare dirt around the burn area to limit the danger of a grass fire. It would be weeks before the brush was dry enough to burn so there was no hurry to get the tiller out. He also cut a few small trees, which were beginning to obstruct his view out over the river bottom, and added to the burn pile.

That evening he became aware that the small brown birthmark on his left hip had begun to itch. The brown spot was only half the size of a playing card and had never been a problem. He rubbed it a few times then got a tube of ointment and rubbed it into the spot. It seemed to alleviate the itch but it never did completely stop it. This was a problem which would continue until the middle of August when it completely stopped. He would discover over the coming years that the itch would recur every year from late April to mid-August. He just learned to live with it.

May passed in a blur. Chris discovered that tending to a one acre garden amounted to very nearly a full time job. Between weeding and watering he spent nearly half of every day with the garden. By early June he was beginning to have radishes, lettuce and green onions and the other vegetable plants were thriving.

In July Chris began to have thoughts about the next year. For some reason he felt the urge to travel and thought only of going west. He thought of driving or flying but came to the conclusion that both were too risky and finding fuel might become a major handicap. That left only the option of walking and the west was a vast area in which to go for a walk. In August the garden came to fruition and Chris was nearly overwhelmed with the amount of produce he had to deal with. He scoured the deserted stores for freezer containers and by the end of the month he estimated that he had at least a two year supply of frozen vegetables. He even went back to the appliance store and brought home two more upright freezers.

With his food supply taken care of for the foreseeable future Chris began his preparations for the coming summer. He walked everywhere he went. He was aware that the coming winter would put an end to the walking and that he would have to start again in the early spring to be prepared for the summer. After a month of walking everyday he found he could easily cover thirty miles a day. If he pushed he thought that forty miles would not be out of reach. He found a child's coaster wagon at a store in Perry. He took the wagon to his shop where he lengthened the handle and built a box to increase the carrying capacity. The wagon went everywhere with him. He tried several pairs of boots but in the end he decided that old fashioned tennis shoes would best suit his purpose. They were available everywhere and were light enough that carrying an extra pair was no burden. He found a light weight backpack with large pockets with a number of straps and rings for attaching items. He also picked up a pair of two quart canteens and a large supply of water purification tablets. A sleeping bag, small tent and grill were the last items put into the wagon and he went home feeling prepared for the trek next summer. 2106 ended with a series of snow storms which followed each other in rapid succession and extended into the new year.

Chapter 5 --- 2113

HOME

Chris went out to feed the dogs before having his own break-fast. He discovered that Lady had died during the night. He was overwhelmed with a sense of grief and loneliness which he had not felt since he had buried his parents. The great dog had been his constant companion and guardian for more than six and a half years and he felt he would never find another one which would compare to her. In a little clearing behind the barn was a twelve by sixteen slab of concrete which had been poured when the other buildings were erected. It had been poured at the insistence of Grandpa John who had laughed and told Chris he could call it the "God knows what" building until he decided on a use for it. By lifting the hinged roof of the dog kennel Chris was able to get the body out and onto the sled. He shoveled the snow clear of the concrete slab then began gathering wood. He had four cords of dry wood for his fireplace which hadn't see a fire for several years. He hauled a cord of firewood to the slab then gathered every loose scrap of wood he could find around the shop, barn and other building. He placed Lady's body in the center of the slab then covered her with the wood and set it ablaze. Chris kept the fire burning for over two days thinking about the past and making plans for the future. He decided that in the coming summer of 2114 he was going to walk to Seattle. It was too far to go and come back in the same season so if he found no people on the way or in Seattle he would spend the winter there then return home in 2115 and travel no more. He would become a full time farmer. He had a team of horses, access to a pair of tractors, if he could get them running, and a small herd of cattle. He thought he could trap and re-domesticate some of the feral hogs and perhaps some of the chickens which were still hanging on at some of the abandoned farms. He made a trip to check on the horses and cattle at his "other place" as he had begun to think of Charlie's farm. The horses, as usual, seemed happy to see him. Even the third one nosed his way in to get his neck patted and scratched. Chris considered the fact that he didn't know what Charlie had called the animal and decided on the spot that he would call him Junior. He also decided to return to the farm store and look for a collar and harness for the horse. On his way home Chris came across a flock of wild turkeys beside the road. The birds didn't flee when he got off the snow machine so he sat down with the 20 gauge shotgun he had brought in hopes of spotting a pheasant. At a range of less than fifty feet it was a simple head shot and Chris was on his way home where he plucked and cleaned the bird and hung it outside to cool until bedtime.

Next morning Chris mixed up cornbread stuffing, packed the bird and put in on the spit of the outdoor grill. He then spent some time with the two dogs before letting them out of the yard for a run. They were gone for a long time and twice Christ thought he heard them barking. When they finally returned and came up on the deck Chris could see blood on both of them. When Chris went out to check them he discovered bite and claw marks on both of them. His first thought was "another grizzly" but then decided there would be more serious injuries from a grizzly. He washed the wounds and then applied a generous amount of anti-bacterial ointment from his medicine cabinet. Chris feasted on turkey with instant mashed potatoes and seven year old cranberry sauce which didn't seem to have suffered much from spending at least seven years in the can.

As usual he went to sleep that night with a serenade from the wolf pack in his ears. When he was on the deck cleaning the grill the next morning he began hearing a new, strange sound. He finally looked down the driveway and was amazed to see a cougar walking toward the house. The animal was limping on its left front leg and swinging its head from side to side in a strange manner. The cat commenced pacing up and down the yard fence while it cried out and continued to swing its head from side to side. Chris didn't relish the thought of killing the big cat but he couldn't risk having the sick or wounded animal prowling about the house area. He fetched the Marlin from the house and with two shots dispatched the cougar. On examining the cat he discovered that the shoulders and hindquarters had several bite marks and the left eye had been blinded. Apparently the dogs had tangled with the cat yesterday and had given at least as well as they had gotten. He dragged the body to where he had dumped the grizzly and the coyotes, vultures and now wolves would soon dispose of it.

After having a turkey sandwich, at noon, Chris went out to the slab where he had burned Lady's body. Using a coarse screen he sifted the ashes and found only two teeth and a few bone fragments. He put the teeth and fragments in an aluminum cylinder and come spring he planned to bury the cylinder and mark the spot. That afternoon Chris sat down with his maps to determine what route to follow on his way to Seattle the following summer. Since he had been over the route before he decided to follow I-80 to Cheyenne, go north from Cheyenne to Billings and then stay on I-90 the rest of the way to Seattle.

After supper that evening Chris bundled up and sat out on the deck for a couple of hours. When he first went out it was clear and the stars were brilliant in the sky. There was even a trace of the Aurora Borealis flashing pale colors from the north. At about 7:30 the clouds rolled in and it began to snow. Chris called it a day and was in bed by nine pm. Before falling asleep he vowed to return to the journals in the morning.

Chapter 6 --- 2107

JOURNAL

2107 came in as 2106 had gone out, with one snow storm following another. He spent three weeks virtually snowbound but reasoned that he didn't have a need to go anywhere even if the snow hadn't been so deep. Chris decided that he was going to go across North Dakota and if the weather held and he had enough time he would go to Billings and then turn south to return home. By the end of January it had turned unseasonably warm and much of the snow melted. When the roads were clear he started walking. Pulling the wagon slowed him down and he found that twenty miles per day was about all he could expect to travel. To compare the difference he walked two days without the wagon and found he could travel thirty-five miles in the same amount of time. Wavering between the added comfort of the tent and the increased miles he could cover without it Chris decided he would start out with the wagon and make the final decision later. Searching through a store in Perry Chris found a supply of high energy protein bars. He carried two cases home and though he didn't realize it at the time those bars would become his standard mid-day fare when he was on the road. He had always worn long trousers year-round but wondered whether shorts might not be more comfortable in the summer heat. Consequently he went to several stores and eventually had a dozen pairs of shorts. They were different styles and colors but essentially similar.

March alternated between weather which was raw and cold or balmy and spring like. Chris carried a poncho and rain coat both of which he used often but he wore the shorts every day. By March 25th his arms and legs were as brown as mid-summer and his feet were toughened by the daily pounding. He felt ready to start the trip but was still leery of the weather and he wanted to start this trip on the one year anniversary of the beginning of his odyssey which would be April 7.

His planned route was to take Iowa 141 to Sloan, get on US 29 there and follow 29 to Fargo where he would change to US 94. US 94 would take him all the way to Billings.

Chris spent April 5th and 6th cleaning house, doing laundry and removing everything from the refrigerator which might spoil. On the morning of the 7th it was lightly raining but Chris donned his rain coat and was on the road by 6 am. The rain was coming from the west and thus was directly in his face. Chris made it only as far as Bagley that first day. He found shelter at a farm just east of town. The house still smelled of the two bodies he found in the kitchen. He carried a twin sized mattress from the house to the garage and made his bed in the back of a small truck parked there. It took him nine days to reach Sloan rather than the six or seven he had estimated. He was wet and cold most of the time but he did manage to find shelter every night. On the fifth night he went into a small service station/convenience store beside the road and discovered a small stove with a supply of coal and dry wood. He soon had a fire started and all of his damp clothing hung to dry. In a back room he found a small cot plus a second stove. In the grocery section he found a small canned ham. There were a few pans in the back room and he had his first hot meal since leaving home.

On the day after leaving Sloan the wheels literally came off of his wagon. They had started squeaking on the second day and he had been oiling them twice a day. One of the wheels was broken at the hub and another was about ready to do the same. As he thought about it he realized that he had pulled the wagon several hundred miles while he was in "training" in February and March and the wagon was never intended for that kind of use. He removed the lighter food items from the wagon and found room for them in his backpack. He left the wagon beside the road and realized he would need to start looking for shelter earlier in the day unless the weather was warm and dry so he could sleep outside. He stopped that night at Sergeant Bluff just south of Sioux City. He found a small motel just off the highway and had to resort to kicking in a door to gain access to a room. It must have been connected to a solar array which was still operating because the lights were working and there was hot water. He found the utility room and put his still damp clothing in the dryer. He also washed and dried everything he had worn so far. He decided he needed a day off after ten days of travel. He spent the morning looking through the stores in the area and found a new supply of energy bars which went into his pack. During the afternoon he cleaned and oiled the Marlin and the Colt pistol. Chris was in bed early and up early the next morning which he noted was April 19. He was past Sioux City by mid-morning and when the road came close enough to observe it the Missouri River was an awesome sight. It was in full flood and the low lying areas on the Nebraska side of the river were covered with water for as far as he could see. He was in South Dakota and the day had turned pleasantly warm. He was making good time and was hoping the weather stayed nice because he was sure he was going to sleep out that night. By late afternoon he had covered 36 miles according to the highway mile markers. He was debating whether to put his sleeping bag in the roadside grass or lay it out on the roadway to reduce the chance of a rattlesnake trying to join him in the bag. As he topped a low hill there was a sign announcing a highway rest area in two miles. As he approached the area he couldn't believe his luck. There were lights burning which meant a solar powered electric system and the possibility of hot water. The lobby was open but there were at least a dozen bodies scattered about. The sight of bodies no longer bothered Chris but the smell of death was still almost overpowering. He checked the offices behind the lobby and found at least one body in every one of them. Both employee restrooms were empty but the smell, while much less than the other rooms, had penetrated here as well. The public restrooms both contained several bodies and were not useable. There were several partial skeletons scattered about the grounds and Chris supposed the coyotes had scavenged the bodies perhaps with the help of vultures. He looked about and saw a medium sized motor home in the truck parking area. He walked out, tried the door and found it unlocked. Thankfully, all he could smell was year old stale air. He went inside where he found nothing but a year's accumulation of dust. Chris unrolled his sleeping bag on the made up bed. He found a small canned ham and a can of pork and beans in the kitchen cabinet and made his supper of those two items. He also found a can of apple pie filling which made a good dessert. He found a hydrant outside the office building which had pressure and after letting the water run for five minutes refilled his canteens and a large pitcher from the motor home. The propane stove still had gas pressure and he brewed a big pot of coffee in an old fashioned percolator. It was the first coffee he had made since leaving home. He filled a large insulated cup and took a folding chair outside. He sat beside the motor home and watched a full moon rising in the east while he pondered the past and wondered what the future might hold for him. Chris slept well and was walking again by 6:00 am the next morning. Over the next five days he averaged over forty miles per day. The weather remained mild although there were rain showers on the second and third days which slowed his pace but were not heavy enough to drive him from the road. He managed to find indoor shelter every night but thought that would not be the case when he turned west and headed out into the North Dakota prairie. Chris slowed his pace and began spending time investigating at least one little town every day. He discovered nothing he hadn't seen countless times in the past year. He did manage to find supplies of frozen foods and juices which improved his diet and saved the travel food in his pack. In the little settlement of Summit he had been forced to kill a large mixed breed dog which had forced him to climb into the back of a small truck parked on the street. The dog was thin with prominent ribs and hips. Chris had no doubt the dog saw him as prey and was determined to get into the truck to attack him. Chris spent a good half hour fending the dog off with a sturdy walking stick he had picked up in western Iowa. Chris finally took the 22 Colt and killed the dog with a shot to the head. He quickly returned to the highway and resumed his journey. On the first of May Chris entered North Dakota and two days later was on the outskirts of Fargo. He didn't spend any time exploring Fargo but got on US-94 and headed west. He began to limit himself to twenty to twenty-five miles per day which gave him time to explore more of the small towns and settlements along US-94. He had started carrying the Marlin 30-30 in his hand when entering these small towns. He was no longer going to risk being attacked by a former pet which now saw him as a possible meal. On May 6 Chris crested a small hill overlooking a narrow river valley. Crossing the highway in front of him was a herd of perhaps five hundred buffalo. There was nothing to do except wait for them to pass so Chris sat down to observe them. The herd milled about on the roadway and in the median until three or four of the big bulls began to attack the fence on the south side of the highway. Using their horns and massive necks they pulled at the wire until it was loose from the posts or broken and on the ground. The animals walked through the opening and the rest of the herd followed. A few of them became tangled in the downed wire but all managed to get free and soon the herd was well south of the road and continuing their journey to some unknown destination. That night Chris stayed in a motel on the bank of a stream identified by a sign as the Sheyenne River. It was early when Chris stopped and on a whim he went next door to a sporting goods shop. He found a spinning rod and reel already set up with line plus he selected four minnow like lures and returned to the motel. The motel had built a small boardwalk which extended out over the river and Chris walked out to the end and began casting. It was as if the fish had been waiting for him. In a matter of a half dozen casts he had landed three fish. They were all Walleyes of perhaps two pounds each. He cleaned them there on the dock and went searching for a working stove. He found a propane range in the motel manager's living quarters plus cornmeal and flour in the cupboard. The fish were soon in the pan and Chris couldn't remember food he had enjoyed as much. He wrapped what was left over for his supper the next night.

It was raining the next morning and Chris chose to stay over another day. He had comfortable shelter and the river seemed to be full of fish waiting in line to grab a lure. It rained steadily for three days and Chris stayed in the motel where it was dry and warm. He was thankful for the solar powered electrical systems which were still operating. He found frozen chicken and strawberries in a nearby market plus canned peaches, beans and other staples. He reflected that he hadn't eaten this well at home and resolved to change that when he was home again. The fourth morning was sunny and clear and although Chris got a late start he made good time and covered over forty miles that day. Two days later he was about twenty miles east of Bismarck when he noticed that a frontage road along the highway was graveled rather than paved. Backtracking for a half mile he got off the highway and onto the frontage road. He thought the gravel might provide some relief from the pounding his feet took day after day from walking on concrete. After he had traveled seven or eight miles he became aware of what sounded like a large dog barking. The barking was mixed in with a chorus of yipping from a number of coyotes. As he approached a small ranch place with buildings set back fifty yards from the road he could see the coyotes, at least a dozen of them, circling a small shed near the house. As he moved up the road he could see a large dog standing in the open doorway. The coyotes were darting at the dog then jumping away. When the dog lunged at a coyote it stumbled half way out the door. When that happened one of the coyotes dashed into the shed and immediately came out again with something in its mouth. By that time Chris had the Marlin out and leveled. Through the four power scope sight Chris could see the coyote was carrying a puppy which was still moving. He immediately shot the coyote with the puppy in its mouth and in rapid succession shot two more. As the coyotes began to scatter he shot a fourth one as it slowed to get through an opening in a board fence. Chris held the rifle up and ready as he walked into the yard. After what the dog had just experienced he didn't know what the reaction would be to his presence. He scuffed his feet in the gravel to be sure the dog could hear his approach. He heard one loud bark and then the dog bounded, in reality staggered, out the door. Chris could see at once that the dog was a nursing mother. She was huge with a gray shaggy coat and even with his limited knowledge of dog breeds he was sure she was pure Irish Wolf-hound. As soon as she spotted Chris her demeanor changed and she began to wag her tail. She was extremely thin with her ribs protruding through her shaggy coat. Chris approached her with his hand extended. She sniffed the hand, then licked it and rubbed her head against his leg. She then turned and walked into the shed with Chris following. Inside he found a nest she had created from a stack of burlap grain bags, some of which were still piled in a corner. In the nest were two puppies whose eyes were not yet open. They had to be only a few days old. When they sensed the presence of the other dog they started to whimper and stir about. The big dog lay down and nosed the puppies which crawled around and began to nurse. Chris felt that given the condition of the mother there wouldn't be much milk for them. While the puppies nursed Chris went outside to check on the puppy which had been grabbed by the coyote. It was dead with obvious puncture wounds from the predator's teeth and a crushed rib cage. His first thought was food and water for the dog. He doubted whether she had seen either for some time. This was another place with solar power which meant there might be frozen meat in the freezer. He found the bones of at least two people scattered in the yard. There were two skulls so he assumed there were only two people unless there were others in the house. The house was not locked and he walked into a neat and tidy kitchen. He searched the house and found no more bodies. In the basement he found a chest freezer which contained numerous packages of both beef and pork. He selected two packages of ground beef and went back up to the kitchen. He put one package in the microwave to thaw and left the other in the sink drainer. When he turned on the kitchen faucet he heard a pump start up. For some time there was only air blowing from the tap but eventually there was a trickle of water and finally a steady stream. He let the water run for some time then found a two gallon pail in the entry-way and filled it. He carried the water out to the shed and put it down in front of the dog. She struggled to her feet and then drank until Chris was afraid she would burst. He assumed that she was probably as hungry as she was thirsty so he returned to the house to check on the ground beef. It was almost ready and two more minutes in the oven had it thawed and slightly warm. Chris found a mixing bowl in the kitchen cabinet and crumbled the meat into it. He didn't want to over feed the dog and make her ill so the small package of meat was all she would get tonight. Chris then searched the house and outbuildings for dog food and finding none he assumed the dog didn't belong on the place but had wandered in and found the shed open and convenient as a place to birth her puppies. Chris filled the water pail again then closed and securely latched the shed door. The water heater was still working so Chris had a long hot shower and slept between sheets that night. In the morning Chris availed himself of sausage patties, orange juice plus biscuits with butter all from the basement freezer. He had fed and watered the dog again and found he had a dilemma on his hands. If he went on his way the coyotes would surely be back for the puppies and the mother dog which he had started to think of as Lady would starve before she would leave the babies. He couldn't think of a way he could travel with all three animals so it was a choice of staying where he was or deserting the dogs. The summer was passing and he knew he had to get moving or else abandon his travel plans. He finally told himself he would stay for two weeks until Lady was in better physical shape and then decide what to do. In the machine shed he found a nearly new, small electric truck. The truck was plugged into a charging grid and the gauges indicated that it held a full charge. He remembered from old ads that this model would travel two hundred fifty miles on one charge. He locked the dogs in the shed again then after testing the brakes on the truck he set out for Bismarck. On the east side of town he found a farm supply store which wasn't locked. There were numerous bodies lying about but by now he simply ignored them and went about his business. He soon found the pet food section and even bags of food designated for nursing mothers. Grabbing a four wheeled flat cart Chris loaded three fifty pound bags and wheeled them out to the little truck. He also loaded two cases of canned dog food to provide variety. Chris returned to the house and put a pan of dry food in front of Lady. She first sniffed at it then finally began to eat. After his own supper that night Chris checked the home's entertainment system. During the evening he watched several videos. One which grabbed his attention was a short comedy featuring three inept characters called "The Three Stooges." They were named Curly, Larry and Moe. As soon as he heard the names he decided on the names of his newly acquired dogs. One of the puppies had a medium length wavy black coat. That one had to be Curly. The other pup was short haired with marking resembling a Harlequin Great Dane. He was left with the title of Moe. Curly, Lady and Moe had a nice ring to it even if the names were from a silly movie over one hundred fifty years old.

Chris had dragged the dead coyotes to the edge of a field beyond the buildings. When he did so the sky had been clear of any birds but now there were several vultures circling overhead and beginning to spiral down to the dead animals. He didn't know whether it was by sight or smell that they located a potential meal. Perhaps it was a combination of both. He took a shovel, dug a shallow hole and buried the puppy beside the barn.

The days passed and it became July. The puppies were walking albeit on legs which were still shaky. When Chris saw them sniffing around lady's food dish he went back to town and brought back a large bag of puppy food. He even set out bowls of canned milk which they seemed to relish. Chris had made up his mind to try to take the dogs home with him. His primary concern was transporting Curly and Moe. Lady was capable of walking the distance but the two puppies were not. He finally began to consider the little electric truck. If it would really travel two hundred fifty miles on a single charge, Chris felt he might be able to find enough charging stations to take them all the way home. Over the years the charging connectors had become standardized and a single type had been mandated by the federal government. Not wanting to transport the dogs in the open bed of the truck. Chris went into town in search of plywood. Instead he found a building supply store with an assortment of panels produced in the Dallas Center plant of his family. He also picked up a rotary saw and charger plus adhesive, screws and two small sliding windows. He searched for a commercially built canopy for the truck but found nothing which would fit. Returning to the ranch he set about constructing a cover for the truck. He had forgotten clear panels for front and back windows so he robbed two vehicles in the machine shop of their back windows. The windows were some type of thermoplastic which was easily cut with his carbide tipped saw blade. The cover was essentially a rectangular shaped box. The roof sloped up from front to back to cut wind resistance. When he finished it was a crude looking box but it was solid and bolted securely to the truck bed. The composite panels he used were of three different colors so it was a strange looking vehicle which he was prepared to put on the road. The construction had been a slow process as he was not particularly adept with tools but he was satisfied that it would hold together for the trip home. He fastened two five gallon water containers in a back corner and added a wooden box in which to carry food for the dogs. After a few tries Lady would jump in the truck on command. The puppies had to be lifted in but with their mother present soon settled down. He had tossed a number of burlap bags in and left it to Lady to arrange her bed. Two nights before, he had determined to leave, he left the dogs in the truck all night. He checked on them before going to bed himself and found all three asleep and apparently unconcerned about their new accommodations. It was August 17 when he set out. It was a cloudy and cool day for August which would make it less stressful for the dogs. He tried to hold his speed to 15 mph which would allow him to cover more than one hundred miles in less time than eight hours of walking. He planned to stop at mid-morning and afternoon plus at noon as well. It would give the dogs a chance to exercise and him to stretch his own legs. He didn't think Lady would go very far from the truck and the pups would not get far from their mother. Chris gave the dogs water at every stop but only fed them night and morning. Lady used the stops to relieve herself outside the truck but the puppies were not so fastidious. At every stop it seemed there was a puddle or pile of puppy droppings to clean up. In two days of this leisurely pace they arrived in Fargo. Chris located a charging station operating off of solar power. There was a major drawback however. The control panel of the charger demanded cash in advance before it would start dispensing electricity. It had been so long since he had needed cash for anything that Chris was momentarily stunned. He quickly recovered and simply walked into the convenience store and pried open the cash drawer. He took the required amount of bills fed the machine and was relieved to see the monitor indicate that his battery was being charged. Thinking about what had happened he returned to the store and removed all the cash from the till. He would be better prepared for the next charging station. Chris walked next door to a small motel where he kicked open three doors before he found a clean room. It seemed as if breaking and entering had become a way of life and he didn't give the act a second thought. He went back to the store, found a canned ham, some vegetables and ice cream. He ate it all without heating and even though it tasted of being in the can too long, was delicious. Chris had fed the dogs earlier but he gave each a treat of canned food when he went to check on the battery charger. Lady walked over to a small patch of grass and relieved herself. Both pups imitated her and he hoped it was a sign they were learning that the truck bed was not the place to go. Back at the motel Chris stripped the blanket and sheet from the second bed and dropped them in the corner. Lady immediately scratched them around and lay down with the puppies. Chris was awakened from a sound sleep by Lady's barking. It took him a moment to remember where he was. When he looked over she was standing at the window with her head up under the curtain. When he lifted the curtain and looked out there was a black bear with two cubs strolling through the parking lot. Chris continued to watch as the bears walked next door and approached his truck. The mother bear sniffed at the tailgate a couple of times and batted at it with a paw then walked on. Chris assumed she smelled the dog food but wasn't very hungry. Remembering that the door was held closed only by the safety chain Chris pulled the Marlin out of its scabbard and laid it on the floor next to his bed. The rest of the night was uneventful and Chris slept late the next morning. He was wakened by Lady's prodding nose. When he opened his eyes the dog began to whine and went to stand by the door. When he opened the door she trotted out with the pups galloping behind her. He fed the dogs and had one of the energy bars for breakfast. Because of the late start Chris upped his speed to eighteen mph. He made the usual three stops and at all three he noted there were no puppy messes in the back of the truck. He as in Watertown, S.D. by five pm and found a small market close by the highway. It had a charging station which was working and which accepted his cash in exchange for pumping the electricity into his battery. He slept that night on a picnic table in a little city park. He left the dogs in the truck with the tailgate open counting on Lady staying close even if she left the truck and knowing the pups would not stray far from their mother. When Chris reached Sioux Falls the next day he left US 29 and got on US 90 headed east. He stopped that night in Worthington at a large truck stop which advertised free bunks and free charging of electric vehicles. There were so many bodies in the store and bunk areas of the truck stop he chose not to stay there. He was lucky enough to find an empty motor home close to the charging station. He also found frozen food in the store area and ate well again that evening. He again left the dogs in the truck and left open the door and all the windows of the motor home. All of the openings were screened so bugs wouldn't be a problem. It reminded him that he needed to put flea and tick collars on the dogs. Before he went to sleep that night it occurred to Chris how thankful he should be for the progress made in the technology of generating electricity with solar power. The next day he drove to Albert Lea, Minnesota. It was a cool overcast day which made the driving pleasant and more comfortable for the dogs in back.

He again found a small market with a cash only charging station. The store was free of bodies and he found a cot in a back room. He and the dogs slept inside that night and were up and moving early the next morning. He was close enough to home that he was becoming anxious to arrive. Chris left early in the morning and boosted his speed to 20 mph determined to get home that night even if it was at a late hour. He was pleased to notice that the puppies hadn't made a mess in the truck for the past two days. It had to be a strain for them and they were always in a hurry to get out when he stopped. They had begun jumping out by themselves but still needed help getting back in. Chris went south on US 35 then west on Iowa 141 at Perry and was home by 6:30 pm. The place had never looked so good to him and the idea of sleeping in his own bed that night seemed like a special treat. The dogs were busy exploring while he opened the house to air it out. He stood on the deck watching the dogs and noticed as Lady stopped and bristled up at something. He decided it was most likely a coyote had marked the place. He locked the dogs in the shop that night after pulling the burlap bags out of the truck and putting them down for a bed. It was a warm evening and Chris sat out on the deck with old music playing softly. He began to lay plans for the immediate future. His freezer and pantry were well stocked with enough food to get through the coming winter. His first priority would be to build permanent housing for the dogs. He had already decided they were not going to be house dogs. They were just too big and he didn't want to live with the odor they would create. Chris slept well that night and after breakfast the next morning took the dogs for a walk down to the river. He could see where the beavers had been cutting the young willows and the bank on the far side looked as if it had eroded ten or twelve feet in the spring high water. Remembering the fresh Walleyes he had eaten in North Dakota he resolved to try fishing for them here. He had never been an angler but circumstances had changed and living off the land, at least partially, was becoming a necessity. As they approached the river a deer burst up out of the willows and fled toward the timber. All three dogs were in instant pursuit but one sharp whistle stopped Lady and the outdistanced pups soon gave up the chase and returned as well. After returning to the house Chris sat down and sketched what he planned to build as shelters for the dogs. The next day he took the ATV to pull his large trailer and drove to Perry to look for materials. In a building supply store he found a large supply of the composite sheets he had used on the little truck. This time he was able to pick sheets of the same color which came close to matching the house color. He also picked up several pieces of metal ducting plus cement and tape to seal the joints. In another store he found a half dozen large stainless steel bowls to serve as food and water containers for the dogs. He picked up tree fifty pound bags of dog food, still getting puppy food for the young ones. When he was a mile from home he discovered the dogs coming up the road to meet him. When he arrived home he found the yard gate standing open. He realized that he had not latched it securely. He put the dogs back in the yard and flipped the switch which would electrify the gate and fence. It carried a very light charge of current and would startle rather than harm any creature which touched it. After two or three contacts the dogs would learn to avoid the fence. It took Chris two weeks to finish the dog houses. The floors were off the ground for dryness and all three had vents from the heating/cooling system which served the house. The tops were hinged for easy access and he placed their food and water dishes inside to encourage them to push open the swinging doors to enter. Lady was the first to accept the idea that this was her new home. The pups tried to share their mother's house but there just wasn't room and eventually both of them started sleeping in the other shelters. Chris went out and examined his garden plot and found it overgrown with weeds. He put the tiller on the tractor and ploughed everything under for mulch.

On September 15 the temperature was 75 degrees. On September 16 it snowed six inches. In two days the snow had melted and the temperature was back to 70. The early snow left Chris with a sense of foreboding and he hurried to prepare the place for winter. He cleaned all the gutters and downspouts plus the filter in the heating/cooling system. He inspected the dog houses to make sure the snow had not filtered through a crack somewhere. Chris went to town and brought home a thousand pounds of dog food in fifty pound bags.

The solar array, which powered the place, was set up in four sections, only one of which was required at a time to supply the needed electricity. Chris turned the switches to put a new quadrant on line and watched the gauges to insure that it was operating properly.

The coyotes were becoming a nuisance. Chris knew they did the job of cleaning up the animals which died or were injured and that they posed no real threat to him. They had, however, begun to patrol the fence around his yard. He saw them at least once a day and often more than once. He took an old .250 Savage out of the gun safe and over a period of two weeks shot thirteen of the wild canines. This seemed to discourage them from visiting the immediate area around the house. The vultures had apparently migrated south which was normal so the bodies of the coyotes were not being consumed. The coyotes seemed reluctant to scavenge the bodies of their own kind. Chris noticed that feral hogs were frequently rooting in the corner of his nearest field. He built a tree blind which would put him within fifty yards of the area they most frequented. On his first day in the blind the hogs appeared. He shot a bigger animal of about one hundred fifty or sixty pounds and a very young one of no more than thirty pounds. To preserve meat he shot both animals through the head. He field dressed both animals where they lay, then hauled both carcasses to the shop. He left both to cool overnight and the next day trussed up the smaller one and put it on the spit of the outdoor grill. After eight hours on the rotating spit it provided a tasty, succulent change of diet for the next few days. The larger animal was cut up using an axe and band saw. He had no experience at butchering but he got the job done and the meat wrapped, labeled and in the freezer. Chris had no intention of traveling the next summer as he would need to plant a garden again for provisions for the next two years. He still walked seven or eight miles nearly every day to keep his legs in shape. He often walked more than that to visit the nearby small towns. He maintained a faint hope of finding someone else but by now it had become very faint indeed.

The young dogs, they couldn't be called puppies anymore, seemed to grow and fill out more every day. Moe had become the dominant of the two and Curly usually gave way when there was a dispute over a bone or a sunny spot on the deck. Thinking back to the old videos he had watched in North Dakota Chris chuckled and thought history was repeating itself. The days passed and 2107 ended with a raging blizzard which lasted three days into 2108.

Chapter 7 -- 2108

JOURNAL

The weather for the first two months of 2108 was terrible with one howling snow storm after another. Chris snow-shoed through the timber for a mile in both directions from his house during lulls in the storms. He found three spots where the deer were yarding up in sheltered areas and he also found several places where the wolves had made kills. There was little left at the kill sites except pieces of hide and a few bones. What the wolves didn't devour was picked clean by the coyotes and crows. Chris considered shooting a deer for a change in his diet but after thinking it over came to the conclusion that the deer herd was under enough stress from the wolf predation. On still nights it seemed he could hear more wolves howling than in the previous years.

In March he delved into his stash of seed packets and started tomatoes and green peppers in the greenhouse. He also started a couple varieties of onions and cabbage. He planted lettuce and radishes which would mature in the greenhouse and provide him with fresh produce before it was ready in the garden. In the middle of the month he became aware of a large almost snow white wolf prowling around the yard fence. The animal didn't seem to be particularly shy when Chris walked out on the deck and this seemed unusual for an animal which was normally very secretive. Chris understood the reason for the behavior when he finally noticed that Lady had come into her heat cycle. Even the pups were nosing around her. He would have to be careful and keep her confined to the yard until the cycle was past. He certainly didn't want a litter of half wolf pups to deal with. Chris considered shooting the wolf but came to the conclusion there had been enough death in the world without adding to it needlessly. Eventually things returned to normal and the wolf went away. March passed with slowly improving weather and by the middle of April Chris had the garden planted. He went to town in search of potatoes for seed and finally found some which had not spoiled in the two and a half years since being dug. Next year he would plant potatoes before leaving for his summer trip. He could freeze enough of the other vegetables to last for two winters but potatoes could not be frozen and seldom lasted fresh for two years. May was wet and cold and the garden progressed slowly. June came in warm and sunny with just enough rain that he didn't have to irrigate the garden which was green and lush. Chris tried his hand at fishing. He caught a few Walleyes but it was much harder fishing than his experiences in North Dakota. He could always catch a batch of Channel Catfish which were nearly as tasty as the Walleyes. Twice he hooked into giant Blue Cats which he released. He didn't keep any fish which were more than fourteen inches long. The smaller ones would go into the pan in one piece and besides what he ate he had at least two dozen of them in the freezer.

In August and September he was again busy harvesting from the garden and getting the produce packaged and into the freezers. He gave some thought to canning some of the vegetables. He had watched his mother go through the process when he was a boy and thought he could manage. He searched the stores in Perry and came home with twelve dozen pint and quart canning jars plus several hundred sealing lids. Enough, he thought, to last for several years. He had sprayed the little orchard south of Perry three times that spring and summer and he was anxious to see the results. He had more or less guessed about the proper insecticides to use. He would need to research that subject as well as try to find the canning manuals his mother had used. As it turned out his spraying attempts had been moderately successful. There was still insect damage to the apples but the quality of the fruit was much improved over previous years. He added an apple press to the list of things to bring home from his "shopping" trips.

The first hard frost came in the first week of October after which Chris took the tractor and tilled all the dead vegetation back into the ground. Except for a supply of meat Chris felt he was ready for the winter. He remedied that situation by bagging three turkeys, another feral pig and a yearling heifer from his former neighbor's pasture. His meat cutting skills were minimal but he managed to get all of the animals cut up, wrapped and in the freezer. In early November the snow began to fall. By mid-November the river had frozen solid and a blanket of bitter cold air seemed to settle over the area. Chris placed the food and water dishes for the dogs in their houses as the water bowls would freeze over after a very short time outside. In early December there was a respite from the bitter weather and much of the snow melted. Chris began his walking routine again often accompanied by the dogs. They as well as he were going to have to toughen their feet and strengthen their leg muscles for the walk next summer. In the shop he put together three small packs which he started putting on the dogs before their daily hike. Lady accepted the pack with little reaction but the young dogs didn't readily adapt to them. They finally accepted the fact that the packs meant going for a long walk, which they loved doing. Chris began adding a small amount of weight to each pack in the form of sand and came to the conclusion that each dog would carry up to ten pounds without it being a significant hindrance. December passed with a continuance of the mild weather and at the end of the month Chris felt it was time to start making plans for next summer's journey.

Chapter 8 --- 2109

JOURNAL

On January 1, 2109, Chris spread his maps on the counter and began looking at the western half of what had been the U.S. He doubted that it could any longer be said to exist. As his eyes moved over the sheets they momentarily rested on Texas. When they came back to that area he recalled a biography he had read as a teenager on David Crockett. Crockett was a noted frontiersman in the early 1800s whose fame got him elected to the US Congress. He apparently did not fit in well with the usual political types who served in Congress. On his last day in office he made a speech to that august body in which he made several cutting remarks. He ended his address by saying, "and all of you can go to Hell, I'm going to Texas." He followed up on that statement just in time to be killed in the siege at the Alamo in 1836. "Why not?" Chris didn't linger on the question but turned to the maps of Kansas, Oklahoma and north Texas. He settled on a route which would take him west on Iowa 141 then south on US 71 to St. Joseph, Missouri, where he would connect to US 29. 29 would lead him to US 70 which at Topeka connected to US 335 leading south and which became US 35 at Emporia. This route would take him straight south all the way to the Dallas - Fort Worth area. He could return by the same route or take a slightly shorter path across Oklahoma then north through Missouri. Chris settled into his usual winter routine of blowing snow off the deck and walkways and reading. When weather permitted and the roads were reasonably clear he walked with the dogs. He wore his pack on these treks just to become accustomed to it again. He didn't load it as heavy as it would be in the summer. He hiked the Perry to Jamaica stretch so many times he felt he knew every fence post and blade of grass protruding from the snow. He made several trips which entailed staying overnight but the cold weather discouraged very many of those. Neither he nor the dogs enjoyed sleeping in unheated buildings when the outside temperature was below zero. His supply of potatoes was running low and he wanted to save as many as possible for seed. He began eating rice and discovered brown rice cooked with bits of browned pork made a tasty and hearty dish. He experimented in the kitchen and finally made a pie crust by doing exactly what his mother had tried to teach him as a teenaged boy. It seemed so simple once he had mastered the procedure.

February passed and in March the weather turned unusually mild. He expected the other shoe to drop and another snow storm to blow in but none came. He and the dogs covered hundreds of miles of pavement and he felt they were all ready for the long walk. He had considered starting out in the little electric truck but the battery system had gone completely dead and he didn't have the means to replace it. On the first day of April he planted the potatoes and put in onions although he wasn't sure the onion sets were still good.

He planned again to leave on the anniversary of the great die-off as he now thought of it. Chris sorted out the clothing he was going to take. He had three pairs of well broken in shoes. He thought these would not last the entire trip but quality athletic shoes could be found almost everywhere. He planned to wear shorts and included only one pair of long trousers in the event of an extremely chilly day. He hoped to find commercial dog food to feed his companions. If not they would have to subsist on what he could shoot or they could catch.

They left at 6:00 am on April 7 as planned. The young dogs were frisky at the start but soon settled into the brisk pace set by Chris. The four of them plodded into Coon Rapids in late afternoon. Chris found a convenience store with no bodies and a back room containing a cot. He fed the dogs and opened a can of beans for himself. He left the door open so the dogs would have full access. They were all asleep before the sun went down. He was awakened at 3:00 am by the noise of all three dogs barking, grocery shelves hitting the floor and some other animal with a high-pitched squall. He flipped a switch and the solar powered lights came on illuminating a very angry raccoon perched on top of the freezer section and all three dogs trying to jump high enough to reach it. Chris knew he wouldn't sleep again after all of the commotion so he fed and watered the dogs and was on the road by 4:00 am. They made good time and the day passed without incident. That night was spent at a truck stop where 71 passed under I-80. The weather stayed mild and after two more days they were at the little settlement of Braddyville just short of the Missouri state line. They spent the night at a house which appeared to have been abandoned ten or fifteen years before. It was full of dirt, broken glass and soggy wallboard which was falling from the ceiling. Chris put his sleeping bag and pad down on the sagging porch. He fed the dogs with the food he had picked up at a convenience store earlier in the day and ate an energy bar for his own supper. The days and miles passed quickly and they were through Kansas City and into Kansas. Chris continued to look for signs of survivors but found nothing. Feeling foolish and a little bizarre he jauntily saluted the desiccated corpse slumped over the counter in the toll booth when they entered the Kansas Turnpike. Now it would be a divided highway all the way to Dallas. He enjoyed the openness and at times crossed over to the northbound lanes to get a better view of a river or creek bottom. There were numerous herds of cattle of various breeds and twice he saw bands of horses. They were domestic horses gone wild from necessity but he knew that in a generation or two they would be completely wild. The mustang had returned to the plains only now there were no Native Americans to trap and tame them to be used for hunting buffalo. In his mind he could see the great herds with the brown men riding among them shooting arrows from their short bows. Chris had stopped checking the calendar and lost track of the days. Time didn't seem to matter as he walked south into increasingly warmer weather. When he was a day south of Wichita at about milepost twenty he met his first real challenge of the trip. As he came around one of the few curves in the highway he came face to face with a mixed breed bull with lethal looking horns. No amount of shouting or arm waving was able to convince the animal that he needed to share the highway. Chris removed his rifle from its scabbard and was afraid he was going to be forced to shoot the bull in order to get past him. He had brought the little 250 Savage rather than the Marlin he usually carried. Both the rifle and ammunition were lighter in weight than the Marlin but the gun had less stopping power and at the moment he wished for the heavier gun. The dogs resolved the dilemma by all three charging at once. They eluded the horns and went for the hindquarters. When the bull whirled to face one dog another would dart in and nip at his flank or back legs. In very short order the bull decided that discretion was the better par of valor. He charged through the dogs and took up a position on the northbound lanes.

He continued to paw and swing his horns but made no effort to re-cross the median. A couple of whistles brought the dogs back to Chris and they continued on their way. Chris thought the dogs looked a little smug about besting the bull but then he decided that Curly always looked as if he had a silly smirk on his face. With a chuckle Chris continued down the road and began looking for a place to spend the night, preferably a place with a soft bed. On his second day in Oklahoma Chris did what he had feared most since being alone. He stepped wrong on the expansion plate of an overpass bridge and sprained his ankle. At first he didn't think it was serious and continued walking. The pain became worse and the ankle became badly swollen. He left the freeway and hobbled into the town of Perry, OK. He found the hospital right beside the highway and went in. The place was a nightmare. There were bodies everywhere and even though it had been more than three years the smell of death was overpowering. The dogs were reluctant to go in so he left them in the glassed in entry. Chris searched until he found a pair of aluminum crutches and quickly left. He also took a wheelchair from the lobby. It was difficult getting in the chair with his pack on but he compensated by sitting on the edge of the seat and pulling himself along with his good foot. Two blocks down the street he found a motel which was solar powered and hopefully would have an ice maker. He had enough dog food to feed them that evening but tomorrow he would have to find more or shoot something. In the motel Chris found an ice machine which was full of ice that had frozen into an almost solid block. He wheeled his chair into the manager's apartment and searched until he located a hammer and a large screwdriver. He then searched the bathroom and found two stretch bandages, a bottle of liniment and a small vial of pain pills. He only carried aspirin in his pack and would try the pain pills only as a last measure. He used the hammer and screwdriver to break up some of the ice. Not having a plastic bag for the ice he pulled a pillow cover off one of the beds and put ice in it. It was going to drip and make a mess but he didn't see any alternative. He rubbed in a generous amount of the liniment, which he didn't have much faith in, and then pulled a plastic office chair out in the hallway. He would at least keep the melt water out of his room. He placed the pillow slip with ice on the chair then put his injured ankle on the ice bag. He then covered the ankle and ice with a bath towel and settled in to wait. After two hours the ice had melted and he was hungry. Chris thought the pain had subsided a little and decided he didn't need the pain pills. He wheeled into the manager's kitchen and found a variety of canned vegetables which tasted of age but which he relished anyway. He also found a supply of heavy duty plastic bags. Returning to the ice machine he discovered it was making fresh ice. He wouldn't want to use it in a drink but it was certainly adequate to wrap his ankle. He fed the dogs then let them out for a while before repacking his ankle with ice. He spent the night in the hall with his ankle wrapped in ice. The wheel chair was not particularly comfortable but he dozed fitfully. As the sun came up the dogs were pacing with the need to go out so he let them out then sat and watched the morning. Chris heard the goats before he saw them. There were perhaps fifteen of them browsing in a little park across the road. He wasn't ready to eat goat meat but thought the dogs would not be hesitant to do so if he couldn't find dog food that morning. His breakfast that day was canned apple pie filling. The ankle was swollen and badly discolored but he thought he would wrap it and take the wheelchair in search of dog food.

As a precaution he slung the Savage across his shoulder then began to propel the wheelchair along the street. Twice he saw groups of dogs which he assumed were hunting packs formed of necessity. They were all medium to large sized dogs and again he assumed the smaller dogs had been killed and eaten. After four blocks of labor moving the chair Chris found a market which had dog food. He looked at the bags and wondered how he was going to get them back to the motel. He finally pulled over a grocery cart and put two twenty-five pound bags in it. It was a struggle to get the cart and chair out of the door and it promised to be a herculean task to get back to the motel. After he was out of the parking lot and into the street the job became easier. It was then Chris realized it was up hill all the way from the motel to the market. Going back the cart very nearly rolled on its own. With the problem of feeding the dogs solved Chris returned to the liniment and ice routine. He swallowed aspirin on a regular basis but the pain never reached the point that he resorted to the pain pills. After a week Chris resorted to pouring a drink from the bottle of Jack Daniels in the manager's office. It went down so smoothly and tasted so good he had a second one. He awakened the next morning with a big puddle around his foot rest plus a hangover. He remembered the three Kentucky coal mines and vowed no more Jack Daniels. He emptied the bottle in the sink and went back to the aspirin when the pain required more than ice. By the end of the second week the ankle was greatly improved but was still too tender to bear his weight. After three weeks Chris realized his Texas trip was ended so he got out his maps and began plotting the shortest route home. Chris knew his progress on the way home was going to be slow and at times painful. After being off of his feet for so long he would not be able to cover the number of miles he had been walking. He would take US 64 east from Perry to connect with US 412 then to US 44 which he would follow to Joplin, Missouri and get on US 71 headed north. He set off on a warm sunny morning and had covered less than half of the seventeen miles to the junction with 412 at Morrison when he realized he wasn't going to make it in one day. He slept in a rundown barn that night and the second day was more or less a repeat of the previous one. He struggled everyday but each day his leg became a little stronger. By the time he passed through Tulsa he was managing to walk fifteen miles a day without undue strain. When he reached Vinita he stayed over for a day to rest his ankle. It no longer was painful but it tired early in the day and he didn't want to risk additional injury. He had shot a deer the day before to feed the dogs but in Vinita he found dog food and let them eat their fill. He added all the dog food he thought he could carry to his pack plus filling the packs of all three dogs. It was enough food to get them to Carthage where again he stayed over for a day. It was now August and he was beginning to feel an urge to get home. The country here was hilly and his daily progress was slower but he was gaining strength every day as he walked. It took him nine days to reach Kansas City plus another day to pass through the city. The wreckage and destruction here was the worst he had seen anywhere in his travels. He was forced to backtrack several miles at one point when he came to a bridge which had been taken down by a pile up of big trucks which had knocked down the supports. He got on US 29 and followed it to just north of St. Joseph. When he got off of US 29 and on to US 169 he relaxed somewhat. 169 would take him within seven or eight miles of home and if things went well he would arrive before September 1. The days and miles passed quickly and on August 25 he passed through Adel, the county seat of Dallas County. He had to sit down across the street and admire the old, red brick and stone County Courthouse. In all of his life and all of his travels he had never seen a prettier building. He had never been able to pass without stopping to admire the structure. He spent the night at a motel on the north side of Adel and expected to reach home before supper time the next day. He considered making the short side trip to Dallas Center to look in on his parents' home but the attraction of his own house was too strong and he continued on his way. They arrived home before 5:00 pm that evening. The dogs seemed to be as anxious to be home as Chris. When he opened the gate all three of them went straight to their kennels before Chris even had a chance to remove their packs. Chris opened all the windows to air the place out although with the A.C. operating all summer it really wasn't bad. He got a piece of pork out of the freezer plus a package of peas and carrots. He called the dogs for their suppers and removed their packs while they were eating. They returned to their kennels as soon as they had eaten as though determined to make up for the nights they had slept on the ground. Chris ate an enjoyable meal at his own table for the first time in months, had a long shower and went to sleep with the sound of his wolves singing their nightly lullaby.

Chris encountered his first at home emergency when he discovered that Lady had come into her heat cycle again and the two young males were bristled up and ready to fight over the right to claim the prize. It didn't matter that she was their mother. The smell told them she was ready to breed. That was all it took to trigger their instincts. He solved the immediate problem by locking Lady in a stall in the barn. She complained bitterly for three days and the young dogs paced the yard fence looking for a way out.

In the second week of September Chris harvested his potatoes and onions. He had a bumper crop of potatoes but the onions were sparse and not of good quality. He vowed to find onion seed and start some in the greenhouse in February. He harvested a yearling cow, two more of the feral hogs and four turkeys. He had all of the meat prepared and in the freezers by the first of October and after cleaning the gutters felt he was ready for winter again. He spent two days gathering and burning all of the dead limbs and twigs which had fallen during the summer and felt the place looked neater and better cared for.

As he sat on the deck one morning savoring his first cup of coffee his thought went to the dogs and the problems involved their maturity and Lady's continuing heat seasons. If there had been a vet available he could have Curly and Moe neutered but that was not an option. He finally concluded that if he could put the dogs to sleep he would do it himself.

Chris made up his mind to try and rehabilitate the little electric truck. Using the fork lift he removed the battery pack. He began searching nearby dealerships looking for a replacement. He had no success until, on a trip to Dallas Center, he went on into West Des Moines and found two exact models of the old one. He also found a supply of battery acid plus the maintenance manual for the truck and battery pack. At home he placed the battery in the truck, put in the required amount of acid plus distilled water. He connected the truck to his charging system and two days later was rewarded with a full charge indication on the meter. He now turned his attention to the dogs.

He searched the nearby pharmacies until he located an over the counter medication which was essentially a tranquilizer. He fed the pills to the dogs, hidden in bits of meat, until he reached the dosage which would put them out for an hour. Chris didn't like experimenting with the dogs but saw no other way to resolve the problem. He found latex gloves, disinfectant and several scalpels. On the day he finally worked up the nerve for the operation he took the dogs to the shop where he fed them the pills until he was sure they were completely out. He put on the gloves, painted the scrotums with antiseptic then did the cutting. As a boy he had witnessed cattle and hogs being castrated so he had an idea of how to proceed. After he had finished he painted on more antiseptic and waited for the dogs to awaken. When they were up and steady on their feet he fed both of them two of the pain pills he had carried home from Oklahoma. Both dogs had a stiff walk for a few days but neither of them showed any other ill effects.

As in the past couple of years the snow started in the middle of October and Chris knew he was in for a long winter. He didn't need to plan for a trip the next summer so he spent much of his time listening to music and audio books of which he had a large collection. He also spent considerable time snow-shoeing in the timber and river bottom. Chris became aware that there were moose in the area. He didn't know if moose had been native to the area before white men had come to the area some three hundred years ago. He assumed that, like the wolf, the

moose population was expanding rapidly with the disappear-
ance of man and the young ones were seeking new territory
to claim. The year ended with a stretch of warm weather and
Chris began to think of projects beside the garden to fill his time
next summer.

Chapter 9 --- 2110

JOURNAL

January came in with a continuation of the mild December weather. Chris was considering taking the little truck and looking through some of the small towns in south-central Iowa. He didn't really expect to find any people but there was always the hope that he would find others. Those plans were put on hold when the snow returned in the second week of the month. The snow and wind continued off and on for three weeks and Chris was essentially snowbound the entire time. He snow-shoed out to the road one day and found drifts eight and ten feet high across his driveway. The outer roads would be just as bad so he didn't even consider taking the snow machine out. Now that he could make an edible pie crust he experimented in the kitchen. He made apple pie from his frozen apples and a cherry pie from canned cherries. Chris thought both pies would taste better with a dollop of ice cream added. Chris had canned pumpkin in his pantry and decided to try making a pumpkin pie. He made the crust but when he opened the can the pumpkin had spoiled. He resolved to add pumpkins to his garden that summer. With that in mind he went to the greenhouse and put a half dozen pumpkin seeds in pots to see if they would germinate. While he was doing this he also planted tomatoes, green peppers and onions. By the end of February all of the seeds had spouted and were growing vigorously. The dogs had recovered and were seemingly unchanged except that Moe seemed a little less aggressive. In March the weather alternated between warm and sunny then snowy and cold. It was late March before the frost was out of the ground and Chris could use the tiller to prepare the garden for planting. It was mid-April before Chris thought it was safe to start planting. He transplanted the pepper and tomatoes and planted seed of the other vegetables. Cutting up the potatoes and getting them in the ground took a full three days. The onions he had started in the greenhouse were the last to go into the garden and he hoped they would survive the transplanting shock. Chris even planted two hills of watermelon seeds although he had not checked the viability of the seeds in the greenhouse. With the garden planted Chris tried his hand at fishing again. The river had not yet started its annual spring flood and Chris found the Walleyes apparently starved after a long winter. In a matter of a few days he had three dozen tasty fish in his freezer and put his rod away. He was soon busy in the garden with his hoe. By the time he finished on one side it was time to start again on the other side. It seemed the weeds never took a day off. Chris noted that Lady had not been in heat for over three months. He wondered if it was because of the change in the male dogs or whether perhaps she had passed the age for bearing young. She had been a mature dog when he found her and he had no idea what her age might be. He had noticed that the hair on and around her muzzle was turning white. Chris made a trip to Dallas Center and picked up his mother's big canning pot plus her canning instruction manuals. August and September passed in a blur as Chris was kept busy picking, freezing and canning the produce from the garden. In October he butchered another yearling heifer plus two hogs. He omitted the turkeys because they didn't seem to age well in the freezer. When he wanted turkey he would shoot one and eat it fresh. In later October the snow began and continued through November and December.

Chapter 10 --- 2111

JOURNAL

t had now been almost five years of being totally alone. In the summer when he was busy the solitude didn't weigh quite so heavily on Chris but in the winter with so much idle time the silence became oppressive. He spent more and more time talking to the dogs and at times wondered whether he was losing his grip on reality. He had home videos of his parents and friends including Carol but could not bring himself to watch them. He dug out the trumpet he had not played since his first year of college. The dogs protested so much at the trumpet's blare that he was unable to force them to endure it. The trumpet went back into the closet.

On January 15, Chris put the maps out on the counter again. He began to scan the western states but stopped and gave thought to traveling to the East this year. As he considered this possibility all he could see in his mind were hundreds of dead cities and towns. At least in the West there were great open vistas and he thought, a better chance of someone surviving over the years. He finally settled on Salt Lake City. He had never been there and had never seen the Great Salt Lake except from twenty thousand feet in the air. With his destination settled, Chris began to plan his schedule. If the weather allowed he would plant his potatoes and onions and be on the road on April 7. That date for departure had become part of his routine and he didn't wish to change it. Through January and February he resumed his walking routine with the dogs. When the snow prevented walking on the highway he snow-shoed through the timber and to neighboring farms. Three miles south of Dawson he found a farm where a flock of chickens were apparently thriving. There must have been at least one hundred of them in a poultry house with only one small opening for them to get in or out. There were bones and feathers lying about the yard indicating that some predator had been at work. Close by the poultry house was a grain storage building which was leaking both corn and oats. This explained the chickens' food supply and why they had survived for five years. He marked the place as a future source of both eggs and chickens. As March approached the weather relented and Chris got into a serious walking routine with the dogs. They often covered thirty-five mile in a day and he felt their feet and legs were ready for the summer's long walk.

By April 1, Chris had the garden prepared and spent three days planting potatoes and onions. On April 7, they left early and went straight south from Dawson until they hit I-80 just east of Dexter. They spent the first night there and on the fourth day they were across the Missouri River in Omaha. The weather across Iowa had been warm and sunny but now turned chilly and damp. It spit a little snow on two occasions but not enough to force them off the road. For five days they averaged only about twenty miles per day which took them to the interchange just south of York. The weather improved and in two long days they arrived in Kearney. After Kearney, Chris lost track of the days but knew from the mile markers that they were averaging about thirty miles per day. On three occasions he saw sizeable herds of buffalo. They were grazing some distance from the road and Chris assumed they were left over from some commercial breeding operation. They now owned the prairie again without the Red Man or White Buffalo Hunters of history to harass them. Chris also saw a large herd of cattle in a mad stampede. He stopped and watched to insure he and the dogs would not be caught in the crush if the cattle crashed through the fence onto the highway. As Chris watched he became aware the cattle were not blindly stampeding but were being herded by a sizeable pack of wolves. Eventually, the cattle would be slowed or cornered by fences or trees and the wolves would move in for the kill. It was interesting to Chris that the wolves had developed this hunting technique in the five short years that man had been gone from the plains. He pulled his rifle from its case in the event the wolves' attention became diverted from the cattle to he and the dogs. After his episode with the bull in Oklahoma two years ago, Chris was again carrying the Marlin with its heavier fire power. The wolves ignored the man and dogs and swept past behind the cattle. The days and miles blended into one long continuous walk and soon Chris and the dogs were on the stretch of highway where it was parallel to the two Platte Rivers where they ran side by side for miles before joining to form one stream. He saw many deer everyday and now began to see scattered bands of antelope. It seems the wildlife wasn't wasting time in reclaiming the prairies. When he arrived at the intersection with US 26 Chris wished he had the time to take that route. He had never seen Chimney Rock or historic old Fort Laramie both of which were important mile-posts for the pioneers crossing the plain two hundred fifty years ago. The distance to Salt Lake and back precluded such a lengthy side trip so he stayed on I-80 and was in Wyoming in four more days. As they passed through Cheyenne, Chris recalled flying over the city and observing the wreckage on his way home from Fort Collins in 2106. He didn't explore the city again but went to the west side of town and finally found a solar powered motel with a clean, meaning no bodies, room. It was such a pleasant location that Chris stayed the next day. He found a lawn chair and spent the day sitting in the shade of a large old willow tree. He watched two eagles fishing in a nearby creek. Their fish weren't very large but they seldom dived without coming up with a fish. They flew off to the northwest after each catch and Chris assumed they were feeding young ones nearby. A group of eight or ten cattle wandered along the grass at the edge of the parking lot and Chris, with a sudden urge for fresh meat brought one down with the Marlin. He found a charcoal grill on the back of a camper van in the parking lot and a bag of charcoal in the van. There were human bones scattered around and one skeleton inside the vehicle which was not locked. He cut off two slabs of beef for himself and several chunks to feed the dogs that night and in the morning. He grilled both slabs and wrapped one of them to carry for his supper the next day. They got a very early start the next morning. It was uphill all the way from Cheyenne to the Medicine Bow summit. Chris stopped at the top to look at the brooding bust of Lincoln which had stood there for over one hundred fifty years. The drop from the summit into Laramie was very steep and much more noticeable than the climb from Cheyenne. However, Laramie sat one thousand feet higher than Cheyenne and Chris could feel the effects on his heart and lungs. The air was clean and crisp and it seemed as if you could see forever. They spent a chilly night in a campground on the east side of Laramie. Chris ate his beef from the day before and the dogs looked envious as they munched their dried dog food. Chris relented and fed each dog a bite of the meat. They settled in for the night with Chris sleeping on a picnic table and the dogs on the grass surrounding it. They left early in the morning and it promised to be a good day for walking. Moe was in the lead by his customary fifteen yards and they had just passed the last motel on the west side of Laramie when disaster struck again. From the far side of an abandoned car a great grizzly roared out and with one swipe slapped Moe to the far side of the highway. Before the dog stopped rolling the bear was on him biting and slashing with its front paws. Moe couldn't even get to his feet as the bear continued to attack. Chris snatched the Marlin from its case and as quickly as he could work the lever fired the entire magazine into the bear. One of the shots hit the bear in the spine just behind the head and the attack was instantly over. The bear had fallen clear of the dog and when Chris got to him he could see the dog was seriously injured. There were gashes in the shoulder from the bear's first blow and deep puncture wounds from teeth on the dog's back and neck. Moe was moving but was unable to get up and Chris hoped there had been no injury to his spine. The dog was going to need medical treatment which Chris was not equipped to provide. Chris stood looking around and wondering how to handle the situation. He spotted a low flat luggage cart in front of the motel they had just passed. He dropped his pack then reloaded the rifle before doing anything else. He jogged to the motel and brought the cart back to where the dog lay on the edge of the road. The other two dogs were sniffing and growling at the dead bear but it was no longer a concern for Chris. As gently as he could manage he got the one hundred fifty pound dog on the cart put his pack back on and rolled the cart back to the motel. Chris parked the cart in the shade of the entrance and went to see what he could find. The first two rooms were open and empty. A cleaning cart sat on the sidewalk between doors. The beds in both rooms had been stripped and were unmade. Not a problem he decided as he pushed the cart with the dog into the first room. He tossed the blankets on the floor and eased the dog off the cart. The dog was conscious and aware but wasn't trying to move. He put the other dogs in the room and moved the cart to block the door. Chris went to the motel office and into the manager's apartment behind it. He went directly to the bathroom ignoring the three desiccated bodies in the kitchen and living room. He was looking for disinfectant, pain pills and material for bandages. He found the first two items but no bandages. There were several rolls of adhesive tape and a large tube of anti-bacterial ointment. Once more the predominance of solar power proved beneficial. In the kitchen freezer he found a two pound package of ground beef. Chris returned to the dogs and when he entered the room was rewarded with a tail wag from Moe. He then began to clean the wounds with antiseptic which brought a whine and groan from the dog. As he cleaned the shoulder wound, Chris decided that it was primarily a surface wound and that the muscle underneath was not seriously damaged. He also determined that a bandage was not going to hold the wound closed. He returned to the apartment and after putting the meat in the microwave to thaw began searching for the sewing equipment every woman keeps. He found it in an oak box by a chair in the living area. He took the two largest needles in the box plus a spool of heavy thread. He also thought to take a metal thimble. He searched the freezer and found two more packages of frozen beef which he put in the oven when the first one was thawed. He again returned to the dogs. As he examined Moe again he could see that the pack he carried had probably saved the dog's life. It was punctured in several places by tooth marks which would have gone into the dog if not for the pack. He began stuffing pain pills into bits of ground meat and offering them to the dog. After Moe had eaten four of them he offered just the meat. Chris had no idea of what would amount to an effective dose without killing Moe or even if the old pills would work. After a half hour Moe began to relax and in a bit it appeared as if he was asleep. Chris returned for the rest of the meat, fed and watered Lady and Curly then turned to Moe. The dog was breathing but had no reaction when Chris cleaned the wound again. Chris soaked the thread in the antiseptic, threaded the needle and began pulling the wound closed. It took him most of an hour and when he finished it was an ugly sight. It was the best he could do and now it was up to nature and Moe's body to do the rest. For supper Chris had two very stale energy bars and a pint of water. He put his sleeping bag on one of the beds and went to sleep. He woke once in the night at the sound of Moe moaning but the dog settled down and he went back to sleep.

In the morning the dog was awake and alert but showed no interest in trying to get up. Chris closed all of the dogs in the room and walked a quarter of a mile to a convenience store where he had to break a glass door to get in. He found a twenty-five pound bag of dog food and carried it back to the motel. He found Moe standing on his feet but not wanting to move much which was understandable. The dog finally hobbled out the door and relieved himself on the cleaning cart which was the closest vertical object. Moe came back in the room, briefly nuzzled the hand which had put him back together then lay down on his bed with a groan. As he sat on the bed watching the dog he realized he was not going to see the Great Salt Lake this summer. Chris took the bottle of antiseptic and washed Moe's wounds again then slathered anti-biotic ointment on them. He considered bandaging the wounds but felt it just wasn't practical.

As Chris was trying to decide when he could start the trip home the other two dogs which were outside began a furious barking. Stepping to the door Chris was startled by the appearance of two half grown grizzlies. They were headed for the dogs and didn't show any intention of stopping. The bears were twice the size of Lady and Chris didn't want any more dogs chewed up. He picked up the Marlin and in a matter of seconds killed both bears with head shots. Now Chris realized he had another problem. The bears were too big for him to move by himself and they were going to smell very bad before Moe was well enough to travel. By the next day the bear carcasses were bloated and Chris was sure he could smell them. He pushed the baggage cart back into the room and was able to get Moe to step onto the cart then lie down. Chris put on his pack, shouldered his rifle and started back down the road toward Laramie. After about two miles he came to a motel with a lighted neon sign. He turned in and found two adjacent rooms with unlocked doors and no bodies. He made another bed with blankets and coaxed Moe off of the cart and onto the blankets. He went again to the manager's apartment to see if he could find anything useful to him. Someone here had been a hunter. There were half a dozen weapons in a gun rack. He didn't need another gun but he found two boxes of ammunition for his rifle. He had left home with one box of ammo but had expended a good bit of it on the bears. He found juice and meat in the freezer. He didn't want the meat but knew the dogs wouldn't object to it. Three doors down the street he found the ever-present convenience store. He found both dry and canned dog food so that problem was taken care of.

He knew he needed to maintain a daily walking routine but he also was reluctant to leave the injured dog alone for extended periods. The next day after feeding the dogs he closed them in the room and set out by himself. After three or four miles he came upon a strip mall just beside a highway. He looked at the stores and decided he didn't want his hair and nails done, nor his taxes prepared. He was, however, interested in the hardware store. He had to break the glass door to gain entry. Inside Chris found a spool of light chain and cut two fifty foot lengths. He also picked up two heavy dog collars and a spool of light weight wire. He found a small hand axe with a leather holster and fastened it to his belt. He was nervous about kicking in doors and felt that eventually he was going to get cut.

Chris returned to the motel and fitted the healthy dogs with collars and chains. He attached the free ends of the chains to a lamp standard just outside the door. It allowed the dogs access to the room yet they could get outside to answer nature's call. He was sure he would have to untangle the chains from time to time. He thought both dogs were giving him reproachful looks when he tethered them but saw no alternative to the problem. Moe seem to be improving every day but still limped badly and cried out if he bumped the shoulder. Chris cleaned the wounds every day and kept them covered with ointment. He now began a routine of walking with his backpack for five to seven miles every morning and again in the afternoon. He alternated between the two healthy dogs, also with their loaded packs, morning and afternoon. Chris explored Laramie and all of the roads leading out of town. He was amazed at the quantity of wildlife he saw on these daily walks. He saw deer, elk, antelope and even the occasional moose.

July passed in to August and Chris was beginning to get antsy about starting for home. Moe continued to improve and his limp was much less noticeable. One day as Chris was fastening the pack on Curly for the morning walk Moe walked over to the table where the packs were stored, picked up his own pack and dropped it by Chris's foot. Chris looked at Moe, shrugged, and put the pack on him. At this point Lady was up from her corner and dancing to be included. Chris slipped her collar off, strapped on her pack and for the first time in more than a month the four of them set out together. Chris kept the morning hike short. They only walked three miles and Moe was visibly tired when they returned. When it was time for the afternoon walk all three dogs were eager to go and Chris lengthened the distance to four miles. The scar on Moe's shoulder was not a pretty sight but didn't seem to be a handicap to him. Chris had removed the crude sutures after two weeks. He had drugged the dog again and after cutting the threads he had pulled them out with a pair of pliers. There was some bleeding but it wasn't excessive and the wound remained closed.

After ten days of walking with the dogs Chris reasoned that it was time to start for home. Even if they averaged only twenty miles per day they could be home by mid-September. They left Laramie with each dog carrying its own food for the next three days. The road to the summit wasn't long but it was brutally steep and they arrived at Lincoln's bust completely spent. Moe was limping slightly but otherwise seemed to be in good shape. Chris slept on the same picnic table he had used on the way west. In the morning the dogs seemed eager to get moving. Moe wasn't limping and Chris took that to be a good sign. Chris took out his map and after looking at the miles they had to cover, consoled himself with the thought that it was downhill from where he sat all the way to the Missouri River at Omaha. They made it into Cheyenne by later afternoon and spent that night in the same motel they had used on the way west. Chris decided to limit each day's travel to Moe's endurance. If the dog started to limp they would stop for the night. He was surprised at the dog's stamina and in two days they were in Kimball, Nebraska. They traveled on with no incidents to slow them down. Chris set a goal of thirty miles per day which they maintained until three days of steady rain forced them to stay over in Grand Island. He found a working dryer at the motel and on the fourth day and with dry clothing again they set out under sunny skies. He saw the buffalo again, this time on the opposite side of the highway and wondered if they had access to an underpass or if they had simply walked through the fence as he had seen them do in North Dakota. As they progressed across eastern Nebraska the eagerness to get home seemed to transfer from Chris to the dogs. Every morning they were anxious to get started. The other two dogs even developed Moe's habit of picking up his pack and presenting it to Chris to put on.

On the day they crossed the Missouri River, they all broke into a trot as if touching Iowa soil again had some special meaning. Chris increased his pace and the length of their travel day and in three and a half days they were home. When they turned into the driveway the dogs broke into a hard run and left Chris behind. When he arrived they were all waiting at the gate. Once in the yard the dogs waited until he removed their packs then immediately dived into their kennels where they remained for most of the next week, coming out only to eat and relieve themselves.

Chris spent the time airing out and cleaning the house, listening to an audio book titled "Wagons Westward." The book was so old Chris didn't even recognize the name of the actor who was reading it. He hiked down to the river several times and on the first trip was surprised to see that the river had changed its course over the summer. The main channel now ran across the middle of what had been a willow covered sandbar. It was now less than half the previous distance from the bottom of the hill to the edge of the river. What had been the main channel was now a still pool which was full of fish which would surely die this winter when the pool froze over. In the meanwhile, it was most likely a great fishing hole for the minks, otters and raccoons which frequented the area.

On October 1, he began harvesting his onions and potatoes. The onions had produced better than he had expected and the potato crop was tremendous. He was forced to go into Perry and scour the stores to find slatted crates in which to store them. After his crop was in the root cellar he returned to the orchard south of Perry in search of apples. There were very few apples left and he noticed a lot of broken branches in many of the trees. He was disappointed at the lack of apples and after looking around found droppings and tracks that had to have been made by black bears. He probably had enough apples in the freezer to last until next year. He would spray the trees again then try and beat the bears to the harvest. He also vowed to plant his own apple trees and learn how to properly prune and spray them.

Chris turned to his annual autumn chores around the house. He cleaned gutters, picked up downed limbs and cut back brush around the buildings. He also brought home wire and posts. If he was going to put in an orchard, it was going to need to be fenced from the deer and feral hogs. The first snow fell on October 17. It wasn't much and didn't last long but it depressed Chris. It seemed that winter was coming earlier and lasting just a little longer every year. The serious snow began early in November and one snowfall followed another for the rest of the month. The only way to get around was by snow-shoe or the tracked snow machine. On one of his few trips to Perry Chris noticed that several older flat roofed buildings had fallen in. He assumed it was caused by years of no maintenance and a heavy load of snow. He would need to be aware and cautious about entering such buildings in the future. December came in much like November and Chris settled in for the long winter.

Chapter 11 ---2112

JOURNAL

With the beginning of January it continued to snow and Chris was pretty much confined to the immediate area around the house. In the shop he found a two by three foot by one quarter inch stainless steel plate. He had forgotten his original purpose for the metal and decided it could be a useable and long lasting marker for his parents' grave. Using the inert gas welder he printed their names and their birth and death dates. He welded several short cross pieces to the bottom edge and would set it in a concrete base. With the grave marker completed and ready to be put in place in the spring he turned to planning the orchard.

He thought he would place it adjacent to the garden and thus only need to fence three sides. He also decided to put fencing around the barn, hog and poultry houses. If he ever acquired livestock he would need fenced areas next to the buildings. After examining his sketches he realized he would need to get more wire and several gates. Most of the field which was closest to the house would have to be converted to pasture but he didn't see that as a large task. In February, the weather cleared for two weeks and warmed up. He took the dogs and walked the surrounding area. He had been over the territory many times but now he was looking with a purpose. If he was going to acquire livestock and poultry he was going to require hay and grain for feed and straw for bedding. After two weeks of searching for several miles around he was convinced there were enough of those basic items to satisfy his needs until he could plant and harvest crops of his own. He would need to acquire a full set of farming equipment but there was more than enough of that sitting idle at neighboring farms. It might be rusty but was still useable. In late February, he started a variety of vegetables in the greenhouse. When he first arrived home in September, he had planted tomatoes, lettuce, radishes and peppers which were now bearing and which provided a welcome variety to his diet. The greenhouse vegetables didn't have quite the taste of the sun ripened variety but were a welcome addition at the table. March came in like, well, March in Iowa. It alternated between warm and sunny then cold and wet with a couple of light snows. The frost was finally gone from the ground and on April 5, Chris began in the garden. He transplanted the vegetables from the greenhouse and put in seeds for the rest. It took him three weeks to finish the garden then undertook his fencing project.

He went to town and found more wire, posts and gates. The livestock wire didn't need to be as high as the deer fence around the garden and orchard. Chris remembered watching the young men who erected the original fences and thinking they made it look to be an easy task. He found that setting posts, stretching wire and fastening it in place was the most physically demanding job he had ever undertaken. Before he finished the fences, the garden produce was ready to harvest. He managed both tasks and finally finished the fences a week before the first snow fell in October.

November and December passed with no unusual events. December's weather was unusually mild. He drove the little truck to Dallas Center to check on his parents' house. The grave had settled and he thought on his next summer he would need to fill it to even the ground. He went to the airport and entered the hangar. His airplane was covered with a heavy layer of dust. It looked ready to fly but he knew it would take a major inspection and some engine work to be airworthy again. He was resigned to the fact that it was unlikely that it would ever fly again. December ended with a week of warm, sunny weather and it gave Chris hope for a mild, open winter.

Chapter 12 --- 2113

HOME - JANUARY - OCTOBER

In the first week of January the weather was so mild Chris took the ATV and went to Perry on a shopping trip. He needed shoes, socks, underwear and hiking shorts. He found all of them although they were all covered in a heavy layer of dust. One cycle through the washing machine at home would take care of the dust so he wasn't concerned. He did consider the fact that the cloth would eventually deteriorate to the point where he would not be able to replace clothing as it wore out and wondered what he would do then. He decided he would worry about it as that time drew closer. He searched for and found a new backpack. His old one was stained and had several small holes and wear spots where sharp corners had rubbed through. This pack was larger but also lighter in weight than the old one. He had decided that he was going to Rapid City, South Dakota, this summer. He wanted to see the Mt Rushmore Memorial before it started to fall off the face of the mountain from neglect. As if making up for lost time winter set in again with a series of snow storms and bitter cold temperatures. Chris was kept busy just keeping the foot paths between buildings open and passable.

February brought very little improvement over the January weather. The roads were too snow clogged for walking so Chris spent much of the daytime hours reading and watching old videos. He had a fondness for the old Western movies and watched dozens of them. One film which touched him deeply was titled "Cheyenne Autumn." It involved one tribe of the Cheyenne Indians who had been forcibly removed from their ancestral territory and placed on a reservation in Indian Territory, now Oklahoma. Their yearning for their old home was so strong that they eventually packed up their homes, children and old people and marched back to their former home. In defiance of the US Government represented by the US Army they completed the trek and were allowed to remain. Chris thought this love of home explained his annual return to his home rather than moving south where winters were much milder and the growing season longer. Chris had viewed this video several times and every time he was deeply moved by the love those people had for their homeland. As February turned to March the weather gradually improved.

Chris began thinking about the garden and frequently checked the plants in the greenhouse. He began the ritual of walking with the dogs and on days when he was late getting started all three dogs often prompted him by presenting him with their packs accompanied by a playful yip. The potatoes, onions and peppers were in the ground by April 1. He even added two hills of cucumber seeds, not really expecting to reap a harvest from them.

They departed as usually on April 7. His plan again was to take Iowa 141 to Sloan, get on US 29 there and follow it to I-90 at Sioux Falls. I-90 ran all the way to Rapid City and unless he chose to make a side trip those roads would be his route for the entire trip. The first few days were uneventful and when they reached Sioux City the Missouri River was again in full flood. Chris stopped to observe the river and as he stood there watching an entire house came floating around a bend. It was standing straight up and was submerged to the second floor windows. For some reason it reminded Chris of an old steamboat headed downstream for Saint Louis. They continued north and being able to find shelter every night made their trek feel like a pleasant summer stroll.

After heading west from Sioux Falls, Chris began to see more and more herds of cattle. They were grazing in fields which had once produced corn and wheat but which were now reverting to prairie grasses. He noticed in many places there were ponds and marshes which could not have been there when the land was being farmed. It had been the same around his home in Iowa. Over the past two years there were ponds and wet places where none had existed before. What Chris didn't know and thus had not considered was that Iowa and the other prairie states had once contained many ponds and marshes. Man had been draining the prairies of excess water for almost two hundred years. A network of open dredge ditches and underground tiles led the water to the natural creeks and rivers in the area. After seven years of not being maintained by the various counties and states the system was beginning to break down. Before many more years the prairie would look much as it had in 1800. They continued west seeing many cattle along the way. They also sighted numerous horse herds, many of them showing the ancestry of the spotted Indian ponies of the past. Wild game was everywhere and not particularly startled by the appearance of the man and dogs. Mule deer and antelope were the most common but elk were also seen quite often. The elk had once been an animal of the plains but the white man had hunted and harassed the herds until they had retreated to the high country in the west. A few miles east of Mitchell they had their first real excitement of the trip. A small creek passed under the roadway at that point and with no warning the biggest hog Chris had ever seen burst out of the bushes and up onto the highway. Chris happened to have the rifle in his hand because he had been thinking fresh venison might make a welcome change in diet. The hog, a boar as it turned out, was popping its long and wicked looking tusks and seemed on the verge of charging so Chris raised the rifle and fired three quick shots without waiting to see their effect. The hog staggered to the side of the road and collapsed. Chris regretted killing the animal but didn't want another dog injured. Chris estimated the weight of the hog to be at least six hundred pounds and perhaps more. The dogs were edgy the rest of the way to Mitchell where they spent the night.

Two days later they crossed the Missouri at Chamberlain and climbed to the top of the hill on the west side before stopping for the night. Chris was in awe of the scope and magnitude of the open spaces of this part of the west. When he reached the top of the hill it seemed he could see all the way back east to Minnesota or west to the Rockies. His mind told him it wasn't possible but his senses said otherwise. Six days after passing through Chamberlain Chris got off I-90 and onto South Dakota 240 which now ran through the north edge of the Badlands National Park. It took them two days to cover the thirty mile walk to Wall back on I-90. He camped beside the road in the park and by the time they reached Wall they were out of water. Chris chose to stay over for a day in Wall. What had once been one of the biggest tourist stops on I-90 was now just a small, dead town with buildings full of useless junk. Chris obtained three more canteens and even though it gave them an awkward appearance he strapped the new water bottles to the top of the dogs' packs.

On June 1, they entered Rapid City. Chris searched for and found a solar powered motel with a two bedroom suite with a kitchen. He planned to stay for some time and he wanted to be comfortable. He found detailed maps of the area and began to plan what he would see. It would be a two day trip to see Mt. Rushmore and the same to visit Crazy Horse Monument. He added Deadwood to his sightseeing tour and that also would entail an overnight on the road. They rested for two days before starting the trek to Rushmore. The walk was uphill most of the way. For the first time he saw Bighorn Sheep and Mountain Goats. He had trouble controlling the dogs when they saw the sheep which were right beside the road. They reached the Rushmore visitor's center in late afternoon and had time to view the Presidents before dark. Through his binoculars Chris could see that a large chunk of granite had fallen from Jefferson's nose and there were visible cracks in the other three heads. Chris camped that night on the overgrown lawn in front of the visitor's center. In the morning he took a last look at the monument and started back down the road. He thought that in his lifetime the great monument would become unrecognizable. Back in his room he waited a day before starting the walk to the Crazy Horse Monument. He used the day to explore the area around the motel. He found a multitude of shops but little of interest to him. He did replenish his supply of dog food and found a canvas hat to replace the worn out and soiled baseball cap he had been wearing for years. Much of the hike to the Crazy Horse Center was over the road they had previously traveled to Mt. Rushmore. When they arrived Chris concluded the view was well worth the walk. The great stone carving was magnificent and well worth the uphill walk. Chris and the dogs camped out once again and were up and traveling shortly after dawn. Back in Rapid City the motel was beginning to feel like home. They lounged about the motel for a week, making short trips around the city and Chris determined that he wouldn't make the trip to Deadwood after all.

On the 25th of June it snowed. Chris knew it had turned cold in the night but was totally surprised to look out in the morning and see four inches of snow on the ground. The snow convinced him to start for home as soon as the roads were clear. It snowed again that day and the day following. Chris was beginning to think he should find someplace with a heat source and prepare to spend the winter. The situation was puzzling to Chris. It just didn't snow in June and July. It took Chris two and a half months to get from Rapid City to Sioux Falls. The snow continued to fall. He would walk for a day or if he was lucky two and then wait out the snow in a cold motel room for three days or even a week. He finally arrived in Sioux Falls on September 15, and felt thankful to be there. From where he had started this seemed to be almost in sight of home. He chose a new route from Sioux Falls to home. He followed I-90 east to US 75 then south on 84 to Le Mars. From there he took Iowa 3 east to US 71 then south towards Carroll. The weather situation didn't change. He spent more time huddled in some room trying to stay warm. He lucked out only once. He stopped at a small country store with rooms where the owner had lived in the back of the building. There was no electrical power but there was a small stove with a supply of wood and several buckets of coal on the back porch. He was leery of the stove pipe which was rusty and hoped that birds hadn't nested in the chimney. He soon had a fire burning and he and the dogs slept warm for the first time in months. Two days later as he was approaching Carroll the snow began again. It was late afternoon but he was determined to reach Carroll so he continued on.

Chapter 13 --- 2114

January and February brought weather which seemed to have become typical. There was much more snow than he remembered from pre-2106 winters. When the weather cleared he hiked the roads with the dogs and checked the horses as often as possible. He had locked them out of the barn but they had access to the open sided shed used by the cattle. The horses always expressed their eagerness for human contact by crowding around him for the petting and neck scratching which went with each visit. They had even learned to accept the dogs as part of the routine of a visit. The cattle also had become less edgy and no longer fled the barnyard at his approach. Chris considered moving the horses to his place but that would entail moving a large quantity of hay and grain. The animals seemed content where they were and they had survived seven years on the place so in the end Chris decided to leave them where they were until after his trip to Seattle. Since he didn't plan to return home for the next winter Chris saw no reason to put in his usual planting of potatoes. They would just rot in the ground. The March weather improved enough that he and the dogs hiked for many miles. Chris felt they were in good physical shape for the long walk in the summer and on April 7 they set out.

His plan was to go south from Dawson and get on I-80. 80 would take him to Cheyenne where he would change to US 25 which would lead to Buffalo, Wyoming. At Buffalo, 25 merged with I-90 which he could then follow all the way to Seattle. This trip was not for searching or sightseeing, the goal was to cover as much ground as possible and to arrive in Seattle on the earliest possible date. Chris set a fast pace and walked for long days. Most of the time the weather smiled on them and they averaged over thirty miles per day. On April 25, as they were approaching Ogallala, Nebraska, Chris changed his route. Instead of going to Cheyenne and then north he turned off on US 26. This would give him a chance to see Chimney Rock and Fort Laramie. This would cut a few miles off their distance and thus make up for some of the time lost at the two historic places. They reached Chimney Rock on the third day and Chris stopped for an hour just to admire and to savor the view of the majestic spire. They arrived at Scotts Bluff on April 30, and Chris stayed there for a day to rest himself and the dogs. They had traveled hard and fast for more than three weeks and both he and the dogs needed a little rest.

They reached Fort Laramie on the second day out of Scotts Bluff and Chris spent four hours looking at the old buildings and reading the many plaques telling the history of the place. He camped that night on the banks of the North Platte River. It was the first night since leaving home which they had spent outside. It was warm enough but the mosquitoes were a plague so Chris spent a restless night. They were off to an early start next morning. They had gone no more than three or four miles when a movement off to the northeast caught his eye. He stopped to look and was utterly amazed by what he saw. Coming over a low hill perhaps two miles away was a line of people stretching back out of sight. Taking out his binoculars Chris could see that some were on horseback, others were walking and some were driving horse drawn vehicles. Eventually, a herd of three of four hundred horses appeared on the hill top. They were being herded by four or five riders on horseback. Still the stream of people continued to appear over the distant hill top. Chris dug a shirt out of his pack and began to wave it frantically. In a short time three riders broke away from the stream of people and headed his way at a gallop. As they drew near Chris could see they were brown skinned and that each of them was carrying a rifle.

The entire scenario was etched in his mind and Chris could think of nothing except to recall a scene from the old video disc he had at home. It was as if the moment had been lifted form "Cheyenne Autumn" and brought to life here in Wyoming. As the three riders approached Chris could see one of them was a young woman. She was in front of the two men and she was the first to speak. She opened the exchange with a rather brusque, "who are you and why are you here?" Chris replied that he was a traveler on his way to Seattle and was just passing through. He also added his name and the names of his dogs. In a somewhat softer tone she commented that their Chief would wish to speak with him. The three riders dismounted and Chris noted all of them kept their rifles close at hand. They carried on a rather stiff conversation while they waited for the body of people to approach. The three were dressed in a hap-hazard mixture of clothing. All three were wearing blue jeans. The two men wore beaded buckskin vests with no shirt. One of them had an eagle feather in his hair and all three of them wore beaded moccasins on their feet. Four more riders broke away from the main group which continued on its steady march. They had started crossing the road some distance away. Chris had seen several of them out in front of the group cutting the fence wire and pulling it back out of the way. The four riders arrived and dismounted. There were some hand signals exchanged between them and the three earlier arrivals. One of the four stepped over to Chris, extended his hand and said, "I am Gray Eagle, elected Chief of the Cheyenne Nation." He then told Chris that they planned to camp along the North Platte River for several days to give the old people and the very young a chance to rest before they pushed on south and into Colorado. He then invited Chris to stay with them for a day so they could compare future plans and events which happened since "The Day of The Red Star," Chris had always thought of the event as "The Day the Earth Died," but he knew exactly what day Gray Eagle meant.

By afternoon the camp was set up. It spanned almost a mile of the river bottom and was composed of canvas tents, lean-tos and even a few of the conical teepees seen on the plains before the white man appeared in the 1800's. Chris was invited to eat the evening meal with Gray Eagle and his family. The tribe had happened upon a herd of cattle the day before and had killed enough of them to provide food for several days. The young woman who had first spoken to him was with the family and Chris noticed that out of the brown face shone a pair of vivid blue eyes. After they had eaten Chris was asked to talk about his survival and the years since. As quickly as he could do so Chris told of his ordeal on the plane and the several days of blindness which followed. He then talked about his air search and then his summer walks in search of other survivors. He spoke of his home and the adopted horses, how he planned to travel to Seattle this summer and if he found no other people to return home the next year and remain there. Chris was so unused to speaking that soon his voice was hoarse and raspy and he had to stop speaking.

Gray Eagle then took up the story of the Cheyenne people. His group was made up of the survivors from several bands and settlements from across the country. Some of them were individuals who had straggled in from all over the country with nowhere to go but home. There had been many cases of blindness as Chris had endured and more than a few suicides by people who had given up hope. After three years when it appeared no more survivors were going to appear they met in a conclave and moved as a group to the Northern Cheyenne Reservation in Montana. The winters became so severe they moved again to the Cheyenne River Reservation in South Dakota which was little better. They had sent scouts all over the west and finally agreed they would move to the Rio Grand valley in New Mexico and become farmers. They were on their way to New Mexico now and hoped to arrive before winter. They had drafted a simple Constitution with few laws beyond what common sense dictated. Anyone who chose to live with the tribe was required to abide by those laws and any major infraction was cause for banishment for as little as a year or as much as a lifetime. They elected a Chief for life who served at the pleasure of the people and who could be removed from office by a simple majority vote by all members sixteen years and older. There was a Council of Elders who really ran the tribe and its day to day affairs. At present there were roughly one thousand eight hundred members. There were a relatively high number of college graduates in the group, many with advanced degrees. Two of these had Doctorates in micro-biology. The opinion of these two experts was that the basic DNA of the Cheyenne held some anomaly which made them immune to whatever had destroyed most of mankind. Their genealogists had determined that every survivor carried fifty percent or more Cheyenne blood. After the meeting was over Chris explained that he needed to be on his way early the next morning as he did not want to get caught in a snow storm on one of the mountain passes he had to cross. Chris retired to where he had spread his sleeping bag and was busy re-arranging his pack when he became aware of the blue-eyed young Indian woman standing nearby watching him. He didn't know her name but spoke to her and invited her to sit. She told him her Cheyenne name was Gray Dove but her birth name was Melinda Johansen. Her father's father had been Swedish and her mother a full blooded Cheyenne. She was twenty-eight years old and lacked only the residency requirement to become a certified M.D., obviously fulfilling that requirement was never going to happen but she had been serving as a doctor with the tribe.

Out of the blue, she asked if she could go to Seattle with him. She then explained that she had hopes that her husband had survived and might be in the northwest. She had been married at eighteen to a Cheyenne boy of the same age. He had gone to the University of Washington on a scholarship to study medicine and she had been given the same opportunity at the University of Chicago. They had agreed to put their marriage on hold while they finished their educations. Chris was concerned about the reaction of Gray Eagle and asked about her relationship to the Chief. She explained that the Chief was her uncle, her mother's brother, and while he might not approve of her decision she didn't think he would try to prevent her from going. He had allowed her to live with his family because he was her only living relative. Chris tried to impress on her how difficult the walk would be but she countered with the argument that she had walked from Chicago to South Dakota and most of the distance from there to where they were now sitting. Chris insisted they discuss it with Gray Eagle who was still sitting by the fire and who apparently had been watching them. He asked them to sit and before either Chris or Melinda could say a word Gray Eagle spoke. In a cultured voice which sounded as if it belonged in an Eastern college classroom he said, "Yes, my dear, you may go to Seattle with Chris."

With a stammer, Melinda asked how he knew what she wanted to ask. Gray Eagle replied he that he could see it in her eyes from the first moment Chris had told them he was going to Seattle. It was, he said, the first time they had looked alive since she had made it back to the tribe four years earlier. He went on to tell them there was a time he would have walked that far to be with his now dead wife. He concluded by saying he thought Chris was an honorable man and she would be perfectly safe with him. Gray Eagle insisted they stay in camp another day so a proper pack could be prepared for her. Chris went to his sleeping bag that night still amazed at all the voices he had heard that day. Going from being totally alone for seven years to suddenly being surrounded by so many people was a shock to the senses. He wept a little before going to sleep but they were tears of joy. If he found no one in Seattle he knew where the Cheyenne people were going to be and had been told he was welcome to join them.

Putting Melinda's pack together became a community affair the next day. She had offers of enough items to equip a dozen hikers. The only thing lacking was footwear. She finally had four pairs of moccasins which Chris thought would last as far as Douglas if need be. Once they found a shoe store he was positive they could outfit her with athletic shoes to complete the trip. It was only sixty miles to Douglas and about that much further to Casper so he wasn't concerned.

Early the next morning, Chris wasn't sure of the date as he had somehow lost or misplaced his watch, they were on the road. It soon became apparent that the dogs enjoyed Melinda's company and perhaps felt protective of her. They marched on either side of her, never more than two feet away from her side. It was unusual because Moe had always insisted on being in the lead by ten to fifteen yards. The first day they only went as far as the intersection with US 25 where they camped under the bridge. Gray Eagle had insisted that Melinda carry a little .22 semi-automatic rifle and she had proved her marksmanship by bagging two Grouse with it that day. They cooked the grouse over an open fire then went to their sleeping bags at dusk. The next day took them to Orin which was little more that the proverbial "wide spot in the road." They slept inside that night with solar power providing lights in the abandoned store. The next day found them in Douglas where, after searching for some time, they located a store carrying athletic shoes. Melinda was soon equipped with two new pairs of shoes and they decided to spend the night. Chris had been wondering where the bad weather had gone. That night he found out. It had followed him. There was lightning and thunder then torrents of rain. The street in front of the store where they were holed up became a lake and Chris thought it might reach the level of the store. Fortunately, the water didn't rise that high and by morning the street was almost dry. It continued to rain for two days with occasionally some wet slushy snow in the mix. They stayed where they were and Chris began to worry about the mountain passes and the passage of time. Melinda didn't seem concerned but Chris felt the responsibility of getting them to their destination. The third day dawned bright and clear and they were underway early. They arrived in Casper after two days of steady walking. Melinda's new shoes proved a good fit and she had no trouble with sore feet. Emptying their bowels and bladder started out as a minor problem which they had solved by the other person walking ahead for a few yards and waiting for the other to catch up. The dogs proved to be a minor nuisance as they didn't want to leave Melinda's side while she took care of such matters. Chris solved that by slipping a cord through their collars and leading them away. They finally got the message and would follow him without the leash but they were anxious until she rejoined them. They were now into the long barren stretch from Casper to Sheridan and Chris pushed hard to average thirty miles per day. After five days they passed through Sheridan. It was beautiful country but they didn't slow much to enjoy the scenery. Chris found his watch which had slipped off and worked its way to the bottom of his pack. He noted that it was now June 6, and felt the need to pick up the pace even more. They had five hundred-fifty miles of Montana to cross and wanted to cover that distance before July 1.

They left Sheridan on June 7. It was a cool, sunny morning and promised to be a good day for hiking. By mid-morning however, there were dark, threatening clouds building up in the west. They reached the Montana state line in the early afternoon. A rest area had been constructed astride the state line and had been jointly maintained by the two states. They stopped for a break and planned to camp outside further along the road. There were remains of bodies in the visitor's center but after seven years in the dry air they resembled pictures Chris had seen of Egyptian mummies. There wasn't much odor to them, just a dry musty smell, so they sat on a bench in front of the center. A few raindrops began to fall. They retired to the shelter of the covered area in front of the center to wait out the shower. There were dozens of Cottontail rabbits hopping about the grounds. Melinda took out her little rifle and shot two of them then cleaned them and hung them up to cool. Chris was surprised by the quick efficiency with which she cleaned the animals. She replied that when you grew up on the reservation you learned such tasks if you wanted to eat regularly. There were several camping vehicles in the parking lot and Chris had noticed a charcoal grill on the back of one of them. By now the rain was a steady drizzle and they had agreed to spend the night where they were. Chris found a bag of charcoal and set the grill up under the overhang of the roof. They cooked the rabbits which Melinda had quartered and while they were eating Chris mentioned that he always hungered for something green while he was on his trips. Melinda assured him that on the next day he would have greens. They went inside and found the caretakers apartment in the back. There was only a kitchen and a very small bedroom which held two cots. Chris was reluctant to suggest they sleep in the same room but she assured him it would not be a problem. He could step outside while she put on her flannel pajamas. Besides she added there was no one around to gossip. The power for this rest area was generated by wind turbines which had ceased functioning so they went to bed at sundown.

They lay in the dark and talked for an hour or so. Chris asked Melinda about her husband. She told him that Brad had grown up with a handicap. His left hip had an abnormality which caused him to limp and walk with an odd gait. With the cruelty of youth the other boys began to call him Running Turtle. Eventually, that became the name by which he was known. At times it was shortened to just Turtle but only to his closest friends. He was extremely brilliant, finishing high school by the time he was four-teen. He had many scholarship offers and accepted the one from Washington to study medicine. He was slated to begin his residency in Family Medicine when the end came. He had wanted to return to his people and spend his life tending them. She had intended to follow a similar path but her residency was likewise cancelled on the day the earth died. She stayed in Chicago for three years assuming her people were gone but the pull of home was too much and eventually she returned home to find that the Cheyenne had survived the day of death. Her mother who had been her only living relative had been killed in an accident and her uncle Gray Eagle had taken her into his family. With very limited resources she had been practicing medicine for her people ever since. Melinda then asked Chris about his background. He told her of his Great-Grandfather Dallon starting a company on a shoestring and borrowed money and in ten years building it into an ever growing billion dollar a year concern. By the time Chris was born the business was a giant among composite plastics companies. Chris had worked at various jobs at the company and at some time in the future was slated to take over the presidency. He had graduated from Iowa with a degree in Manufacturing Economics and what amounted to a minor in Manufacturing Engineering. His first love, which was encouraged by his grandfather John, was flying. John had bought a plane, had it retrofitted with new engines and presented it to Chris. It was listed as a company plane but in reality it was a very expensive toy for Chris. He spent much time in the air on company business but to those who took note of such things Chris was the only one who ever piloted the craft. Chris told her of John contracting to have his house and all of the accompanying buildings built.

In the morning it was still raining so they became resigned to spending another day at the rest stop. Chris became amused at the possessiveness Moe had developed with Melinda. Moe seldom left her side and if Chris stood, what the dog deemed too close to her, Moe would try to shoulder Chris aside. There was no overt or aggressive behavior but a firm reminder that the woman belonged to Moe. Melinda giggled at the interplay between the two and commented that she hadn't had two boys arguing over her since she was fifteen. She didn't discourage Moe when she gave him a little extra neck scratching. Chris had the feeling that when he and Melinda parted company he was going to lose the dog as well. After two days of rain the weather cleared and they took to the road again.

It was June 10, and Chris was anxious to travel. Chris had been skeptical of Melinda's stamina on a long walk. She had quickly proved those fears groundless. She matched him stride for stride and never requested an extra rest stop. It was his habit to stop for a twenty minute break morning and afternoon. They reached Lodge Grass the first day and went all the way to Hardin the next. Nothing of an unusual nature occurred either day although they did observe a sizeable herd of buffalo grazing on the hills above the Little Bighorn Battlefield. Melinda commented that her ancestors would have been pleased at that sight. From Hardin to Billings was a forty mile stretch which they covered in one day. Now the road became relatively flat and even as it followed the course of the Yellowstone River. They maintained a steady pace and with good weather all the way arrived in Bozeman on June 17. They found shelter in a motel and were fortunate to do so because the weather changed once more. At about 10:00 pm it began to rain and by midnight it turned to snow. They spent the 18th and 19th in the motel trying to stay warm. On the 18th Chris shot a yearling heifer which had wandered into the area with a group of cattle. Melinda skinned out a hindquarter with more skill and dexterity than Chris possessed. She told Chris that if they had a few days to stay she would make beef jerky they could use as travel food rather than having to shoot something every day. They didn't have the time and were on the road again on the 20th. The weather stayed clear and after three days of steady walking they arrived in Butte on the 22nd. The climb up Pipestone

Pass had been a lung and leg burning ordeal so they opted to stay over the day in Butte. As they left Butte on the 24th, Chris noted the mile markers and thought they would not meet the goal of July 31 to be out of Montana but they would be close and he was content with their progress. It took them seven days to travel from Butte to Missoula but it was, for the most part easy walking.

On July 30, they arrived in Missoula with only about one hundred ten miles left in Montana. They used four days at an easy pace to reach Lookout Pass on the Idaho border. That climb had been another long hard trek so they camped that night on the pass. It was cold but it stayed dry so they were comfortable. They spent an almost leisurely three days crossing Idaho and stopped for the night of August 6, in Coeur d'Alene. Now that Chris was within reach of Seattle he spent time pondering the future. He really didn't expect to find survivors in Seattle but he was confident he could survive there for the winter. He also considered Melinda's future. If she didn't find her husband Brad would she attempt to return to her people who by next year would be settling in New Mexico or would she become a nomad wandering aimlessly? He and Melinda had become such good friends he could not see any romantic developments between them. Perhaps she might return to Iowa with him and become a farmer. There were certainly enough houses and farms from which to choose. They left Idaho at a leisurely pace; it was just too hot for hurrying. They left on August 7, and six days later arrived in Moses Lake. They spent that evening sitting on the deck of a lakeside home enjoying the cool breeze. Again, they adopted an easy pace and on the 15th of August they were in Ellensburg. In two more days they were at the summit of Snoqualamie Pass. Seattle was no more than two days away so they stopped for a day to gather themselves for the final push. They spent considerable time discussing their friendship and their future plans. Melinda was effusive in her thanks to Chris for allowing her to travel with him. Chris in turn told her he could not have picked a better traveling companion. Chris who didn't believe they would find any survivors extracted a promise from Melinda that she would return to Iowa with him if that proved to be the case. He, in turn, promised to help her

get back to her people in New Mexico. On August 18, they headed out on the last leg of their seventeen hundred mile hike. As
they rounded the last curve on the mountain and could see out
over the valley below their lives changed, forever. Parked in the
middle of the roadway was a large van with the back doors open.
When they were fifty yards from the vehicle a man stepped out
and walked toward them for a few feet then stopped. He stood
with his hands clasped behind him, very much at ease. He was
wearing a military style short sleeved shirt and matching shorts.
His hair was bright red. Chris depended on Melinda to control
the dogs which were bristling and putting forth low growls. He
walked forward to meet the man who extended his hand with
a smile and said, "Hello, you must be Christopher Weddle; we
have been waiting for you," after a pause he added, "for seven
years." Still grasping Chris by the hand the man added, "If you
go back five generations we are cousins, your grandfather and
my grandmother from that generation were twins." The man
also added, "My name is Brendon Hintz, welcome back to the
family, cousin." Chris was stunned, unable to speak; he stood
with his mouth open looking from side to side as if looking for
an escape route. The red headed man laughed and asked who
his blue-eyed companion might be and added that they had expected Chris to be traveling alone. Chris finally was able to blurt
out Melinda's name and added the names of the dogs as well.
Chris finally managed to ask how Brendon knew his name and
why they were expecting him. Brendon replied that Chris was
on the list and was, in fact, the last one on the list. He went on
to say everything would be explained by the indoctrination team
when they arrived at Mount Vernon. He then explained that
there were around thirty-five hundred people and that they had
settled in Mount Vernon because of its proximity to the rich farm
land of the Skagit Valley. Brendon then asked if the dogs were
used to riding in a vehicle and seem surprised when Chris said
yes. They all climbed into the van where a driver had been dozing behind the wheel. He smiled, said hello and started down
the hill. Moe, as usual, would not be separated from Melinda.
He insisted on lying in the aisle where he could rest his head on

her feet or she could reach down and touch him. As they drove, Brendon explained that he had pulled strings to get the job to watch for his distant cousin to appear. The watch had been maintained through the late summer months for the past three years and was scheduled to end permanently on August 31. All else, he said, would be explained over the next several days. Melinda entered the conversation at this point. She explained that her maiden name had been Johansen and that was the name she had been using but that actually she was married and her husband's name was Brad Sweet. She added that he was most likely working in some capacity in the medical profession. Neither Brendon nor the driver knew of him but assured her that if he was in the community he would be found. When they reached the Seattle area, the driver exited the freeway and went north on smaller state roads. Brendon explained that the city had been ravaged by four earthquakes over a three year period and most of the city was in ruins. They had to make several detours to get around bridges which had fallen from the quakes but eventually they arrived in Mount Vernon. They drove into a parking lot and parked in front of a building still bearing the sign which said, "Fabrics and Sewing Supplies." As the group alit from the van the door to the store opened and at least a dozen people rushed out and gathered about the van. Chris could control his pent up emotions no longer. He broke out in tears and wept uncontrollably and unashamedly. A matronly woman of perhaps sixty years clasped him in a hug, patted his back and said, "Let it out, almost all of us have been there."

Chapter 14 -- 2114

When the initial excitement had subsided Chris and Melinda were shown to rooms in a nearby building which had been converted to a dormitory. The restrooms and showers were pointed out and they were invited to shower and put on fresh clothing if they had any. Brendon, who continued to act as their guide, told them there was a supply store next door and he was sure they could find suitable attire there. When they had showered and changed they went outside. They found five people, including Brendon, sitting in the shade of the awning talking. Four of the five were going to work late that evening and invited Melinda and Chris to eat with them at the community kitchen. There was a single cook on duty and he told them to order anything they would like to eat. Melinda opted for roast beef, baked potato and a green salad. Chris studied the reader board and asked for ham, hash browns, eggs and toast then added a green salad as well. All seven of them sat at a large round table and most of the conversation centered around questions about the hike from Iowa to Washington. Brendon told them he had to leave as he was a farmer and had been neglecting his fields for several weeks. In a few days he would come back to town with his wife and they could talk about family and future. One of the women from the office told Melinda to come in at nine the next morning and she, her name was Paula, would search the records to see if Brad Sweet was listed among them. The two travelers said goodnight and agreed to meet for breakfast at eight. As Melinda started for her room she turned and grasped Chris in an embrace. It was the first time they had touched each other except a touch of hands or arms in passing. With tears in her eyes Melinda again thanked him for allowing her to come along on the great trek they had made. After Chris went to bed he found himself weeping again for no apparent reason. He finally realized the tears were for the great friendship he had developed with Melinda. It was the first he had known in eight lonely years. Partly he knew that some of the tears were for the simple fact that he could hear muffled footsteps in the hallway and quiet voices bidding each other goodnight. He had become accustomed to being alone but it had not blotted out that need for human companionship. The dogs were in kennels provided by the group and he was assured they would be fed, watered and exercised until he returned for them. Chris slept very well that night. He didn't know what the future would bring but he was no longer alone. He was pleased to have a cousin, a very distant one to be sure, but a cousin all the same. The next morning he had breakfast with Melinda. While they were eating she told him when she was a young girl her best friend and only her best friend had called her Mel. She then told him she would be pleased if he would use that name. Chris teared up again but managed to finish his breakfast. Melinda left to begin the search for her husband and Chris went to meet the panel which, hopefully, would answer his questions and start to plot his future.

There were four people in the room, three men and a woman. All of them were older and looked to be in their 60's or 70's. The oldest looking of them introduced himself as Jack Wilson and the other three as Martha Brown, Steve Prejean and Gunter Smidt. He advised Chris that any questions about the community could be asked of any of them and he could have an immediate answer. Jack then asked Chris if he had any questions before they started the meeting. Chris said he had only one. "What happened?" Jack smiled and said, "The answer to that will tell you all you need to know." Jack then proceeded to narrate the story. In 2038 one of the space telescopes detected an unknown body well beyond our solar system. It appeared to be on a trajectory which would bring it into our system so it was closely watched. After two years the experts were positive it would intersect with the sun and orbit somewhere within the system. It was also noted that this body was giving off particles which glowed and gave the body a red appearance. By 2042, the Air Force had developed a rocket with, for lack of a better description, a plasma drive. It was capable of velocities approaching two thirds of the speed of light. The rocket was launched on a mission to intercept the body, by then commonly called the "Big Apple," sample the atmosphere around it and return the sample to earth. One year later a second rocket was launched on the same mission. It took two years for the first mission to return. When the rocket was recovered it was a disaster. When the first sample module was opened everyone in the room was dead in less than two hours. The lab was sealed for three weeks then put under negative air pressure and entered only by people wearing pressure suits. When the second sample module was opened and the contents analyzed it was found to contain a virus which was completely new to the scientists. It was tested on lab mice and rats with no ill effects at all. It was tested on birds and reptiles with the same results. Several species of domestic animals were tested and again nothing. Finally, a monkey was exposed and like the humans it was dead within two hours. Several of the lab monkeys were tested and all died. There were no symptoms displayed. The animal was alive and then it was dead.

When the second rocket returned in 2045 the results of the testing were identical to those of the previous year. It was then discovered that the virus could live for an indefinite period in a vacuum but could live only sixty hours in an earth atmosphere. It was also determined that the "Big Apple" was on a collision or at best a near miss course with earth. All of this information was held in the closest secrecy and somehow remained secret. A highly secret crash program was set up to develop an effective vaccine for the virus and it was not until 2065 that a reliable vaccine was developed. A major drawback to the program was that the vaccine was terribly expensive and could be made only in minute quantities. It was determined that by the time the "Big Apple" was predicted to hit earth in 2106 no more than thirty thousand units of vaccine could be produced. Now the problem became one of who lived and who died. Chris' father had been one of the chosen and after being sworn to secrecy was told of the plan. He flatly refused telling them he didn't want to continue his life without his wife. He insisted that the condition of his silence on the matter was that the vaccine be administered to Chris who would be a young man when the end of the world came. With each inoculation a homing device was imbedded in each of the recipients. It was smaller than a rice grain and it was supposed to draw the person to Southern California or the Seattle area of Washington. In most cases the device worked but in others like Chris it had failed to impel them to their intended destinations. Many people had died in accidents on the day of death and more than a few committed suicide on finding themselves alone. There were now about twenty-three thousand people in California and with the thirty-five hundred in Mount Vernon they made up the total population of what was once the United States. At this point Chris interjected that there were also eighteen hundred Cheyenne Indians headed for New Mexico. Jack continued his narration. On the day the end came the "Big Apple" approached from west to east orbited the earth twice and then was sling-shotted back into space. It was now out in deep space and perhaps had even exhausted itself and burned out. They would never know whether it was just carrying the virus or had been generating the deadly bug. The names of all those who had received the vaccine were on file but it was impossible to tell which or how many had died from accidents or suicide. At this point, Jack called a halt to the session and said they would meet at the same time the next day. Jack then asked Chris where in Iowa he lived. Chris told him and Jack said he had a brother who lived in that area. Chris said, "If his name was Charlie and he was a loner then he was my neighbor." Jack replied that there was no doubt it was his brother and added that he didn't think Charlie was warm to anyone or anything except his horses. Chris left the meeting room and headed back to the rooming house. He saw Melinda sitting outside the door and knew instantly that she had good news. She was wearing the biggest smile he had ever seen on her face. He knew at once that she had found her Brad. She jumped up from her seat gave him a big wet kiss on the cheek then said she could do that now that they were best friends and he was going to call her Mel. She was almost babbling as she told him Brad was working in a clinic in a place called LaConner and he would be here that afternoon. She said Brad had lost the lower part of his good leg in one of the Seattle quakes but had a prosthetic fitted and could get around just fine. Chris decided he could use a nap before supper and lay down on his bed. He had taken the dogs out for a walk and they were now back in their kennels and he had nothing else to occupy his time. He had barely put his head on the pillow when there was a sharp rap on his door. He went to the door in his stocking fee and there stood a beaming Melinda hand in hand with an equally beaming man who had to be the missing Brad. They insisted that Chris must come out and talk before he went to supper. They sat in the shade and chatted as if they were old friends. Brad asked questions about their trip and Chris in turn asked about the practice of Medicine in LaConner. Brad told him there was a sizeable fishing and construction business and he was busy every day the clinic was open. There were always accidents and a surprising number of pregnant women. They asked what Chris planned to do and he told them he supposed the elders would have some suggestions for him tomorrow. After supper they chatted for some time then Mel asked Chris if she could take Moe with her as she was going home with Brad and would really miss Moe if he wasn't close at hand. Chris agreed and they walked to the kennel. When Chris opened the gate Moe went directly to Mel without so much as a tail wag for Chris. Chris wasn't overly disappointed. He knew Mel had won the dog's heart many weeks and miles ago on the highway. As the three of them walked over to get in the truck Brad was driving Moe trotted back to Chris and gave his hand a wet lick as if to say, "Thanks pal, I'll see you around."

The next morning when Chris met with the panel it was Martha Brown who took the lead. She told him they were formulating plans to move the entire Mount Vernon population east and south. Chris asked why and she explained. When the "Death Star" as she preferred to call it orbited the earth, it had enough mass and magnetic pull to tip the earth off of its axis by a few degrees. Those few degrees of position change were enough that it was going to bring another Ice Age. Already the Arctic ice cap had doubled in size and it was growing at a faster rate every year. In one hundred years the Skagit Valley would have a sub-arctic climate and in two hundred years the area would be uninhabitable. They were looking at moving the group to the midwest and in two hundred years join the California group in a trek to what were now the tropics and which in two hundred years would change to a temperate climate. Chris immediately broke in to suggest his area in Iowa. The farmland was productive and there was an adequate supply of farm machinery which could be re-habilitated even after eight years of not being used. He added that there was already enough grain in storage in the area to sustain them until they could harvest their own crops. At this time, Gunter Smidt entered the discussion. He mentioned Chris' manufacturing degree and asked Chris if he had the knowledge and ability to put part of the composite plant back in operation. Chris replied that with a cadre of skilled men who understood the process he could manufacture composite sheets and structural beams in less than six months. Jack then began to ask questions about Chris' flying experience. Chris replied that he had almost twenty-one hundred hours of total flight time with two hundred of those hours in twin engine small jet craft. He also added that he had a twin piston engine plane at home which had not been in the air for the past eight years. He then said he thought a couple of good mechanics could have the plane ready to fly in a few weeks. Jack's smile had become increasingly broad as he turned to the other panel members and said he thought they had found the man they had been waiting for. He then told Chris that they had a twin jet plane at the Bellingham airport. It had been flown in from California in May and two weeks later the pilot had fallen off a fishing boat and drowned. Jack suggested they go to Bellingham the next day and examine the plane.

That evening Chris had finished his supper and was lingering over a cup of coffee when a young woman wearing hospital scrubs approached his table. She asked if his name was Chris Weddle and if he was from Iowa. When he replied yes to both questions she asked him if he knew a lady named Carol Maginnis. Chris replied that he did indeed know her but that she had probably died in southern Mexico eight years ago. The young woman who introduced herself as Corinne told him that Carol was alive and well and working as an M.D. at the clinic in Bellingham. Carol was sure that Chris had died on the big day but anytime someone came to Mount Vernon she requested that they ask about him. Only today an updated list of residents had been sent to all the clinics. The list wasn't really necessary as anyone who walked into a clinic was eligible for treatment. Carol had developed the habit of checking each new list for familiar names. Chris was up and ready to leave immediately but realized he had no vehicle. He hurried to the group office and found Jack and Martha working late. He explained his urgent need for a car but they turned him down. They explained that driving at night was forbidden except for emergency vehicles. The roads had deteriorated to the point it was unsafe to drive at night. Chris continued insisting they let him take a car and that he would be extremely careful. Jack pointed out they were going to Bellingham first thing in the morning and that Chris could look for Carol after they had examined the plane. Chris replied that the plane would have to wait until he had talked to Carol and knew for a fact she was here and healthy. Jack peered at Chris and commented that he appeared to be a stubborn young man. Jack then asked Chris if he was going to be a difficult citizen to which Chris replied that he was going to be a model citizen except for this one issue. On this issue there would be no negotiation, he would see Carol before he did anything else.

Chris didn't sleep well that night. He couldn't believe Carol had survived and was actually here. He was groggy from lack of sleep when they left for Bellingham. He wanted to tell Jack to drive faster but wisely decided to stay quiet. He felt he had just about pushed Jack to his limit with the outburst yesterday evening. Even at Jack's sedate pace they arrived in Bellingham. It turned out the clinic had been set up in a building just past the airport gate. Jack made a motion as if to turn into the airport and smiled as he heard Chris take a deep breath in preparation for making a protest. Jack was still smiling as he parked in front of the clinic. He then told Chris he had one hour as they had other business after this and the airplane. He also told Chris he would send a car to bring Carol to Mount Vernon in the afternoon if this was, indeed, the Carol for whom Chris was searching. As Chris walked into the clinic he was met by a grey haired lady with a pinched, drawn face wearing a broad smile. It took him several seconds to recognize it was Carol and by then the smile had begun to dissipate. He stepped forward with his arms open and starting to sob, she rushed to him and clung as if she were drowning and he was a lifeline. They both kept repeating, "I thought you were dead." Chris finally stepped back while he held her at arms-length and told her she was the most beautiful woman in the entire world. Suddenly there were applause behind him and Chris turned to see Jack and Martha clapping along with two nurses. Jack finally stopped clapping and said, "I assume this is the young woman for whom you were searching." Jack then added, "kiss her then come along, we have an airplane to check out." Carol spoke up and said she had surgery in five minutes and she still had to scrub. Chris walked out in a daze, still not quite believing what had just occurred. In the car Jack told Chris that he and Martha had sent a message to Carol last night explaining that Chris would be there in the morning. Carol had sent a note back expressing her fear that Chris would be repelled by her aged appearance. He then went on to tell Chris that Carol had been through a terrible ordeal and that Chris would have to be extremely patient and gentle with her. Martha then told Chris that she and Jack were so inspired by the reunion that on their way to the car Jack had proposed, she had accepted and they would like to be married at the same time as Carol and Chris. Chris replied that it couldn't be too soon for him but he still had to ask Carol. He then added that Carol's engagement ring was in the safe at his home in Iowa. Martha patted him on the knee and said she didn't think there would be any question of Carol accepting the proposal and that Jack had a tentative idea which might just solve the ring problem.

By this time they were in front of a hangar where the door was open and two men were inside cleaning the windshield of a twin engine jet plane. Jack spoke to the men and asked if the plane was ready to go. One of them replied, "Yes sir, all we need is a pilot." Jack quietly reminded the man not to use "sir" when addressing him. He said they were all survivors and were all equal. The man replied, "Yes sir, I will try to remember that."

Jack sighed and remarked that he had tried but was giving up. He introduced the two men as Rascal and Jib. Rascal being the one who liked the word "sir." Jib was named for the sail because he was so skinny the wind tended to blow him away. Jack then asked Chris if he was familiar with this particular aircraft and Chris told him he had logged thirty-five hours in this model until his grandfather had bought him his very own plane which was piston engine powered. Jack told Chris that since they didn't have his log book and there was no one to fill the roll of a check pilot they would have to rely on his word. Jack then told Chris that when they returned to Mount Vernon he wanted him to go to the commissary and outfit himself with a complete wardrobe. He then pointed out that the travel clothes Chris had been wearing were stained, worn and not at all fitting attire for the group's new Chief Pilot. To this remark Chris snapped out a crisp, "Yes Sir" then ducked his head so Jack couldn't see his smile. Jack then continued his instructions. Tomorrow Chris was to move to Bellingham where he would find a small apartment already prepared for him. Chris replied to this by saying he hoped there would be a place for Curly because the dog went where he went. Jack mumbled a bit more then continued his instructions. Tomorrow Chris was to get settled then starting on the following day he wanted Chris to start flying four to five hours a day so he was thoroughly acquainted and comfortable with the aircraft again. He wanted Chris to log a minimum of thirty hours in the air over the next two weeks. Then came the bombshell. At the end of two weeks he wanted Chris to fly to Dallas Center carrying six men. Three of them would be experts in manufacturing who would look at the feasibility of starting up the composite plant, two would be the mechanics Rascal and Jib who were to start rehabilitating Chris' plane and the sixth man would be responsible for keeping them all fed. The little jet had ample range to fly to Iowa and back if no fuel was available there. Chris was then to fly to California and pick up a qualified pilot for the jet. After that the two planes would be kept busy ferrying people and essential goods to Dallas Center. One of the most pressing problems would be to provide adequate housing for the influx of people.

Chris replenished his wardrobe, was assigned a vehicle and drove himself and Curly to their new home. He found he had been assigned a three room apartment and that a temporary shelter had been put in place for Curly. Chris drove to the clinic and found Carol, who had asked for the rest of the day off, ready to leave. They drove to the waterfront and parked where they could watch a crew preparing a small ship, of about one hundred feet, for sea trials. They sat on a park bench and talked for the remainder of the day. Chris finally managed his marriage proposal which was quickly accepted. Carol told him marriage wasn't really a necessity that she just wanted to be with him under any circumstances. They decided to have the ceremony on the day after Chris returned from his flight to Iowa and that they would invite Jack and Martha to join them. Curly had immediately taken to Carol and he spent the day as close to her as he could get. If he didn't have his head in her lap he was leaning against her legs and feet. Chris, of course, noticed the interplay between the two. Before the day was over he acknowledged the fact that he had lost his last dog and Curly now belonged to Carol. They agreed they would not live together until they were married but Carol insisted that it had to happen soon. At thirty-two she was two years older than Chris and could hear her biological clock ticking. She wanted children. At least three and perhaps four. She told Chris to be prepared because she wanted to be pregnant no later than two hours after the wedding. They hated to say goodnight but after Carol had inspected his apartment and pronounced it large enough for both of them Chris took her back to her room which was in a small dormitory set up for the single women. As they were walking from the car Carol told him there was something she wanted to say about Curly. Chris told her to go ahead, fearing that she didn't want the dog around. Instead, she said that Curly was so sweet and loving he should become a house dog and live with them. Chris knew for certain that he no longer owned the animal which had been his companion since he was a puppy in 2107.

Chris was at the airport by 7:00 am the next morning and found that Rascal and Jib had towed the plane outside and were just finishing cleaning the windows. They reported that they had started the engines, ran them up and they were operating perfectly. Chris did a visual inspection of the exterior then strapped in to the pilot seat and checked the instrument panel. Most of it was similar to his plane at home. He noticed that it had an identical automated landing system to his plane while thinking it was no longer of any use. He opened the pilot's manual to insure he turned every switch in the proper sequence. He soon had the engines running and every gauge indicating that he was good to go. There was no apparent wind so he taxied to the end of the nearest runway, opened the throttles to full power, released the bakes and went rushing down the runway. At the predicted 85 mph the plane broke free of the ground and Chris was thrilled to be in the air again. At an altitude of two thousand feet he leveled the plane, adjusted the throttles for an indicated speed of 275 mph then turned out to the middle of the sound and headed south. He soon flashed past Everett, then Seattle with its dramatically altered skyline and finally Tacoma which looked normal except for the tangle of wrecked cars at various points. Chris had no destination in mind so he continued south. In less that an hour he was over the Columbia River where he turned west and followed it to the Pacific. At the coast he turned north and flying a half mile offshore he followed the rugged coastline. He saw the wreckage of several small boats which appeared to have foundered on the beach or on rocks. He also saw three large ships which looked as if they had rammed ashore at full speed. Other than the derelict watercraft the landscape was as empty as it had been fifteen thousand years ago, before the first Native Americans had appeared on foot or in their great sea-going canoes. Chris now climbed to eighteen thousand feet. He put on an oxygen mask rather than the cabin oxygen and banked to the right to cross over the Olympic Mountains. It was difficult to tell but it looked to him as if the glaciers on the mountains had grown since he was last here. He noted that he had been in the air almost four hours so he turned north and dropped back down to two thousand feet. This time he flew directly over Seattle and the devastation was depressing to behold. A few of the tall buildings were still standing but most were just heaps of rubbish. He flew low over Mount Vernon and waggled his wings to let Jack know he was following orders. Chris made a low pass over the field and saw that the mechanics had found and hoisted a windsock which indicated calm conditions. He lined up on the runway he had used for take off and touched down with only one small hop. "Not bad after an eight year lay-off," he told himself. He taxied to the hangar and found the mechanics waiting with a tug and tow-bar. After shut down Chris dismounted from the plane and was greeted by Rascal who said, "Good landing sir, how was your flight?" Chris reminded Rascal that according to Jack, "sir" was a no-no word. Rascal replied that he had spent twenty-one years in the US Navy, mostly aboard aircraft carriers and that anyone who gave orders or flew one of the silver birds was automatically a "sir" to him. Jib entered the conversation to say his daddy had been a mean old man who had insisted on being addressed as sir and breaking the habit had not been the least bit difficult for him to break after he left home. The men drove a fuel truck up to the plane, topped off the tanks and assured Chris it would be ready to go at the same time tomorrow. Chris returned home to take a shower before going to see Carol. He walked in to find her waiting for him. She was seated on the sofa trying to read a book while Curly sat at her feet with his head on her knee looking hopelessly in love. Chris told her she would have to marry him now or the dog would surely die from a broken heart. Carol showed him a bed she had made for the dog out of two old blankets she had scrounged from the commissary. She then pointed to the corner and said, "Bed Curly." The dog went to the bed and lay down, never taking his eyes off of his new love. Chris asked her how long it would take her to train him that well. She pointed to her lips and said, "kiss" which Chris proceeded to do, long and well. When they finally came up for air Carol smiled and said, "See, it didn't take long at all but we need to continue the training."

It was still early afternoon so they drove to Mount Vernon to tell Jack and Martha of their marriage plan and ask the older couple to join them. The four of them had supper together and Jack reminded Chris that he needed to be back in Bellingham before dark. Chris asked Jack about the night Jack had sent a messenger on two separate trips to arrange the meeting of Carol and Chris. Jack nonchalantly waved his hand and told them that sometimes they had to make exceptions for emergencies and he couldn't afford to have his new and only pilot die from separation anxiety. Chris took Carol directly to her room because she had a pregnant mother-to-be who was expected to deliver that night. For the next four days Chris averaged five hours of flight time per day. He saw Carol every evening and it was becoming more difficult every day to take her back to her room.

Chris took one day off from flying and wandered down to the waterfront. He went into the small shipyard where the gang of men were working to restore the little ship. In conversation with them he learned that when the work was completed the plan was to take the ship to Asia. There was a theory that a small group of Chinese had survived the disaster and might be living on the coast of China. DNA records showed a genetic anomaly very much like that of the Cheyenne. Chris remarked that it was a small ship for a trip to China and the seaman replied that it was bigger than any of the ships with which Columbus set out in 1492. Besides, he included, we have better navigation equipment and won't have an unknown continent to block our way. One of the workmen then said, "I know you, you're that crazy pilot who is going to fly to Iowa then come back and take off again to Los Angeles. You sure won't find me up in one of those little birds with nowhere to go but down if anything goes wrong, at least we have life boats." Chris had no argument for that remark. He returned to his apartment and took Curly for a walk.

For the following two days he flew, taking Rascal and Jib with him the second day. They both enjoyed the flight and Rascal spent most of the flight in the co-pilots seat. Jib preferred sitting back in the cabin where he could see the wings which were holding them up. When they taxied to the hangar Jack was waiting for them. He asked Chris how many hours he had flown and if he was comfortable with the idea of taking the plane to Iowa. Chris told him he had flown thirty-five hours and that he loved the plane almost as much as he did his own. Jack then asked Chris if he could be ready to leave on the day after tomorrow. He pointed out that Chris would have to fly to California as soon as he was back from Dallas Center and then make yet again another trip to Iowa where he would remain for the winter. Jack wanted all three flights completed before September 15 which was less than three weeks away. Chris said, "Then we need to have a wedding tomorrow, there is no other time in the schedule and we are not going to spend the winter apart." Jack surprised him again. He had already informed the magistrate to be available at 10:00 am the next day. Chris said he would need to ask Carol but he thought the little park on the river in Mount Vernon would do nicely. Chris then asked if Melinda and Brad Sweet could be brought from LaConner to act as their witnesses. Jack said he would see that it was done and they went their separate ways. Chris went to find Carol and tell her the news. He was shocked at her appearance. She had dyed her hair a dark brown. It wasn't the black he had dreamed of for years but it was attractive and took years off of her appearance. Chris had spoken at length to Carol about Melinda and wanted them to meet before the opportunity passed.

The next morning everyone met at the park at 9:30 am. Carol and Melinda had both insisted on bringing their dogs. Curly and Moe acknowledged each other but neither of them strayed more than a few paces form their mistresses. They allowed Chris to give them head pats but for the most part ignored him. Mel scolded Moe for being so aloof to his former owner and companion but Moe continued to ignore Chris. Brad had observed this by-play and laughingly told Chris that Moe ignored him also and he had to feed him and scoop his poop every day. The magistrate arrived at 9:45 am carrying two big bouquets. Chris first thought she was someone Jack had arranged for to act as flower girl. She soon dispelled that idea when she pulled a sheaf of papers from a folder and told all of the people involved to step over to a table and sign their names in the spaces indicated. She told them the information would be scanned into the group computer which could only be accessed at her office because, as they all knew there was no longer an effective internet, in fact, there was no internet at all. The ceremony was short and business-like but Chris didn't care, he couldn't remember being happier in his entire life. After all the hugs and kisses were dispensed with Jack announced that he had a proposition for Brad and Melinda. He told them he knew their dream was to return to their people. He then told them if they would fly to Iowa the next day with Chris and start setting up a dispensary he would make sure they were flown to New Mexico no later than next summer. Carol would be going to Iowa on the second or third flight and the three of them should have a usable clinic set up and running in no time. The Sweets left for LaConner to pack their few possessions. They mentioned a carrier for Moe but Chris told them he didn't think one was needed. He was sure Moe would follow Mel onto the plane and stay by her seat for the five hour flight. Jack and Martha still had to arrange suitable quarters for a couple. They had both been living in rooms at the dormitory/rooming house and felt the need for more privacy than was possible where they were. Chris and Carol took charge. She asked Chris to take her home. She told him she was all packed and they could move before the supper hour. By the middle of the afternoon they had her possessions moved and unpacked. She reminded Chris that she was spending the night, as if he wasn't aware, and she wanted a coffee pot set up and ready to go in the morning. She informed him she was going to the airport to see him off and that it just wasn't fair to separate them less than a day after their wedding. Chris agreed with her but pointed out that within the next couple of weeks there would be no more separation for several months.

There were some awkward moments as they were preparing for bed that night. Carol solved that by announcing that she wasn't going to need night clothing, then stripping and getting in bed. Chris followed her example and their married life began. They could hear Curly complain in the living room about being locked away from his new love but Carol said he would just have to learn to live with it.

The next morning as they were having coffee before leaving for the airport Carol said she had a secret to tell Chris and that he couldn't repeat it for a while. He asked what it was and she said Mel had told her yesterday that she and Brad were expecting a baby. That, however, was only half the secret and Chris again asked for the rest of the story. Carol smiled and said, "Just so you are the first to know, I became pregnant last night with a boy so you need to start thinking of a name for your son." Chris was stunned beyond words. He had no idea how she could know but somehow he didn't doubt a word of what she had said.

They were met at the airport by Jack who asked Chris how much time he would need in Iowa. Chris told him he would stay there two days and return on the third day. Jack told him he could have two days to rest when he was back in Bellingham then he would need to go to California to pick up another pi-lot. Chris agreed and set about pre-flighting the plane. Carol stayed close to him and tried not be a hindrance. She already had tears on her cheeks and made no effort to hide them. The plane was crowded with the two extra passengers and various boxes of medical supplies and food items. It was nowhere near its weight carrying capacity so Chris had no concerns about his cargo. Chris asked Rascal if he would like to make the flight in the co-pilot's seat and Rascal was buckled in before the question was finished. Jack asked Chris about his planned route and Chris told him it would be to follow I-90 all the way to Sioux Falls then a diagonal path across Iowa. He was familiar with every landmark for every mile of the way. Carol clung to him and again insisted this wasn't fair. She finally released him and moved to where others were standing. Chris started the engines and taxied to the end of the runway. When they were in the air Chris leveled off at five thousand feet. He turned on the inter-com and informed his passengers of his intended route and that there was cold water in the small galley and a toilet in the aft section of the plane. As an afterthought he told them if anyone was uneasy about unbuckling and leaving their seat, Jib would be their steward for the flight. As they approached the Seattle area Chris turned on the cabin oxygen and took the plane up to twelve thousand feet. They were soon over the Cascades and then the Bitterroots of Idaho and Montana. He climbed to eighteen thousand feet and maintained it at that level until they had crossed all of the mountains and were over the rolling plains of South Dakota. Here he dropped back to twelve thousand feet which he would maintain into Iowa. As they approached Sioux Falls the cloud cover lowered so Chris dropped his altitude and hoped the weather would hold off until they reached Dallas Center. They were going to have a flight time of almost exactly five hours which made their arrival at 4:30 pm local time. As he approached the Dallas Center strip he had Jib come to the cockpit and he along with Rascal scanned the runway for debris as Chris made a very low and slow pass. Seeing nothing significant Chris turned and landed the plane, then taxied to the company hangar. He told Jib where to find the switch to open the door. When the door was open he taxied inside, then shut down the engines. Everyone dismounted and Moe rushed outside and lifted his leg to a post which held a fire hose at the corner of the hangar. Chris had never been more proud of the dog. It had been a long flight.

The first problem the group faced was one of sleeping space for everyone that night. Rascal, Jib and Chuck, the man who was to be their cook and provisioner could stay in the crew quarters adjacent to the hangar office. The three engineer/plant operators could be accommodated in the small apartment complex near the headquarters complex. All were within a three or four minute walk of each other and the plant itself. Chris then lead all of them to the motor pool where they found ten vehicles plugged into the charging grid. He explained the average two hundred mile range of each car or truck and the necessity of plugging each unit into the charging grid every four days whether they had been driven or not. He chose his usual little truck and suggested a four door sedan for Brad and Mel. Chuck assured them all he would have a meal ready for them in two hours and that it would include fresh steaks he had brought from Bellingham. Chris then asked Brad and Melinda to follow him and he would show them to their quarters. He drove to the home of his parents where he found the yard full of weeds and the grass overgrown. The two people were surprised and delighted. When he told them the place had belonged to his parents Mel protested saying that he would surely like to keep this place for himself. Chris told them his own home was only about twenty five miles away and that he had no intention of moving. He felt his mother would be pleased to know that someone of Mel's character would be living in her house, using her things. Chris told them of his parents' grave in the backyard and that he had a stainless steel marker he wanted to erect. He then asked if he might use the back bedroom for the two nights he would spend before returning to Washington. He was assured the room would be his as long as he wished to use it. They returned to the office complex where Chuck, as he had promised, had a meal prepared. Chuck had brought fresh produce so they dined on steak, salad, fresh green beans and mashed potatoes. Chris told the engineers he would give them the combinations and open the various files on the manufacturing process in the morning as they could get a start on determining the feasibility of starting the plant again. That night everyone rolled out sleeping bags and the next day would be spent cleaning and doing laundry. Chris turned on the water heater and they had turned on all the taps to purge the lines of the old water. Chris left Mel and Brad washing dishes and cleaning house and returned to the airport office. Jib and Rascal had already found a tank truck and refueled the plane. They were busy checking every system to insure it was ready to go whenever Chris wanted it. Rascal wanted to talk about Chris' plane which he had already given a cursory exam. He told Chris there were four new identical engines sitting in a warehouse in California. Chris pointed to a pair of crates in the back of the hangar and told Rascal there were two more of the same engines. Rascal was ecstatic. He told Chris that as soon as he took off for Bellingham they would simply put the new engines on the plane and not have to rush the process of getting the used ones ready to fly again. He also said if they could get the engines from California they could keep the "Ugly Bird" flying forever or at least fifty years.

Chris got the engineers into the files and left them to their reading. He drove back to where Mel and Brad were cleaning house and found them taking a break on the deck drinking iced tea. Mel had discovered three vacuum sealed tins of tea and insisted to Brad they must have a glass of tea on their new deck. Chris choked up when he realized they had moved their chairs to the exact same position where he found his parents eight years before. He didn't mention this to the couple. It provided a view from a mile away of the same Raccoon River that he watched from his own deck. He accepted a glass of tea from Mel and noticed a tear in the corner of her eye. Chris asked if something was wrong and she said, "No, I'm just happy." She then told Chris it was her first real home and her first guest was the man who made it possible. At this point Brad entered the conversation with the comment that she had been this way all morning. He also added that there might be a problem next summer in convincing her to move to New Mexico. Chris told them he had to leave as he was going to his home and wanted to check on the horses as well. They were surprised at the mention of horses so Chris told them the story of Jack's brother Charlie and his pet Belgians. He rolled his sleeping bag and put his pack in the truck.

In thirty minutes he pulled into his driveway and found everything as is should be. He was happy to be home again if only for overnight. He took a pork steak out of the freezer and a potato out of the root cellar. Chris checked all of the buildings to insure there were no leaks or storm damage. He then pulled out a deck chair and just sat. Totally relaxed for the first time in months, he wondered if Carol would be as content here as he was. He considered making a quick trip to check on the horses but decided he would do it in the morning on his way back to Dallas Center. He ate his supper outside on the deck and while he was eating he began to feel that something was missing. He wished Carol was here of course but that wasn't the problem. It finally came to him that it was the dogs. Most of the time he had lived in the house they had been his steady and only companions and he missed them. He consoled himself that Moe was in Dallas Center and Curly would be here with him in a matter of days. Chris had stripped his bed, then washed and dried everything and made up the bed again so it would all be clean and ready when Carol arrived. When they were building the house he had wanted to put in a king sized bed. His wise old grandfather had said, "Son, you don't want to be that far away from the woman you are sleeping with." Chris had opted for a queen sized bed and now thought Grandpa was probably correct. That night as Chris lay on one of the beds upstairs he went to sleep listening to the now familiar wolf song. He hoped Carol would find the sound as soothing as it was to him.

The next morning when Chris stopped to check on the horses he was surprised to find five strange horses in the lot with the Belgians. Three of them were of a size with the Belgians but Chris had no idea of the breed. One was a fine looking mare of same saddle breed with long legs. She was black with three white feet and the remnants of a halter still around her neck. The last one was what appeared to be a yearling filly with Appaloosa blood. She was brown in color with a spectacular blanket of white filled with brown spots across her rump. The Belgians immediately came to the fence to be petted. The other horses didn't approach but neither did they run. Chris opened a bale of hay and put it over the fence for them. By this time Chris became aware of the cattle trotting up the lane from the pasture. Chris thought perhaps they had heard the horses nickering for hay and wanted their share of the treat as well.

Chris drove back to Dallas Center where he found the two mechanics happily uncrating the new engines. Melinda and Brad had arrived and were examining the rooms which had contained the small clinic maintained by the company when it was operating. They were both of the opinion that it would adequately serve their needs until the population increased to at least two hundred. The engineers had spent most of a day and a half reading the specs for the materials and manufacturing process and were confident they could have the plant running at twenty-five percent of its former output in as little as six months with no more than one hundred workers. With an additional crew doing carpentry and construction work they could provide shelter for the entire community now in Washington in as little as two years. Chris pointed out that Perry might be a good center for location of the majority of the group. It was located in the midst of good farmland. In addition a new hospital had been erected in 2104 complete with regional trauma and urgent care centers. This was added to the report being written by the engineers. Chris added that the runways of the Perry airport were of adequate length to handle both his plane and the jet he was now flying. Chris sketched a quick map of the Perry area for the engineers, Mel and Brad. They were going to check out the hospital plus any industrial areas to see what could be rehabilitated. Rascal and Jib assured him they would make sure the Perry runways were clear plus they would find a hangar for his plane. Chris slept that night, for what he hoped was the final time, in his boyhood bed.

The next morning as he was preparing to leave he told Mel she should check out the attic. He told her his mother had never discarded anything and that there were at least a dozen boxes containing baby and toddler clothing. Melinda blushed and then asked how he knew she would need then. He didn't let on that Carol had told him. He simply said, "You have a new glow Mel, you glow."

Chris took off as shortly before nine. He thought with the prevailing westerly winds the flight could take as long as six and a half hours which would put his arrival at 1:30 pm local time in Bellingham. The flight was uneventful except for having to fly around a thunderstorm in central South Dakota. It was a localized storm and the skies were clear for most of the trip. He landed at 1:45 pm and was greeted at the airport by Carol, Jack and Martha. Jack told Chris that he was to stay over a day before making the trip to California. Jack was going to spend the afternoon and evening reading the report on the situation in Iowa and wanted to discuss it with Chris the next morning. Two new mechanics were scrambling over the plane and Jack told Chris they were every bit as capable and Rascal and Jib. Chris and Carol drove to the apartment where Chris was given a cursory sniff by Curly then totally ignored. The first thing Chris did was to ask Carol if she was still convinced that she was pregnant. Her response was an emphatic yes and Chris believed her. She had been relieved of her medical duties in preparation for her trip to Iowa. There was an adequate number of medical staff available so she was expendable and she would be needed in Iowa once the movement of the group began.

The next morning Chris met with Jack and the rest of his executive panel. They asked questions about Perry and Dallas Center and concluded they would settle most of the group in and around Perry and place about four hundred in Dallas Center. Two hundred would be utilized in the plant and the remainder in various support capacities. Jack's plan was to send them off in groups of three hundred to follow the three main cross county highways. This meant that about nine hundred per year would make the trek. By using the three routes of I-70, I-80, and I-90 the surrounding country would not be stripped completely bare. It would take three years to complete the migration and it was hoped the remaining five hundred people could be ferried by the two small planes over the three year period. Jack then asked about the house of his brother Charlie and if it was habitable. Chris told him it was in great shape and only needed a thorough cleaning of the eight years of accumulated dust. Jack then announced that he along with Martha were going to Iowa on one of the first flights. He told them that when he and Charlie were young Charlie who was twelve years older had always taken care of him and he would like to spend his final days under Charlie's roof. Chris thought it was a great idea but reminded Jack that he, Chris, claimed the Belgian horses under right of first discovery. Chris then asked whether, if he was willing, his distant cousin Brendon Hintz could be included on one of the first flights. Chris wanted to get his and Charlie's farm land back into production again. There was a farmhouse only a long mile from his where Brendon, his wife and two children could be comfortable. Brendon and his wife Phoebe were sent for and after Chris quickly explained the situation they enthusiastically agreed to go. Jack told Chris that his destination in California was to be the abandoned Vandenberg AFB. The group had people there working to restore several airplanes to flight condition. They were also working on a short wave radio system which was still a year away from completion.

Chris took off at seven the next morning. He flew out to sea for a couple of miles and followed the coast all the way to Vandenberg and was pleased when it showed in his left side window. As he taxied off the runway he was met by a "Follow Me" truck which led him to a cluster of hangars.

When he parked the plane there was a car waiting for him. He was met at the door of a small office building by a man whose haircut and stance suggested he had been a career military officer. The man introduced himself as Jacob Brown, Chief Pilot for the California group. He said he was expecting Jimmy Brown, his nephew, to be piloting the plane. Chris introduced himself and explained the drowning accident. Jacob's only comment was the he had always told Jimmy he needed to learn how to swim. Chris told Jacob the purpose of his visit and asked if there were any qualified pilots on hand who might be willing to move to Washington and make a couple of flights to Iowa over the next two weeks. Jacob replied there were six men on the field with substantial time in the twin jet and all of them were bored and would fight for the opportunity to be flying again. Chris asked Jacob if he would make the selection and to keep in mind that Chris wished to return the next day. Jacob, or as he told Chris he preferred to be called, Jake picked up a microphone for the paging system and said, "Pete I need to see you in the office." In less than two minutes a man of about the stature of Chris walked into the office. He looked to be about mid-forties in age and the squint lines in the corners of his eyes appeared to be those of a man who had spent many hours in the air. Jake didn't waste time with preliminaries. He asked Pete if he would like to fly to Washington and start shuttle flights to Iowa. Pete smiled and said he hoped they were not in a hurry as it would take him at least an hour to be ready to leave. Chris introduced himself and told Pete he had until the next morning to be ready to go.

Jake then told Chris he had something to show him. They all got in Jake's car and drove up the ramp a half mile to a very large hangar. When they entered Chris was awed by the sight in front of him. There sat a pair of C-130 Hercules cargo planes. The design of these planes was at least one hundred-fifty years old and had been retired by the Air Force around 2050. Chris asked if they were real and if they were flying. Jake assured him they were real but were not flying, yet. They were two of the last planes off the assembly line and had been stripped down to bare bones then re-assembled fifteen years ago. During this operation ten feet of length had been added to the fuselage. The hold-up had been engines and propellers. They had finally re-sorted to removing those items from planes in the aircraft bone yard and rebuilding them. They were still a month away from completing the work. Then there was the problem of qualifying pilots. They had a number of men with multi-engine experience but none in this aircraft. It would be spring before they were able to move people in the big birds. The group had even named the planes. In two foot high letters down each side was printed Survivor I and Survivor II. When they were back in the office Jake told Chris he had two more surprises for him. He opened a box behind his desk and lifted out a shiny black object about the size of a deck of playing cards. It was a two way radio which was limited to forty miles in range although from altitude it would operate up to eighty miles. The California group was using them extensively but they were unable to manufacture more of them. They had used all of two types of microchips that went into the unit and had been unable to find more. They had a dozen of the radios not in use and he was going to send those with Chris to be distributed as the Washington group thought best. His big surprise, Jake said, was a short wave radio. They had one compact unit completed and would send it with Chris. A second unit was near completion and should be ready to use by October. The sets were designed for one frequency only but should deliver good quality sound. Jake suggested that they turn on the set on the first of October and try to monitor it during daylight hours.

Jake suggested they go to the dining hall and eat before the rush started. It was a small affair with about fifteen four seat tables and was set up cafeteria style. They each selected stuffed pork chops plus a variety of vegetables. For Chris the topper for the entire meal was a big helping of orange slices. He had not seen a fresh orange in over twelve years and went back for a second serving. While they ate they discussed their pasts. Chris gave them a quick summary of his education, flying experience and his walks across the West. Jake, it turned out, had been a transport pilot in the Air Force for almost twenty years. He had been flying the latest, and as it turned out, the last of the Air Force jumbo haulers. They had been based at a new field just outside Amarillo when in a matter of two days in 2105 a series of tornados had virtually flattened the base and destroyed all ten of the big planes then in existence. His career had been in limbo while they waited for more planes to be delivered and after April 2106 there was no longer an Air Force for which to fly. Pete modestly said he had started as a fighter pilot and ended it flying VIPs in the same aircraft Chris had piloted into Vandenberg. He had over twenty-five hundred hours of time in the little twin jet transport. Jake continued Pete's story. Pete had been flying the very newest fighter in the Air Force inventory with a squadron based in Germany. In 2097 when France had decided to avenge all of the real and imagined humiliations from Germany, the French attacked without warning. It was a short war which was over in six weeks. Aided by US forces the Germans repulsed the French and peace was restored. The new plane being flown by Pete and his fellow pilots was vastly superior to anything else in the air. Pete personally destroyed forty-two French aircraft and so many tanks and armored vehicles that the total count was unknown. Jake laughed and said Pete had so many medals he had to wear some of them on the back of his uniform when he wore them all at one time. Chris was invited to spend the night in the four bedroom suite shared by his two new friends and two other men.

In the morning Chris told Pete to take the pilot's seat as it was going to be his plane from now on. The last thing Jake told Chris was when the first C-130 arrived in Washington it would be him in the pilot's seat. When Chris climbed into the plane Pete was already going through the pre-flight check list. In the back of the plane Chris noted the shortwave set plus the box of hand-held radios. There were also eight crates of oranges plus two of grapefruit. A note from Jake was attached stating the fruit was a gift to the children of the Washington group. After they had been in the air for about thirty minutes Chris could see that Pete was indeed a good pilot. He flew the plane manually rather than using the auto-pilot and Chris relaxed to the point of being a tourist as he watched the scenery flowing past off the right wing tip. Their flight to Bellingham took less than four hours and they arrived in time for Carol to rush to the airport when she heard the plane while taking her mid-day break. Jack was there as well. He had been pacing all morning as he awaited their arrival. He had heard of Pete and his flying skills and was delighted to have him join their group.

Jack's first question to the airmen was whether they were up to flying to Iowa the next day. Jack was delighted with the oranges and immediately dispatched four young people in cars and light trucks. He directed them to go to every community of the group and present every child under sixteen with four oranges. After thinking about it he added that most of them had never seen an orange and would have to be shown how to peel and eat one. When shown the radios Jack immediately asked someone to fetch Jinx. While they waited for Jinx to arrive Jack explained that he was a twenty-two year old wizard with electronic gadgets. He had no formal education in electronics or engineering but had been obsessed with the working of things electronic since he was ten years old. He didn't have the knowledge or training to create new technology but he could reverse engineer almost anything he saw. There was a stir at the door and Jack's so called "wizard" entered. He was six feet four or five and wearing the most outlandish garb Chris had seen. His feet were huge and clad in torn and stained tennis shoes. He wore a pair of faded jeans that were stained and appeared to been torn rather than cut off just above the knees. His shirt had once been a polo shirt but the arms and collar had been hacked off and the pocket was hanging by a couple of threads. His face and arms were covered with freckles and his carrot colored hair looked as if it had been hacked off in a dark closet. Chris didn't know what the style was supposed to be but it didn't resemble anything he had ever seen. Jack handed the young man one of the radios and asked Jinx if he knew what is was. The reply was, "Sure, it's one of those model KB-231 zip phones which were popular just before the big ball of fire went past." Jack asked Jinx to remove the cover and look more closely. Jinx removed a small screwdriver from his fanny pack and popped both the front and back and looked intently at the innards of the radio. Suddenly, he asked of no one in particular, "Why didn't I think of that?" Jack asked what he meant and Jinx said, "Look at this, they removed two diodes and two chips and replaced them with these two chips. You no longer need a cell tower to send your message you now have a two way radio with a range of twenty to forty miles." Then Jinx added that he could build that radio, all he needed were the phones and there were still plenty of those available in the electronic stores. Chris pointed to the chips and told Jinx the engineers in California had run out of the chips and couldn't find any more. Jinx replied to that by saying the company here in Bellingham which had made sonar for small boats had bought out the market of the chips in an effort to shut out their California competition. He had been to the local plant and there were at least five thousand of each of the chips at their facility. Jack thanked Jinx and asked the young man to come to his office the next morning as he had a new job starting immediately. After the young man left, Jack said he was going to have him look at the shortwave set and see if that could be replicated as well.

Chris and Carol went home after a room had been arranged for Pete. They had set a time to meet for supper. Carol started to smile on their ride and Chris asked her what was funny. Carol told him she was about to undertake her first attempt at matchmaking. One of her nurses just today at lunch had told her how lonely she was and how much she would like to have a companion. The woman was forty-two and attractive and Pete would make a perfect match for her. Chris was dubious. In the few hours they had spent together Pete had never mentioned women and Chris had no idea if he was interested in meeting a new one. Carol insisted that Chris stop at the medical clinic where she went inside and was gone for no more than fifteen minutes. She came back to the car smiling and told Chris they would pick up Jackie at five o'clock. She only lived two blocks from their apartment. After they arrived home Carol informed Chris that she and Curly were slated to be on the flight to Iowa tomorrow. She planned to ask Mel and Brad if she could room with them until Chris was finished with the Washington flights for the year. Rascal and Jib were working on his plane but he wasn't sure they would finish it in time for him to make any flights before they shut down for weather at the end of September. Jackie turned out to be a willowy brunette of about Carol's height with a bright smile. Pete had not yet arrived when they walked into the dining area so they selected a table for four and sat down to wait for him. Carol insisted she and Chris sit next to each other. She winked at Jackie and said it was so the two of them could hold hands under the table while eating. Pete arrived after just a few minutes and seemed surprised to find a fourth person at the table. During supper they all talked of mundane things and of the prospect of getting a copy of the shortwave radio put together and operating. They all agreed it would make communication between the three far separated groups much simpler and obviously much more rapid. It was obvious to Chris and Carol that Pete was attracted to Jackie. He hung on every word she uttered and said "yes ma'am" to her so many times it caused her to blush. When they were ready to leave Pete turned to Jackie and very formally asked if he might escort her home. With no hesitation she accepted and then asked if he minded if they walked since it was such a pretty evening. Chris and Carol stood talking to another nurse from the clinic and both of them noticed the two were holding hands. After they were home Carol said, "I know they don't play baseball anymore but did I just hit a home run or not?" Carol had already packed what she was taking so they had a leisurely breakfast the next morning then drove to the airport with Curly.

Jack and Martha were waiting along with Brendon and his family. An architect was going along as well. His job would be to design a small easily constructed house to be built of the material from the plant. The houses were to be designed so additions could easily be joined to the structure. For all of them except Carol and the architect this was to be their first airplane ride and combined fear and excitement created an almost palpable aura over the group.

As soon as they were in the air Pete asked Chris if he would mind taking the controls for the first two hours while he caught up on a little sleep. Pete then told Chris that he hadn't gone home from Jackie's place until almost four am. The last thing he said before falling asleep was, "I'm going to marry that woman if she will have me." "Home run indeed," thought Chris as he smiled. Chris found a note pad, wrote what Pete had said then waved his hand back toward the cabin until Carol noticed and he motioned her to come to the cabin. She unbuckled and stuck her head into the tiny cockpit. Chris handed her the note while putting a finger to his lips for quiet. Carol returned to her seat and Chris could almost see her smile of pleasure as she read the note. Chris had followed his previous route of following I-90 and they were just approaching Sheridan when Pete finally stirred in his seat. He unbuckled and went back and made use of the toilet. He returned to his seat and when he was strapped in, turned to Chris and said he was ready to take the controls. Chris agreed and Pete took over. Pete then began to speak of his evening and night with Jackie. He began by saying there had been no sex or even heavy petting. They had spent the evening and early morning just talking. Jackie had been named for her great-great grandmother whose maiden name had been Weddle. Spelled the same as Chris spelled his. Chris promised himself to go to the genealogy charts when he was home as that name triggered something in his memory. He had the feeling he had just discovered another long lost cousin. This one even more closely related than Brendon. Chris called Carol on the pager and asked her to come to the cockpit. He wanted her to hear all of this. Carol sat on the floor using a small cushion between and just behind the pilot seats. Pete continued with the story of Jackie's life all the way to Sioux Falls. At this point Carol said her knees and behind were telling her it was time to return to her seat. As they crossed Iowa Chris pointed out the landmarks Pete should look for on his next flight when he would be alone in the plane.

When they landed in Dallas Center everyone was tired and happy to be in their new home. Chris had to laugh when Curly trotted over and used them same post Moe had found on the previous arrival. Rooms were found for the architect and for Brendon and his family. Rascal and Jib reported they were still two weeks away from having the "Ugly Bird" ready to fly. This meant there would be no more flights for Chris until spring. Pete insisted his plane be prepared and ready to fly the next day. He wanted to make one more delivery flight to Dallas Center plus he had urgent business in Bellingham. Brad and Mel came in just as they were sitting down for supper that evening. They had been in Perry working to clean and organize the clinic and ad-joining facilities. They were both enthusiastic about the potential of the place. It had been a state of the art facility when the end came and could be again with the application of a lot of elbow grease and a trained staff. Melinda and Carol were going to be great friends as well as fellow doctors. When Carol announced that she also was pregnant Mel told her she must have all the baby and toddler things she had found in the attic of their new home. They were all handmade, apparently by the grandmother of Carol's coming baby. Mel added that all of the patterns as well as a large supply of well stored material were in the attic also. Mel herself was a talented seamstress and could make all of the clothing their baby would need. Chris' mother had also left a many function sewing machine and Mel was anxious to try it out. Chris and Carol decided that since he wouldn't be fly-ing again this year they would stay in Dallas Center that night and go home the next morning. Chris had in mind to see if the house of his former neighbors, the Browns, would be suitable for Brendon, Phoebe and the children. He knew there was some water damage where windows had been broken in a storm but thought the rest of the house was sound. The place had a solar powered electric system and a good set of out-buildings. They told Brad and Mel they would check in with them at the clinic within the next couple of days and bid them goodnight.

As they were leaving he remembered the radios and called them back. He opened the box, explained what he had and handed them out. Keeping one for himself he passed the rest to Brad, the engineers, Rascal, Brendon and the final one to the cook/provisioner who told them to just call him "Cookie." He told them he was Hungarian and his name was too hard to pronounce. The batteries in the radios were supposed to last fifty years so there was no need for a charger.

That night they slept in a room next to Brendon's family. It had been a long day and everyone retired early.

Pete was the first one up and about the next morning. Breakfast was uncured bacon, grits and stewed prunes. Pete didn't actually ask anyone to eat faster but it was obvious he was anxious to get started. When Carol asked why he was in such a hurry he replied there was no hurry he just enjoyed flying in the early morning. Carol gave him as skeptical look and with a rueful smile he added; "besides Jackie is back in Bellingham by herself and I don't want someone moving in on me."

After Pete had departed Chris took Brendon to the plant motor pool and found a small truck with a stake bed large enough to haul sheets of building composite. He told Brendon he wanted to show him a house which needed some repair but which Chris thought would meet the family needs. Chris took a sedan for himself after Carol assured him she could drive it. They drove directly to the Brown place and Chris warned Brendon not to expect too much as they walked to the house. Chris flipped a light switch as they walked into the kitchen and was relieved to see the power was still on. He showed Brendon the bedroom where the remains of the Browns were still in bed. Brendon's only comment was the couple could be buried under the big maple tree which stood at the back of the yard and which was visible through the bedroom window. They went into the rooms with the broken windows where Brendon slammed his heel on the floor in several places and pounded the walls with his hand.

He announced that all of it seemed solid and unaffected by the rain which had blown in. Brendon wondered aloud what material had been used which seemed so impervious to prolonged soaking. Chris told him it was most likely some of the composite sheeting from his family's plant in Dallas Center. Brendon paced about the house several times then announced it would do nicely for his family. He said as soon as he replaced the windows they could get rid of the mice and rats then start the cleaning and painting. Brendon was sure that he and Phoebe could restore the house to livable condition in less than a month. They went to the electric panel and turned on the breakers for the well pump and water heater which Chris had turned off years ago to prevent a fire. After they heard the pump start they turned on all of the water taps in the house. At first there were only bursts of air from the taps then a trickle of slightly rusty water. Finally, the taps were all flowing clear and cold water and that question was answered. There was a two car garage which they checked next. Inside was a small car and a beat up old truck. They were both connected to a charging grid and indicated a full charge. There were no bird or animal droppings on the floor so apparently the building was critter proof. They went on to a shop/machine shed where they found two medium sized tractors, both electric, and all of the equipment required to operate a medium sized farm. There was a heavy workbench with several tool boxes. The wall behind the bench was covered with a full array of carpenter tools and Brendon commented that he wouldn't have to shop for tools. The barn, swine and poultry houses were all in good shape lacking only livestock to bring life back to the farm. Brendon went back into the shop and returned with a ladder, tape measure and note pad. He started to measure the windows and discovered all five of the broken ones were the same standard size. Brendon asked Chris for directions to a building supply store in Perry. There were two which were within sight of each other. Chris gave him directions and Brendon, telling them he would be back early the next day, headed out for Dallas Center. Chris turned to Carol and said, "Finally, it is time for us to go home."

Chris drove the short distance and parked in front of the yard gate. They sat for a moment looking at the house in silence until Carol commented, "You and your grandfather chose well, this is lovely." Chris opened the gate and Curly, after visiting the nearest bush, went directly to his kennel as if he had never been away. The couple entered the house and it struck Chris for the first time that the place had an extremely masculine décor. They toured the house and Chris explained it had been designed for the easy addition of two rooms off the west side. The balcony space was such that it could be partitioned into two rooms and another bathroom added. All this, of course, would have to wait until the move from Washington and the required carpenters and plumbers were available to do the work. He then told Carol the house had been waiting for her and was now hers. He wanted her to redecorate the place in any way she desired. The only things he wanted left undisturbed were the pictures of his parents and his grandfather which were hanging above the fireplace. Carol was impressed with the quantity of meats Chris had in the freezer and the home canned vegetables in the large pantry. They took a ham form the freezer plus green beans, peas and carrots from the pantry. Chris then took Carol on a tour of the out-buildings. She was impressed with the shop and the vehicles it contained. She immediately spotted the grave marker Chris had created for his parents and insisted they must get it placed before winter. It was a warm evening so they had their supper on the deck. Chris grilled ham steaks outside and Carol prepared the vegetables in the kitchen. They ate in silence while the evening bird chatter went on around them. A squirrel in a nearby oak tree seemed to be scolding them for intruding on his sanctuary. Chris told the squirrel to get used to it as we are here to stay. Carol commented on how wonderful the ham had been and Chris could only say, "Beginners luck, it was my first effort." They went to bed early and Chris had already drifted off to sleep when Carol woke him by grasping his arm and whispering, "What is that, what is that noise?" Chris listened for a moment then smiling in the darkness he told her that it was her lullaby by which to go to sleep. Carol commented that it was too scary for a lullaby and wanted to know what was making the noise. Chris told her it was their very own wolf pack and they would sing for her almost every night.

In the morning while they were eating breakfast Carol told Chris that after listening for a while the wolf song became a soothing melody and she had enjoyed it. After eating, Chris took the tractor and turned the potatoes and onion out of the ground. They would be left to dry until the next day. After putting the tractor away he took out his new radio. He turned it to channel four which they had agreed to use and paged Brendon who answered almost immediately. When Chris asked where he was Brendon replied he and his entire family were at their new house and he was just starting on replacing the third window. Brendon said the family including the children, Mavis who was seven and Brendon Jr. aged five had agreed they didn't want to wait three or four weeks to move in. Today they would attempt to clean two rooms enough to sleep in and then work on the rest, one room at a time, starting with the kitchen. Chris asked if it would be ok for him and Carol to drop by and visit for a few minutes. Brandon replied, "Sure, just don't get in Phoebe's way, she is on a mission and is making the dust fly." At this point, Mel and Brad broke into the conversation to ask if they could come out to see both places. Now Carol took the radio and said all of them were to have supper at her new home. She said her husband had cured the most incredible ham in the world and she couldn't wait to share it. Mel told them she and Brad would be there around four. After the conversation Chris showered to get rid of the garden dust then climbed the stairs and looked over the sleeping areas. He stripped the beds and took the sheets and blankets downstairs to the laundry. Chris and Carol drove to their new neighbors and found Brendon's statement to be true. Phoebe was truly making the dust fly, then scouring everything with hot soapy water. Brendon had carried the beds and ruined furniture outside. The items made of wood he could burn but he didn't know what to do with the mattresses and bed frames. Chris suggested all the iron and steel be saved. He sensed that in the future they would need it. As for the rest he told Brendon he would show him where to dispose of it and told him of the mine shaft. Carol offered to prepare them a noon meal but was told that Cookie had taken care of that. Chris then asked what the family was going to sleep on that night and the foreseeable future. He was told the floor would be clean, and they had slept in worse places. Chris then told them he had a queen sized bed and two twin beds that weren't being used and that he and Brendon could have them moved in less than an hour. By now the usually stoic Phoebe was in tears. She sobbed, "A new house and new beds. We will never be able to repay you." Chris told her no payment was necessary and any thanks should go to his long dead grandfather for creating the place where he and Carol were living. As they were driving home, Carol took his hand and said, "You are a good man Mr. Weddle." They held hands the rest of the way home and Chris was reminded of his parents. At home Chris hooked the ATV to his large trailer then called Brendon to come over when he finished the windows and they would move the beds. He then went to the garden and picked out six large potatoes and two smaller ones. Chris then asked Carol if she liked to bake. She replied that if he had the sugar, flour, spices and apples she'd make him an apple pie her grandmother would be proud to claim. Chris brought three bags of frozen apples from the freezer and put them in water to thaw and reconstitute. He then showed Carol where everything else was stored and said, "Two pies please." He then put the ham on the spit of the outside grill, turned the heat on low and waited for Brendon. When he arrived it took them less than an hour to take down, move and re-assemble the beds. Phoebe was in tears again and Chris was happy to escape after telling them they would be expected around five. At home he greased the potatoes with ham fat, wrapped them in foil and placed them on the grill. He then asked Carol to select some vegetables from the freezer or pantry and felt he was ready for the first guests the house had seen since his parents ten long years ago.

Mel and Brad arrived at four and the two couples visited until Brendon and his family arrived. Mel told them they would have the Perry clinic ready in another week. She also told them she was having second thoughts about moving to New Mexico next summer. She asked the group if that made her a traitor to her people. Phoebe suggested that Mel visit her people and see if she was really needed. If not, there was no reason not to stay where she wanted to be. Chris moved his opinion of Phoebe up another notch and decided there was more depth to her than her farm wife demeanor indicated. Their supper was declared a feast and Carol's apple pie was a perfect ending. Phoebe stated it would be even better with ice cream on it. Brendon chimed in and said as soon as he could corral some of the cows they would have ice cream not to mention fresh milk, cheese and butter. The two children were puzzled never having experienced the things their parents had just mentioned. Chris asked Brendon if he had experience milking cows and Brendon told him if someone would hold her head and let him use a pair of kickers he would milk a buffalo. Chris told Brendon he might have a solution to the cow problem and that they would look into it once the Hintz house was fully restored. Curly had come out of his kennel and was instantly taken with the two children as they were with him. He had never been around young people. He positioned himself between their chairs and didn't move. Chris told Carol it looked as if Curly was about to jilt her as he had done with Chris. Carol watched the inter-play between the kids and dog but said nothing. When they had finished the meal and were beginning to clean the table Phoebe spoke again. She was standing by the kitchen sink when she stopped, looked at the others and began speaking to them. Her words were simple but, as it turned out, tradition making. Phoebe's words were, "Folks it is September 28, we just had a wonderful meal with dear friends in a new land. I propose we establish this as the new Thanksgiving Day and that we celebrate it every year on this date." There was silence for a moment until Brad said he would second the motion and as one they all responded with yes. Thus was born the first tradition of the group. Mel and Brad departed first then as the Hintz family boarded their truck to leave Curly whined and pawed at the gate to follow. When they were gone Curly went to his kennel and would not come out even when Carol called him and rattled his food dish. Carol commented that it was one fickle dog which had deserted Chris and now her.

Next morning when they let Curly out at about nine for his morning run he trotted up the driveway which was his usual route but this time he didn't return. At noon Brendon called to ask if they were missing a dog. Curly had shown up on their doorstep at ten thirty and didn't seem to be inclined to leave. Chris asked him how he felt about owning a dog. Brendon said he wouldn't mind having a dog but he certainly didn't want to take Curly from Carol. Carol took the radio from Chris and told Brendon it really wasn't up to the adults to decide, the kids and Curly had made the choice. She smiled and returned the radio to Chris who could see the tears in the corners of her eyes. She mumbled something about darned fickle dog and returned to picking up potatoes. There were bumper crops from the potato and onion patches and Chris thought he had enough to feed both families plus Mel and Brad.

Two days later the radio crackled to life with Pete's voice. He was approaching Jefferson and would be over Dallas Center in a matter of minutes. He asked if they would mind driving to the airport as he had something to show them. Chris told Pete they would be there within the hour but couldn't stay long because he didn't like driving at night on the deteriorating roads. When they arrived, Mel and Brad were at the airport. They had seen the plane approach and wanted to hear the latest news from Washington. Jack and Martha were there as well as four men and two women whom Jack identified only as the carpenters and the record keepers. Pete finally made his appearance, walking out of the terminal tightly holding Jackie's hand. He walked over to the group and told them, he wanted them to meet his bride. Chris asked Pete what his bride's last name was and Pete replied it was the same as his of course. Chris pursued the matter by saying he had flown at least three thousand miles with him and had never heard his last name. Pete was flustered but he soldiered on. He said, "My last name used to be Brown but now I think you should just call me Lovesick. I had never married, never wanted to be and an hour after I met this woman I couldn't imagine a life without her. Now let's change the subject before I turn silly." Jack asked for everyone's attention and asked them all to be present in the dining room at ten the next morning. He said they had decisions to make and that he wanted the opinion of every single one of them.

On their way home Chris and Carol stopped at the new Hintz home to inform them of the meeting in the morning. Phoebe commented that she had too much work to waste time at a meeting. Carol assured her it was important or Jack wouldn't have asked for everyone to attend. Curly acknowledged their presence but paid no special interest. Brendon told them it was a good thing they didn't spank their kids as he didn't think Curly would allow it. They had filled the back yard fish pond in that morning and Curly would not allow the five year old Jr. within fifteen feet of it.

They were all in Dallas center the next morning and gathered in the dining room. When he was sure everyone was present Jack stepped up to a small podium which had been rolled in. Jack thanked them all for coming and then told them there was one thing to take care of before starting the meeting. He had forgotten to tell them yesterday but he had brought three golden lab puppies which needed homes. Chris and Carol were both on their feet before he finished the word homes. Jack laughed and told them they were first but could only have one of the dogs. The other two were quickly claimed and Jack called the meeting to order. One of the recorders was taking notes as Jack began speaking. He said the board of governors in California had appointed him as Temporary Manager. After the full population had been moved they would hold a general election to name a board and permanent governor. Eventually, their center of government was to be in Perry since that was where the best medical center was located. They were going to stay out of Des Moines because of the number of bodies, wrecked cars and cluttered streets. The first thing we have to do is name this settlement. There no longer is a United States of America as there is no longer a state of Iowa. Today those places are just lines on the map. The governing board members want us to name this place; we are the pioneers even if we are few in numbers. Take some time to think about it. If needed we can do it over the radio tomorrow. When he stopped speaking Phoebe was on her feel. "I may be out of line," she said, "but I don't think we need a grand, eloquent or historic name. Let's call it what it will be to most of us, a fresh start, a New Home." Melinda was on her feet next. She said, "That is perfect, New Home," and sat down. Carol followed Mel and said it was the perfect name. One of the three engineers, no one apparently knew their names except Jack, made a motion for a vote which when it came was unanimous. So a new political entity was born, New Home. Jack then went on with the meeting and told them he had been asked to do double duty by becoming Manager of the composite plant for two years. He then told them Jinx had put together a shortwave radio which was better than what had come from engineers in California. It was capable of broadcasting on multiple channels. The biggest advantage was that now all three settlements could communicate with each other. Jack was sure the California people were going to want Jinx down there but he had left there because they had treated him as a borderline nut so he wouldn't be going back. The plan was to transport the Washington people to New Home over the next two summers. When those folks were all settled an additional five thousand would be moved from California to New Home. As for the present, one of the C-130s was due to arrive in two days with forty people who would be assigned the task of preparing housing for two thousand people next summer with the remainder following the next year. The other cargo plane would arrive a day later with a full load of food and medical supplies. Jack asked Chris if he would give up flying and become Placement Manager. His job would entail matching newcomers to farms and overseeing the rehab of homes so they were ready when the newcomers arrived. Chris was astounded by the offer and looked at Carol who nodded yes. He accepted the appointment still in awe at the magnitude of the job. Of the forty workers arriving ten would be assigned to Dallas Center and the remainder would go to Perry so Chris would be busy right away. The meeting was adjourned and Jack told Chris he would contact him tomorrow as he had to spend the day finding a house for Martha and himself. On the way out, Mel asked Chris if he could talk for a moment. She told him she hated to ask him after he had been so generous but she and Brad had decided their future should be at the Perry medical facility rather than in New Mexico. Would he mind terribly if she offered his parent's home to Jack and Martha while she and Brad looked for a place nearer the hospital. Chris and Carol were thrilled the other couple would be staying in New Home and Chris told her he had a place in mind which should suit them perfectly. They walked back inside together where they explained to Jack who enthusiastically agreed.

On their way home with the puppy in Carol's lap they discussed what their lives were going to be like for the foreseeable future. The best description was hectic. Chris felt he needed to take care of the problems close to home before starting on the larger community issues. He called Brendon and Brad and after giving them directions, asked them to meet him at Charlie's place in one hour. Chris and Carol were waiting when the others arrived. Their first move was to check out the house. Aside from the dust everything was as Chris had last seen it. Mel commented that it was all rather austere. Chris told her of Charlie being a loner, set in his ways. Chris asked the couple if the house would meet their needs. Mel clapped her hands and practically danced. She told him two days of dusting and doing laundry and it would be ready to move into. Chris told them they could take his truck, drive to Dallas Center today and bring back their belongings then stay with he and Carol until the house was ready. Carol suggested they bring all of the baby clothing, crib and material at the same time. "And the sewing machine?" asked Mel. Chris replied, "of course." So it was settled, Chris and Carol had new neighbors. Chris now led the group to the barn area. The Belgians, having heard the vehicles, were waiting for them. Chris gave them their customary hay and soon the other horses were crowding in for a share. Chris was aware that a horse was missing from the group. It was the big gelding he had considered as a teammate for Junior. Brendon asked if anyone had a claim on the other horses. Chris said no and Brendon said it was a fine looking pair of Percherons and he would like to have them.

If he could find harnesses for them they would make a nice addition to the farm. He added that the saddle mare would be suitable for Phoebe who had been a skilled rider in the old days. He also said the little Appaloosa filly would be a nice pet for the kids in a couple of years. Brendon went on to say that all of the horses need attention paid to their feet. He said he could do that including shoeing them if it was decided to do that. Chris asked him if there was anything about horses he couldn't do. Brendon told him not much, in fact, he could even make horse shoes if that was called for. Chris had looked out and seen the little cow herd trotting up the lane. He and Brendon put a couple of hay bales in the feed bunk as the cows came into the lot. Brendon was now all smiles. He pointed out three of the Holstein cows which were obviously pregnant. They were young cows probably carrying their first calves. There was also a pair of cows of predominantly Jersey blood which Brendon was eyeing. He told Chris if they could capture those five cows he would have more milk and cream in four months than all three of the families could use. Chris pointed out that they, primarily Brendon, would have to move a large amount of hay and grain if they were going to move the livestock. Brendon told him he had checked the barn and granary at the Brown place and there was more than enough to feed the animals through the winter. Chris told Brendon the operation was all his and to proceed as he saw fit. Chris told Mel and Brad about Charlie's body in the barn and asked if it would be a problem. They were both doctors and they had seen their share of death so it was not a problem. Brendon told them he would come over in a day or so and use the little backhoe to dig a grave for Charlie.

They returned to Wolf Song as Carol had started calling her new home. She had, in only a few nights, come to love the nightly "Lullaby."

Mel and Brad took the truck and headed for Dallas Center immediately. She was determined to get moved in as soon as possible. The rest of them had an early afternoon ham sandwich. While they were eating Carol commented that she wanted to paint a sign with Wolf Song on it to hang on the gate. The multi-talented Brendon told her if she could wait until winter shut down most of their activities he would carve one from a piece of Redwood he had found at the Brown place. Phoebe pointed out to him it was no longer the Brown place and should be referred to as the Hintz place. Brendon told them he had a plan to use corn as bait to lure wild hogs into a trap. He wanted to capture ten or twelve young ones and try to domesticate them. He was sure that within two generations they would become the placid animals they had all known in their younger days. Chris had been thinking of the same thing and offered to help when he could find time. Brendon asked if he could measure and make sketches of the smokehouse as he would like to build one at home.

After the Hintzs left for home Chris sat down with a sketch pad and began to outline his tasks for the next few days. His first problem was housing for the forty or so people due to arrive the day after tomorrow. As he mentally ran through the facilities in Perry large enough to accommodate the group, he finally settled on the Community College. He knew there were dormitories capable of housing four hundred students so he would start there. He asked Carol if she would like to make a quick trip to town but she was busy mentally re-arranging the house and planning where she wanted to put house plants. Chris jumped in his "North Dakota" truck and headed to town. He went directly to the school which was in the southeast section of town. The parking lot was almost empty and as he entered the administration building he was mildly surprised by how few human remains were present. They could no longer be called bodies. There was nothing there except bits of parchment like skin, patches of hair and the bones. He went into a dormitory to find it completely empty. The doors to the rooms were open and beds sat with only a mattress, pillow and folded blankets on each one. He climbed the stairs to the second floor and found the same situation. Chris counted thirty rooms on each floor. Even if most of the crew wanted private rooms there was more than enough sleeping spaces. There were two beds in each room so there was potential for housing many more people than were scheduled to come this year. Chris went to the cafeteria and found it and the

174

kitchen in good shape, needing only a thorough scrubbing. Chris rushed home where he had left his radio. He paged Jack several times before he finally got a response. It was obvious from his voice that Jack had been asleep. Jack explained that he had been sitting on his new deck and had dozed off. Before Chris could explain the reason for his call Jack began thanking him for the use of the house. He laughingly told Chris that the house made a wonderful Presidential Palace for the recently created country of New Home. Jack then said that Mel and Brad had been there and gone through the house like a whirlwind collecting what they wanted to take with them. Mel had been in a hurry to get back to her new home. When Chris had the chance to speak he told Jack of the accommodations he had located at the college and that if Jack could supply another plane load of workers that there was room for them to sleep and eat. Chris gave Jack directions to the school and said he would be there to greet the newcomers. Jack said he would get on the shortwave radio and see if the people in Washington could scrape up another fifty people on short notice. The weather might determine whether another flight could be made. The increasingly early winters in New Home might prevent it. Jack told Chris he could not be present tomorrow when the new arrivals came in. The engineers were going to make a test run of the equipment at the composite plant and they insisted he be present. Chris went to sleep that night listening to the wolves and preparing his greeting for the newcomers tomorrow.

Chris woke in the morning to find Carol holding his hand to her abdomen. She smiled and asked him if he could feel his son moving. When Chris said no she looked disappointed and told him she could feel Christopher Jr. moving every day. Chris asked her how she could be so sure since it had been less than a month. She told him, "She just knew." Chris heard a noise in mid-morning and went out to investigate. He found Brendon unloading hay and straw into the barn loft. He was using an elevator from the machine shed which Chris had looked at without understanding its purpose. He had told himself he was a pilot not a farmer. Brendon told him he would haul two more loads of hay and straw today and deliver fifty bushels each of oats and corn tomorrow. "After all," he said, "if you are going to keep horses, you need to have feed for them." Chris left Brendon to his work and after kissing Carol goodbye drove to Perry. He was forced to break the door to gain entrance to the City Administration Office. Even after seven years of making similar break-ins he had to force himself not to look around for a policeman. After searching several offices he found a plat of the city. In fact, he found several and took them all. In mid-afternoon he was preparing to return to town to greet his repair crew when he received a call from Jack. Jack told him the plane had been delayed two hours with a mechanical problem. It would arrive too late to transport the crews to Perry so the men and women would sleep on the floor in D.C. as Dallas Center was now referred. They would be brought to Perry in the morning along with their tools and a truck load of food. Jack told him Jinx would be on the plane and had fifty of the little radios with him. Communication would be much easier in the future. Mel called to tell him the clinic was open for business. She and Brad had been busy washing towels and bed coverings plus they had solved the operation of the autoclave and sterilized all the instruments they might need. Chris thanked her and returned to his planning.

Carol suggested that they invite the Sweets and Hintz families for supper that night because starting tomorrow they would all be busy. Carol began preparing apple pies and Chris brought another ham from the freezer and put it on the spit to thaw and cook. When they had all gathered Brendon mentioned that he was ready to start baiting the feral pigs in an effort to trap some young ones. Chris told him it might be a good idea to harvest three or four of the young adults for their winter meat supply. Brendon offered to help tend the smokehouse fire if he could use space to cure his share of the hogs. Chris told him they would process the meat together and all three families share as they needed it. Brad protested not doing any of the labor to provide the meat. Chris simply told him he was a doctor and shouldn't waste his talent butchering hogs. While they were eating Mavis commented that she had heard a strange noise last night. When asked about it she said it almost sounded like someone crying but different. Chris told her it was a lullaby sung for all of them every night. The little girl wanted to know who was singing and Chris told her it was their wolf pack. Mavis continued to ask about the wolves and who owned them. Carol told her the wolves didn't belong to anyone but had adopted the ridge above the river as their home. Ham, onion and potatoes were sent home with the guests. Chris told them all what a pleasure it was to have neighbors again and that he would like to continue the dinner at least once a month. Phoebe said she would host it next time. Mavis chimed in with, "Could we call it the Wolf Song dinner?" So another tradition was born in New Home.

Next day at mid-day three buses rolled into the Community College parking lot followed by two trucks carrying tools and food supplies. Chris noticed that out of the forty people at least fifteen were women. He told them to go to the dorm and select a room with men on the second floor and women on the first. If there were married couples or just couples they could take the rooms at the far end of the first floor. There were toilets in each room and two shower rooms on each floor. After selecting a room they were asked to return to the cafeteria and print their name by the appropriate room number on the chart. When all were seated Chris stepped to the podium but didn't have a chance to utter a word. A man in the back of the room stood up and yelled that he wasn't going to sit through a meeting without coffee. Before Chris could reply to the remark, a deep voice from the kitchen roared, "Shut up and sit down Johnson, we just got here, you will get it when we have it ready." With that exchange completed a tall dignified looking black man stood up at one of the front tables. He introduced himself as Phillip Webster and said he was a former contactor from California and had been appointed foreman of the repair group by the council in Mount Vernon. He had divided the group into eight five man crews of people who knew each other and could work together. They had agreed that one crew would be assigned the job of hauling away trash and bringing new material to the job site. This job would be on a rotating basis with each crew taking a two week turn at it. Phillip concluded that he knew every person in the group and could vouch for the ability of each of them, women and men alike. Chris at last got his chance to speak. He told them his name and that he was the overseer for the project. He stressed that his name was Chris and not Mr. He passed out copies of the plat with about ten square blocks outlined on each. The plan was for each crew to be assigned a block and for them to work exclusively in that block until it was completed. If they determined a house was not suitable for rehabilitation they were to paint a "D" on the front and back doors and leave it. If there was a question of whether the building could be saved they should call on Phillip, he was the expert. If they finished the residential areas they would start looking at commercial buildings but most likely there were enough residences to keep them busy all winter. At this point a giant of a man, who was at least six feet six inches tall and close to three hundred pounds, rolled out a cart holding two coffee urns. The giant looked at Chris for permission to speak. Chris nodded and the giant, whose apron was embroidered with the name, Gentle Bob, announced that the coffee was ready. He then added that if Johnson was the first in line he would get all of his fingers broken. After everyone, who wanted it, had coffee Chris resumed the meeting. He told the group that in the course of entering all of the houses they would be encountering a lot of valuables. At this point they belonged to no one and were there for the taking. He also pointed out that while the gold and jewels were pretty they were of less value than a bag of un-rusted nails or lock-washer holding a machine together. The cook then announced there would be sandwiches ready in an hour and that supper would be ready at six. Breakfast would be at seven and he wanted them out of his dining room before eight. On the way out of the building Phillip told Chris he would have the crews on the job at eight-thirty the next morning. He then asked the question which had been nagging at Chris since he had accepted the job, "What do you want us to do with the bodies?" His only reply was that there were just too many to bury. It sounded callous and uncaring but they would just have to go out with the trash. A gravel pit had been excavated just south of town and that was where they were going to dump the debris.

Chris arrived home to find Pete and Jackie waiting. The first news was that Rascal had asked Pete to tell Chris his plane was ready. Rascal had dropped his radio and Jib had run over it with a tug. Pete then asked if there were any vacant houses nearby. He wanted to base his plane at the Perry airport and he and Jackie wanted to live close to the other three couples. When Chris told him the nearest one was two miles away Pete asked about vacant land suitable to build on and preferably in the timber. The only spot which came to his mind was on the boundary between his property and Brendon's. Chris drove the ATV out of the shop and told the other three to hop in. They passed behind the barn and skirted the edge of the tree line as they drove west. When he got to the property line Chris stopped the ATV and they all dismounted. Chris led them back into the woods and after two hundred yards they approached the brow of the hill and could look out over the river. Chris told them they could move back fifty yards and still see the river. By putting a bend in the driveway the house would not be visible from the road. Pete could see the potential and asked, "How much for five acres?" Chris asked him what currency he was going to use. Pete was stumped for a moment then shrugged. Chris told him all he needed to acquire the property was permission of the Hintz family and suggested they go find the answer. They got back in the ATV and continued along the edge of the trees until they came to the Hintz buildings.

Chris drove around the barn to find Phoebe and the kids in the yard throwing a stuffed sock which Curly was retrieving and dropping at the feet of the children. Phoebe was doing the throwing but the dog was ignoring her when he returned it. It always went to one of the children. Carol laughed and told Phoebe she knew just how she felt. Chris asked if Brendon was around and was told Brendon had driven to the Sweets to play with the horses again. Jackie clapped her hands and pointed. They all turned to look at Brendon coming up the driveway riding the black mare. The Appaloosa filly was following on a lead rope. Brendon dismounted and with a sweeping bow, doffed his cap. Handing the reins to Phoebe he said, "She now belongs to you dear wife." Brendon told them he had named the mare Lady because she behaved like one. He then told the children that naming the filly was up to them as she now belonged to them. Mavis immediately said, "Spot." Brendon told her Spot was a name for a dog and Mavis replied that it was now the name for her horse. Jr. added that Spot was a good name so that issue was resolved. The horses were put in the barn where hay and oats were waiting. The filly had a separate stall but Brendon left her loose so she could stay close to the mare until she settled in to her new home.

When they were all gathered outside again Chris brought up the reason for their visit. They all walked back to the property line fence. Brendon, who was excited at the prospect of new neighbors, suggested that instead of tearing out the fence and replacing it with two new ones they just leave it and build a new one forty feet inside the Hintz property. He point out that the ground was more solid on his side of the fence and suspected that in years past it had served as a driveway or lane for moving machinery. Pete promised that he would help with the fence and road building but reminded them his entire adult life had been in aviation. Brendon told Pete that an occasional airplane ride would suffice to pay him for the work he put into the proposed new house. Brendon intended to fence three acres of garden and in exchange for Pete's labor in the garden they could use the produce next summer to pay for craft-men to work on the house.

October passed without the usual early snows. The three pregnant women were joined by Jackie who announced that she too was expecting. With this announcement Phoebe told them they must organize a school immediately. Jack agreed and appointed Phoebe to head the project. They all agreed that in the beginning it would require small rural schools in each township with elementary through high school in the population centers.

There were buildings in the towns which could be rehabbed but the rural schools would have to be built new. Brendon located a well drilling rig plus pipe and they drilled wells. One was where Pete and Jackie's house was to be. The other was on property beside the berm which had once been the bed for a railroad. The trenches were dug and footings were laid for the house and school. Ditches were dug and drain field pipes were laid for both septic systems. With the electric toilets now in use the drain fields would carry only water so there was little concern for contamination.

Chris and Pete both moved their aircraft to Perry. They found a hangar large enough to accommodate both planes. They towed out the remains of a plane which had been wrecked and which had been in the process of being dismantled. Rascal and Jib were given the job of moving all the tools and parts from Dallas Center. By the end of the month the move was virtually complete.

Jack had called for one more flight of the C-130s and fifty more people. He now had a sufficient number of workers to produce one hundred, four by eight foot sheets of the composite per day. They were also turning out numbers of structural members. When spring came there would be no shortage of building materials.

Jack had requested that two more doctors be sent since two of his three were pregnant and would require more time off. On the fifteenth Phoebe invited the other three couples for the "Wolf Song" supper as Mavis insisted on calling it. Mavis insisted they all go to the barn to see how much Spot had grown. On their way out Brendon told them he had something for show and tell also. After the proper amount of oohing over Spot they were allowed to follow Brendon into the cow barn. There in the stanchions, munching hay and oats stood the three Holsteins and two Jersey cows. Brendon told them the Holsteins would deliver their calves in less than three months and the Jersey in about four. Imitating her mother's habit Mavis clapped her hands and said, "Isn't my daddy smart, I bet he knows everything there is to know about a farm." No one present wished to dispute her statement. Brendon led them to the swine building where they found 12 weanling pigs happily eating a mash of oats and ground corn. Brendon told them he intended to keep five of the pigs for breeding and eat the rest. While they were eating supper Mavis asked if they could stay up late and listen to the lullaby. "After all," she said, "it is the Wolf Song night." Both children were asleep in their parents' laps before the concert began. Chris told all of them to be thinking about next summer's garden and in February they could start planting in the greenhouse. It was late when the guests departed.

Chris invited the Browns to spend the night rather than drive to Dallas Center in the dark. He had just replaced the beds he had given to the Hintzs so they had sleeping spots for guests again. On their way home Chris asked Carol if she had settled on a name for the Lab puppy. She told him she couldn't think of a name she liked so she had decided to just call him Dog. Chris chuckled and remarked that it was an appropriate name but as original as a horse named Spot.

All four of them slept late and went their separate ways after breakfast. Carol to the clinic to give Mel and Brad a break for the day, Chris to check on the progress of the work crews and the Browns to look for living quarters in town so they could end their daily commute from Dallas Center.

Late in the morning Carol had an unsettling experience. One of the workmen came in with a complaint of a sprained wrist. When he signed the register she recognized the name Thad Johnson. She remembered it was a name Chris had mentioned. He said Johnson managed to cause at least one interruption at every meeting Chris called for the work crews. She palpated the wrist and could find no sign of a broken bone. She wrapped it with an elastic bandage and told him to put ice on it for an hour several times a day for three days. By then, she assured him, the swelling and soreness would be gone.

As she turned to leave the exam room he blocked her way and asked her if that was all she was going to do. She told him there was nothing more to be done. He still didn't move out of her path but stood staring at her. She told him it wasn't needed but if he wanted she would put the arm in a sling. While she was adjusting the sling on his arm he touched her breast three times. Each time she was sure it was intentional. Before he left the office he told her she was too cute to be hanging out with a runty pilot who thought he was a construction boss. Carol thought, this creep thinks he is flirting with me. She was nervous and edgy the rest of the morning so at noon she hung a sign on the door which said, "If you need the doctor call on the radio." She then went home. She called Mel and Brad to tell them she hadn't felt well all morning and was now at home. They told her to rest for the afternoon and one of them would go in to cover the office. Carol considered telling Chris about the incident and concluded that might cause more problems than the incident merited.

The repair crews were making rapid progress with each crew completing an average of two houses per day. Phillip told Chris that when the weather turned bad he planned to pull the men out of the houses and have them start on the school. He had already picked a fifteen man crew to erect the rural schools which would all be constructed using the same plan.

On the last Sunday in October Chris and Carol were sitting on the deck discussing the past week. It was chilly so they were bundled in warm clothing enjoying the sunshine. Carol held up her hand and Chris paused in mid-sentence. She asked him if he could hear bells. He said no but he knew too many hours in loud airplanes had reduced his hearing. In a couple of minutes Chris realized he could hear bells but could not imagine what they were. The bells became louder and around the corner of the driveway came Brendon driving Belle and Beau hitched to Charlie's parade wagon. The children were on the seat with Brendon with Curly behind them with his head hanging over the top of the wagon box. Junior was on a lead rope following the wagon. Brendon turned the wagon at the yard gate and stopped the team. The horses were decked out in fancy harness with lots of silver and nickel buttons and buckles. The harness was draped with the bells Charlie had used only for the Christmas parade. Chris was awe stricken and couldn't speak. Carol, who had known what was coming patted him on the back and led him out of the gate. She said, "It's alright Honey they are real and you get to keep them." Brendon stepped down from the wagon and with his now familiar sweeping bow said, "Squire Weddle, here are your horses, you are now officially a farmer." Mavis shouted, "Surprise! Happy Birthday Uncle Chris, you are invited to our house for supper and a cake." Chris was stunned; he spent several minutes standing with his head pressed into the neck of Belle while he stroked her flank. It had been so long since he had celebrated a birthday that he had completely forgotten it was today. Mavis had climbed down from the wagon and began tugging at his shirt. When he looked down the little girl said, "Don't cry Uncle Chris, this is a happy day. This is your birthday and we are going to have a party." Chris reflected on her words and concluded yes it was a good day, a very good day. He had Carol, he had survived the dark days and he had several very good friends including this sweet little girl determined to cheer him up. He turned to the little group and thanked them. Brendon told him, "No, thank you" and wiped his eyes.

Brendon told him it had been Carol's idea. Carol, close to tears herself, kissed him and told him he was the one to be thanked. He may have saved them all by bringing them to New Home and by extension to their little community of Wolf Song. They arranged the vehicles in the shop until there was room to park the parade wagon. Brendon told Chris to come to the barn and watch him un-harness the horses. He then told him to do each step in reverse when he wanted to use the team. Brendon then told him this was show harness and that he would need heavier duty gear if he was going to work the horses. Chris related that he had heavy work harness in the shop store room and asked Brendon if he would help him fit and adjust it to fit the Belgians. Chris told Brendon of the harness sets at the Farm Supply store and Brendon replied he would check as he wanted to bring the Percherons home. The party for Chris was a huge success with the Browns and Sweets attending also. The cake was a spice cake with walnuts picked up by the children from the back yard. Phoebe told them the recipe was from Carol who said she got it from a cookbook which had belonged to Chris's mother. There had been a notation in the margin, "favorite of Chris."

The party was held at a fortuitous time because the next day winter began with a fury. The wind blew and it snowed more or less constantly for a week. There was a break of clear weather for four days then the snow began again. The only vehicle which could move was the snow crawler. Chris used the snow machine to check on his two neighbors but otherwise everyone stayed inside.

November passed with no pause in the series of storms. The only communication was by the radios and that traffic increased as cabin fever began to settle in. Chris was somewhat surprised at the quantity of manure created by the three horses. He soon had a sizeable pile heaped up outside the barn. When he mentioned this to Brendon the only reply was to be thankful that he didn't have five cows to clean up after as well.

As November turned to December Chris made a delivery of beef, ham and fresh pork to the Sweets. He also took both canned and frozen vegetables. They were effusive in their thanks but Chris waved them off telling them that next year they would have their own garden and meat in the freezer. Mel hugged him, gave him a sisterly kiss on the cheek and told him that she, Brad and the baby all three thanked him. She then told him she had wanted a brother all of her life and he was filling that role very nicely.

During the bad weather the construction crews completely redid the school. They not only cleaned and repaired they also painted most of the rooms. The men were then given township plats with every building located and labeled as to its purpose. Chris had chosen a three tier block of nine counties to be prepared for the people who would be arriving. They would start with Dallas County then move west to Guthrie. They would then move north to Greene and Calhoun, east to Hamilton and Hardin, south to Story and Polk and finally to Boone County. The construction people would be given first choice of the farms in Boone County and by that time it was hoped that a large number of newcomers would be capable of doing their own rehab work. They were all going to be required to scavenge the old farms for the equipment to work the land. The problem of seed was foremost in the minds of everyone involved. There were millions of bushels of all kinds of grain in storage around the mid-west. The question was whether, after eight years, it would be viable as seed. Chris and Brendon planted corn and oats in the greenhouse. They used grain from both the Hintz and Sweet granaries and waited impatiently for the results. It turned out the seed was good and they estimated the germination rate was over seventy-five percent. They had seed for their grain crops but Brendon cautioned that they must find alfalfa seed and test it. If they were going to keep livestock they must have hay as well as grain. A trip back to the farm supply store netted them sixty pounds of alfalfa seed plus two sets of work harness for Brendon's horses.

They immediately planted the seed and while they waited to see if it would sprout Brendon worked with the horses. He was sure they had been in harness before but they had not been the pets as Charlie had made his Belgians. They eventually accepted the harness. Brendon drove them around the barnyard several times with nothing behind them. When he finally led them to a wagon he had dragged out of the machine shop they each took their places on the sides of the tongue with no coaxing. These were obviously the positions to which they had been accustomed to in the past. Brendon left the horses hitched to a gate and called Chris to see if he would pick him up in an hour to go to Sweets to pick up his truck. Chris told him sure and was in the shop cleaning up and putting tools away when he heard horses' hooves and wagon wheels on the driveway gravel. He stepped outside to see Brendon driving the Percherons which were pulling a wagon equipped with the new synthetic hard rubber tires. In harness, the horses looked even more impressive than they had standing in the barn-yard. Brendon's face lit up with a smile of pride and satisfaction.

The weather relented somewhat in February and by the first week in March the rehab crews were working in the rural areas.

On a warm sunny morning Chris hiked along the timberline to talk with Brendon about planting schedules and where to put the various crops. Carol had opened the house to air out some of the winter mustiness. She was dusting the pictures over the fireplace when she heard a step on the deck and turned with a smile. Expecting to see Chris she was shocked to see a stranger standing in her living room. After a second look she realized it was not a complete stranger but Thad Johnson who had fright-ened her when he had visited the clinic. She said, "What do you want and what are you doing here?" Johnson replied, "I'm here to have some fun and you are going to be my partner. Don't waste time with talk; just get your clothes off now." Carol's response was, "You must be insane, I am six months pregnant and we aren't doing anything together, just leave." His response was to take two steps, grasp the collar of her blouse and with two hard yanks ripped it from her body. He then grabbed her bra which proved to be of sturdier material than the blouse. After two yanks failed to remove the bra he pulled a sheath knife from his hip. With one slash he cut the short strap in the center of the bra. In doing so he also cut her breast. The pain shocked Carol but as Johnson stood there staring she grabbed the fireplace poker. When he stepped toward her again Carol took a two-handed swing and hit him solidly across the ear. He staggered back two steps and then holding the knife out he said, "Bitch you will pay for that." At this point Chris, who had returned and entered through the back door walked out of the hall and roared, "What is going on here?" Johnson bolted out the door only to meet Phoebe and Brendon on the steps. Johnson lunged at them and stabbed Brendon in the right shoulder just as Chris came out the door.

Chapter 15--- 2115

Brendon had tumbled backward off the stairs and Phoebe was staring open mouthed at her husband wondering what had happened. By now Chris had the little .22 Colt pistol in his hand. Johnson apparently didn't see the pistol. He grabbed Phoebe by the hair lifting her up on her toes. Brandishing the knife Johnson said, "If you come any closer I am going to cut her bad." Chris didn't hesitate; he lifted the pistol and shot the man squarely in the middle of the forehead. Johnson fell backward off the steps, hit the ground and didn't move. Chris rushed back into the house to see to Carol who was still standing by the fireplace staring into space. Chris grabbed a clean kitchen towel to try to stop the bleeding. He pressed it into the wound as Phoebe and Brendon came through the door. Phoebe pushed Chris aside and said she would take care of Carol. He should call Mel and Brad to see if either one was at home or whether they would have to drive to the clinic. Mel answered the radio and confirmed that she was home. Chris told her they had an emergency and needed her at once. Phoebe had lifted the compress to look at the wound and told Chris to advise Mel the wound was going to require sutures. Mel said she would be on her way in two minutes. True to her word she arrived in less than ten. Mel took one look at the wound and commented that most of the bleeding had stopped. She told them Brad was on his way. She had called him while on the road and said she wanted him to do the stitching. "He makes such a fine seam the scar will be all but invisible," Mel commented. Mel administered a pain shot to numb the area while they waited for Brad. Chris finally remembered that Brendon had been stabbed and told Mel she should have a look at his shoulder. Brendon said he had suffered skeeter bites that were worse but Mel told him to take off his shirt. The bleeding had slowed to an ooze and the wound was no wider than the knife blade. Brendon had full motion in the arm so nothing crucial had been cut. Mel told Brendon there was no telling where the knife had been so she was going to administer a tetanus shot to both he and Carol as a precaution. She put a bandage over the wound and told Phoebe to make sure he changed it every day plus he was to limit the use of the arm for a few days. When Mel approached Brendon with the needle and reached for his arm he fainted. Luckily he was seated in a big chair and didn't fall. Mel administered the shot and Phoebe began rubbing his face and neck with a cool cloth. Brendon soon came around and with a sheepish grin asked if he had missed anything. Phoebe said, "I'm glad your daughter didn't see that, she thinks you are invincible." Brad arrived and after looking at the wound and checking to see that it was suitably numb he had Carol lie on the couch so he could sit in a chair and be close to his work. He told everyone except Mel to go outside and stay there until he called them. They all took coffee and sat on the deck. As they waited Chris called Jack and told him he needed to come at once. Jack wanted to know what was so important it couldn't wait until morning. Chris was beginning to shake now that Carol was being cared for and he had relaxed a little. He told Jack tersely that he had killed a man and didn't want to discuss it over the radio. Jack told him he was on the way and forty-five minutes later he drove in. Just as Chris completed his call to Jack, Phoebe jumped from her chair with a cry of "Good grief the kids are home alone." Twenty minutes later she drove in with the children and Curly in the car. That will never happen again was all she had to say. Brendon told them all that Chris had just left to walk home when he realized he had forgotten to ask about obtaining fencing for the garden. The kids had been in bed for their afternoon nap and he had asked Phoebe to ride along, not expecting to be gone more than ten or twenty minutes. Never again he said, repeating Phoebe's statement. "We were playing fetch with Curly," Mavis added, "I knew Mom would be right back."

Jack and Martha arrived and taking one look at the body in the yard Jack muttered, "I should have known." He went on to tell them he had received two separate complaints from women on the rehab crews about Johnson's aggressive approach to them and frequent comments of a sexual nature. There had also been reports of insulting remarks directed at two women involved in a Lesbian relationship. Jack had talked with Johnson twice about the reports and Johnson had remarked that people were just overly sensitive about a little adult bantering. Jack listened to the accounts of all four of the adults including Carol who was woozy from a sedative administered by Brad. Jack's rage was barely contained but he told them he would hold a meeting the next day for every adult in the area. Martha would do the same in Dallas Center. The message to be delivered would be identical and very specific. Jack asked Chris if the body could be placed in the shop overnight and said he would send two men at eight-thirty the next morning to carry it to town.

The older couple departed and the others prepared to do the same. Brad, before leaving, told Chris that Carol was to have complete bed rest for at least three days and for a week she was not to move unless someone was at her elbow to prevent a fall. They were in the bedroom when Brad told them this. Carol immediately protested. She said her husband was not going to carry a bedpan for her. She was a doctor also and she was capable of walking six steps to the bathroom. Melinda spoke up and said she intended to stay with Carol for at least two days and perhaps three if she determined she was needed. She said that since she and Carol had the same body shape she could wear something of Carol's for a day or so. Phoebe announced she would cook for all of them. Brad left for home, Phoebe went to the kitchen where pots and pans began to rattle and Mel took up her station in a chair beside the bed where Carol lay.

Chris and Brendon wrestled the body onto a trailer and carried it to the shop. The two children had been placed in the video area with a selection of cartoons and old comedy movies to watch. Phoebe announced that supper was ready and placed a large pot of vegetable soup on the table. It was laced with bite sized pieces of fried pork and accompanied by fresh bread. Everyone declared it was a great meal. Chris and Brendon offered to clean up but Phoebe just shooed them out and told them to leave her to her work. The two men walked to the greenhouse where the corn and oats were thriving but there was still no sign of alfalfa sprouting.

Brendon and Phoebe took the children home but not before Mel told Phoebe to drop them off in the morning. She said they were too young to understand and didn't need to hear what would be said at the meeting. Mel and Chris settle in for an all night vigil. Mel dozed in a chair beside the bed and Chris tried to sleep on the couch. He gave up on sleeping and prowled the house in his stocking feet. He was terrified at the thought of infection in the wound or the chance of Carol losing the baby. The night eventually passed and Carol woke at eight looking better than did Chris. Mel had managed enough sleep that she could function.

Brendon and Phoebe had arrived while the two men were there to collect the body. After Phoebe had a look at Mel and Chris she announced she was going to stay and look after Carol while Mel and Chris got some sleep. Brendon told them he would explain the absence of Chris, Mel and Phoebe and Jack could accept it or not.

At eight-thirty people began to filter into the cafeteria to find coffee and their seats. Promptly at nine Jack went to the podium and addressed the gathering. "Yesterday, we were reminded of something we all knew but didn't take the time and effort to acknowledge. All of the people saved eight years ago are not good people. We, as yet, do not have written laws. In three years when our full population has arrived we will convene a convention of elected delegates and write a constitution complete with a code of criminal laws. Until that time, this will be the law and I will be the judge, jury and if need be the executioner. For minor offenses such as stealing or simple assault the guilty person will be shunned for ninety days. They will be restricted to their primary residence with no contact with anyone except their immediate family. For more serious crimes they will be banned from our community for one year and must stay a minimum of fifty miles from our residents. A breach of a shunning sentence will result in banning. A breach of a banning sentence will result in the death penalty. We do not have jails nor even the manpower to staff them so that option has not been considered. Yesterday this man whose body lies before you attempted the rape of a woman who is six months pregnant. He was caught in the act. He used a knife in the assault and the woman was badly cut. He also managed to stab a man who walked in on the event. Both of the victims will recover. Fortunately he was shot and killed by a second person at the scene so there is no need for a trial. This is the law effective now. For the crimes of murder, kidnapping, rape or attempted rape the punishment is death by a pistol bullet to the head. The sentence will be carried out immediately upon conviction and there will be no appeal process. This body is to be left at a secret location to become carrion for the coyotes and vultures which is a much as it deserves. Jack then said his statement was over and asked if there were any questions. There were none but then the giant cook came out of the kitchen and said, "Sir, if you need an official executioner I wouldn't relish the job but I would do it for the sake of the community." Jack then told the people to take the day off from work and perhaps spend some time discussing and meditating on what had been said this morning.

Carol followed Brad's directions and remained in bed for the three days prescribed but she was clearly anxious to be up and about. Mel checked on her twice a day and was satisfied the wound was healing with no infection. The wound was still sore and the surrounding area tender to the touch, as was to be expected and the two doting doctors were pleased with her progress.

Brendon was anxious to start farming and was busy going over every piece of equipment to be sure it was ready for the field. He brought the tractors and equipment from Charlie's shop and since he would be doing most of the farming took it to his place. One day he and Chris hitched their teams to the wagons and drove to town. They loaded sixteen apple and pear trees at the local nursery and carried them to the orchard area Chris had fenced in. The trees were large and overgrown from years of neglect but

Brendon was sure they could be restored with careful pruning. The next day they drove a tractor with a large trailer and brought home the fencing material Brendon would need for his garden.

One morning Chris heard aircraft engines and went out to see the two C-130s overhead on a course for Dallas Center. Jack had decided to risk the weather and called for the planes to deliver fifty people and food supplies. Chris drove to Dallas Center to see a group of people waiting to board buses to their new homes. Jack handed Chris a clipboard while telling him if he would accept it there was a new job for him to assume. Jack told him Phillip could handle the duties Chris had been doing. Jack explained that Chris was to become Commissioner of the north part of the former Dallas County. Phillip would consult with him to insure placement of families into homes and farms of the proper size to hold and support them. Chris was to see that the newcomers received a property deed and that it was recorded. They wanted to place families with children close to the schools which were being built. Chris would also be the arbitrator in any disputes over land or its use. Jack also told Chris that eventually they would have to address the problem of the drainage system and he would be responsible for that as well.

There were three new doctors in this group of newcomers and three educators prepared to open the new schools immediately.

Chris met Rascal and Jib who seemed to think they worked for him as both addressed him as "boss." They were excited to show him what they had found. It turned out to be four small planes. There were two four seat aircraft and a pair of two-seaters. One of the two-seaters was an open cockpit biplane which looked as if it had been lifted from a video of the 1930s except, Rascal said, it was brand new. The other was a STOL which the book said could take off and land in three hundred feet. The other two planes were high end pleasure craft and both mechanics swore that all four planes were ready to fly today if Chris wanted to do so.

As March ended Brendon's three Holsteins dropped the calves. After a week they had more milk than the three families could consume. Brendon began making deliveries to the two families in town who had five children between them.

In early April the gardens were tilled and planted. Brendon even tilled a small plot for Brad and Melinda but because of the deer he didn't hold much hope for its success. He promised them he would fence an area for them for next year.

One morning Chris heard a strange engine and drove out to find Brendon plowing the sod in what had once been a field of Timothy hay pasture. They had agreed to plant forty acres of Brendon's land in alfalfa with the other forty plus the eighty of Chris and Carol's farm in soybeans. The one hundred twenty acres of what had been Charlie's farm would be planted to corn. Chris thought the old diesel tractor made a wonderful sound but he was not so sure about the smell.

Chris was busy visiting the new farmers and advising them where to look for seed and equipment. Without fail he was asked about the livestock which was running loose in large numbers. He told them if they could catch it then it belonged to them or if they wanted beef or pork to eat by all means shoot what they needed. He even offered them limited amounts of grain to use as bait. Most of the farms held grain in storage so he didn't get many takers of the offer.

Phoebe called Carol one day and asked if she could use some fresh eggs. Carol told her of course but asked where they were coming from. It turned out that Brendon, without telling anyone, had trapped wild chickens at other farms. After two weeks of being confined and fed they began using the nest boxes and were now producing eighteen to twenty eggs per day. Brendon, with forty hens and four roosters, felt that number would go up. Meanwhile, Phoebe was faced with what seemed like an avalanche of eggs. Carol told her they would be priceless as trading goods.

By the end of April the gardens were up and thriving and the crops were planted. They had "borrowed" forty acres of land from a vacant neighboring farm and seeded it to oats. It should yield enough to provide feed through the winter and seed for next year. Because of the size of Brendon's garden they had searched stores as far away as Boone and Ames looking for canning jars and freezer containers. Several of the women on the rehab crews had offered to help in the preparation of the produce in trade for a share of the food. Since all three of the women were going to be caring for new babies at harvest time in the gardens they gladly accepted.

On May twenty-eight Mel and Carol went into labor within two hours of each other. After six hours of labor Mel delivered a baby girl. Brad looked at his daughter and commented that she was as pretty as a Pearl. Mel said, "Then that will be her name, Pearl Janine after my new sister." Three hours later Carol delivered a girl. The doctor commented that they were on a roll. Carol almost wailed as she said it was supposed to be a boy. The doctor replied, "Let's not be hasty here, I don't think we are finished yet." Two minutes later Christopher Elliott Weddle, Jr. was wiped dry, swathed in a blanket and placed in his mother's arms beside his sister. Chris who twice in his life had faced down enraged grizzly bears, was so shaken that one of the nurses led him to a cot and had him lie down. The little girl was named Kathie Lynette and was so registered in the hospital log. Chris revived and said he wanted to hold both babies so he knew they were real and not part of a fantasy dream. He was told the babes were nursing and didn't want to be disturbed. Thirty minutes later Chris, who was sitting by the bed holding Carol's hand, was told he could now hold the babies. Both of them were asleep. The moment was so emotional for him that Chris began to leak tears. The nurse who put on a gruff, no nonsense air when she was working also had moist eyes when she took the babies and placed them in their cribs.

Over the next two weeks Jackie then Phoebe gave birth to a boy and girl in that order. Pete was ecstatic over his son and Brendon commented that he was lost now that he was outnumbered by the females in the family. The doctor who had helped in the deliveries suggested that since no more babies were due, that the mothers and infants stay at the clinic for ten days. "Just to be sure everyone is off to a good start," he said.

An older doctor, who had arrived with the last group to fly in, had noticed Brad's limp and asked Brad if he would submit to a series of x-rays. The doctor whose name was Combs was a skilled orthopedic surgeon. After viewing the pictures he told Brad with two hours of surgery he could eliminate the limp and the pain which went with it. He drew sketches to show Brad exactly what he would be doing and Brad quickly agreed. They would not do the operation until November when mother and baby had settled in and Mel had recovered her full strength.

Four young women from the new group volunteered to move in with the new parents to be combination nannies and household help. Pete who had been flying one of the four seat planes discovered by Rascal and Jib was kept busy moving people, machinery parts and in several cases one of the doctors to an emergency scene.

Brendon and Chris harvested a bumper crop of oats in late June and Brendon put an old baler back in operation to bale the oat straw. The alfalfa was slow to grow and Brendon predicted they would only get one cutting that year. Brendon by working eighteen and twenty hour days managed most of their farming. His common sense approach to problems had resulted in his becoming the answer man. He had, in fact, become the de-facto agricultural commissioner. Jack, who missed nothing taking place in New Home, asked Brendon to accept the post of Agricultural Boss. Brendon told him he simply did not have the time. He was tired and thin and looked fifteen years older than his thirty-two years. Jack promised Brendon he would pick three very capable men to take over his farm and machinery restoration work and that Brendon would have the final word on any matter relating to his farm. Brendon agreed and on hearing the news Chris came up with a suggestion. If Brendon would allow Pete to give him flying lessons he could use the STOL plane to cover the area being settled. He could reach outlying areas in minutes compared to hours on the road and would seldom have to be gone overnight. Brendon turned out to be a natural pilot and soon the stubby winged little plane was a familiar sight all over central Iowa, now called New Home.

Mel made it known she wanted to make her promised visit to New Mexico. Contact was made over the shortwave radio which had been delivered to the Cheyenne and Gray Eagle advised Chris to land at the airport outside Socorro. The runway would be cleared and if needed, fuel could be provided. They arranged the date and the old twin engine plane Chris had flown in the past would be used. Mel was still nursing so Pearl would have to make the trip with her. It was decided the nanny would go along to look after the baby when Mel was occupied with people or meetings. Chris asked Mel if she would like to sit in the co-pilots seat for at least part of the trip. She told him yes and was in the cockpit when they took off. Chris told her it would be a three and a half hour trip at their speed and if she became tired or the baby needed to nurse she could unbuckle and go back to the cabin. As they leveled out at five thousand feet and headed southwest, Mel commented that the landscape was passing just a little more quickly than it had on their trek across Wyoming and Montana. After an hour in the air the nanny whose name was Carolyn put her head in the cockpit and announced that Pearl appeared to be hungry. Mel, who said she didn't want to miss any scenery told her to just bring her the baby and she would feed her. Chris kept his eyes fixed out the windshield until Mel laughed as she patted him on the arm. As he turned she told him not to be afraid to look her way. She said, "It's only a breast and it is feeding the baby you made possible." They continued their conversation about the walk west and the changes which had come to both of their lives since completing it.

Chris found the field at Socorro and upon landing they were greeted by Gray Eagle. The plane was pushed into a hangar and Chris was assured there were people on hand who were competent to refuel and have it ready for the return flight. Gray Eagle's transportation was a spirited team of Pinto horses pulling a rubber tired farm wagon. They drove to an adobe house on the outskirts of Socorro which looked to be two hundred years old. Gray Eagle told Mel he didn't know she had a child or a husband. He said he would send for a crib and have it set up in their room at once. She told Gray Eagle that Chris was not her husband but her best friend. Her husband was Brad for whom she was searching when she left her people. Chris, she said had safely led her to the far northwest where she had found Brad.

After a simple supper they settled in chairs on a covered patio and Gray Eagle began to speak. He thanked Melinda, or as he referred to her, Gray Dove, for returning. He told them the tribe had sufficient doctors to meet the needs of the people so she should not feel compelled to stay for that reason. He then told them his people were not happy here. The land along the river is fruitful and supports us well but they miss the turning of the seasons, the great open vistas and even the bitter cold of winter. Gray Eagle then asked the three visitors to describe their land. He had never been to the mid-west and wanted to hear about it. Mel was the first to speak. She told her uncle the winters would certainly be cold enough to satisfy anyone. The vistas were not as long or as wide as the Great Plains but from any little rolling high point you could see for miles. Chris added that the soil was so fertile you could almost grow metal fence posts. Anyone who chose to work the land could reap ample rewards for their labor. There were also small industries being started and there was always going to be a need for scientists, engineers of all types and most of all educators for all levels. Gray Eagle asked if the red people would be accepted as equals and was told that the New Home community contained almost every race existing in the U.S. at the time of the disaster. Carolyn spoke up she said, "Look at me, my great grandmother was white as Chris, now I have predominantly black and oriental genes. My mother always said we were mutts and someday the whole world would look like us. When I am finished helping tend to Pearl, I have a job teaching at a school which will almost certainly contain all white children. There will no doubt continue to be individual cases of racism but your people will be accepted if they are good citizens.

Next morning, Gray Eagle told them he wanted to consult his people but he anticipated that they would want to join the people in New Home. Chris told him that with only two planes for transport it would take at least two years to move the Cheyenne to New Home. Gray Eagle replied that the Cheyenne had walked to New Mexico and if they chose to go they would most likely prefer to walk again. It might take them two years to make the trek but he thought they could make the thousand mile journey in one. "We have discovered that when a people are united in purpose they can accomplish great things." As a bonus, Gray Eagle added, "I have fifteen young engineers and scientists working on a wind turbine which will revolutionize the generation of electricity. We have several prototypes in operation now. They mount on any tall post. We have been using street light posts for the prototypes. The rotor is a small finned cap which makes no noise and turns in the slightest air current. One of these turbines will power four average homes. They can be erected anywhere and we are prepared to share the technology when we are in our new home. Where ever that may be." On the flight home Chris invited Carolyn to sit in the cockpit with him for part of the flight. After they were in the air she came forward. As soon as she was buckled in she thanked Chris for bringing her along. She then told him that "Cheyenne Autumn" was her all-time favorite video and that she had probably watched it a hundred times and always cried. Chris told her it was one of his favorite videos as well and that he had watched it many times also. She then told him she had never expected to meet a Cheyenne Indian and she had just found out she had been working with two of them for almost three months. Now she had spent two nights with the entire tribe and had even spoken to the Chief. "How cool is that?" she asked. When they arrived home Chris and Mel wasted no time in talking to Jack and Martha. Jack asked if they thought the Cheyenne would make good citizens. When they said yes he immediately got on the shortwave and contacted Gray Eagle. He told him New Home would be expecting them next August or September. Jack said his people would try to have adequate housing prepared for them. He added that New Home would be prepared to provide them food with the exception of meat which was readily available on the hoof. After breaking the radio connection Jack asked Chris if he had a plan for locating the Cheyenne. Chris said his idea was to offer them all of Carroll County. It would give them a chance to settle as a group and pick the location each family wanted to occupy. Jack told Chris he thought that a good plan then he told Chris he had assigned a crew to put up Pete and Jackie's house. He told him that when Jackie really wanted something she could nag the bark off an oak tree unless she got it yesterday. He had also assigned crews to build three houses for the men or families who were going to do Brendon's farming, adding, yours as well of course. There would be ten acres fenced for each house for the residents to do with as they wished.

Carol was actually pouting when Chris arrived home. She was sitting in her rocker with her arms folded and a hurt look on her face. He asked he what was wrong but received no answer. When he asked a second time she replied that she was never going to have another dog. They were fickle creatures which had no love or respect, even for the hand that fed and bathed them. When Chris asked what she meant she told him to go to the bedroom and see for himself. In the bedroom there was Dog on the bed, which was forbidden, with his eyes fixed on one crib then the other. Chris snapped his fingers for the dog to get down and was ignored. Taking Dog's collar Chris tugged him off the bed. Through all of this, Dog never took his eyes off the cribs. Chris dragged the dog, only a puppy, to the front door and put him outside. Dog simply sat in front of the door and whined with an occasional yip thrown in. Chris went out and took the dog to Lady's kennel, which he had been sleeping in, and locked him in. When he went back inside Carol said, "That dog is only a puppy, what will he be like when he is grown?" After a moment Chris replied, "Protective, I think, protective." Dog at last quit crying around two a.m. This routine went on for two weeks. If Dog was loose he waited at the door. When the door was opened he shot it and went directly to the cribs. The dog was finally trained to understand that he was to enter the house or the bedroom only by invitation but it was very clear he didn't like it. He paced, either on the deck or in the living room. Trespass meant banishment to a locked kennel. At times Carol allowed him in the house while she was nursing or rocking one of the twins. This was heaven for Dog. He stayed close as he could get without actually touching the baby. Chris predicted that when the dog was grown and the kids were old enough to be outside it would be a fool who tried to interfere with them.

The soybeans were harvested in late September and a single alfalfa cutting went on at the same time. The old combine and baler which Brendon had put together worked well. The beans filled two of the bins at the Sweet's farm and the barns were bulging with hay. They shelled what corn remained in Charlie's crib then ground it to use for livestock and chicken feed. Brendon had found a supply of commercial feed for laying hens and hauled a ton of it home. He didn't know if it was still effective but the hens liked it so it couldn't hurt.

In late October they began picking corn. They picked enough on the ear to fill the crib then combined the rest and put in bins. The bins had heated blowers to complete the drying. The gardens had kept the women busy picking, canning and freezing through September then the potatoes and onions were dug and put in the root cellar. Brendon's smokehouse and a root cellar had been built during the summer and were full. Both teams of horses had been used to haul grain and Junior had proven invaluable for dragging hickory and maple trees out of the timber to be used in the smokehouses.

Pete on his return from a trip to deliver corn picker parts had filled the back seat of his plane with packages of washable cloth diapers. These were welcomed by the women as the disposable ones were becoming more difficult to find and disposing of them was even harder to accomplish.

The disposal problem was eventually solved by the engineers. A pair of them designed a furnace burning natural gas which was plentiful and could be tapped from a pipeline running through the area. The pipeline was connected directly to the wells and the entire system was completely automated which made it easy to use. The furnaces were simple affairs and easy to build. It had started with diapers but eventually was used to dispose of any waste which they didn't want to put into the landfills.

November and December passed with the usual snow storms. In November Brad underwent the surgery on his hip and be the end of December he was walking without crutches with no sign of the limp. He found that he had to learn to walk again. His former mode of walking had involved compensating for the deformity in his hip. The new freedom of motion of his leg required a new approach to his movement.

There were still five hundred people in Washington to be moved and that would be done as soon as the weather cleared enough to make the flights safe.

The Wolf Song dinners continued every month and now included the Browns who had moved into their house as soon as it was closed in from the weather. Pete discovered that he was handy with tools and was doing much of the finish work and all of the painting. The house was sparsely furnished but livable. Jackie had insisted they host the December dinner and her only request for outside help was for a ham from the Weddle smokehouse.

After the crops had been gathered Brendon had fenced ten acres at the Weddle place for Chris and seeded them to pasture grasses. The grass had sprouted and showed a green fuzz on the land before the snow covered it.

Word came over the radio that one thousand people in California were going to leave on February 1 in three groups by different routes and head for New Home. The same week a radio message from Gray Eagle informed the people in New Home that the Cheyenne planned to leave the banks of the Rio Grande on March 1 and to expect them by the end of May. That would mean an influx of almost thirty five hundred new residents next summer and it spurred the New Home people into a flurry of activity. The rehab crews in Polk, Boone and Carroll Counties worked in weather that should have seen them inside their homes keeping warm. 2115 ended with unprecedented activity for the winter months.

Chapter 16 --- 2116

In January Mel and Carol both announced they were pregnant again. Both of them wanted three children and they both said they wanted them as soon as possible. Phoebe told them three were enough for her as she wanted to be able to devote the time each child deserved. Jackie said she was forty-three and didn't want to take the risks involved with older women's pregnancies.

Brendon presented Chris with twenty hens he had trapped. The hens were kept inside the chicken house until they were able to obtain netting and stretch it over the chicken yard. In two weeks the hens settled down and with a steady food supply began to produce eight or ten eggs per day. Brendon was taking eggs to town every week. A Farmers' Market or more properly a swap meet had been established in a former insurance office. Tables and chairs were brought in to accommodate about thirty people. There was no money involved of course but people traded every imaginable type of goods and services. It was a lively place and many people came just for the social aspect of such a gathering. Mavis loved sitting at the table and dickering over goods while her mother visited. She was a sharp bargainer and always managed a fair exchange for her mother's baked goods, her father's wood carvings or the hams and bacon from his smokehouse. There was already talk of moving the meeting to a roomier location.

When Carol and Chris returned home one day they found a large sign fastened to posts at the end of their driveway. It was at least two feet wide and ten feet long. It was carved in deep relief with the letters painted white. It said Wolf Song. At each end was a wolf with its nose pointed to the sky and also painted white. They stopped to admire what was a work of art and at the same time both of them said, "Brendon." They drove into the yard and there, fastened to the gate was a smaller version of the same sign. By now Carol was in tears. "How does he do it, where does he find the time?" Carol spoke these words to the air not expecting an answer. Chris replied that Brendon felt a calling, that it was his duty to do good things for other people. "Plus," he added, "five generations back his grandmother and my grandfather were twins and I believe he feels a strong blood tie. That is why he named the baby Letha Julia." When our next son is born in August I want to name him Craig Allen so the names of those two ancestors will live again. Carol asked how he knew the new baby would be a boy and he could only reply that he just knew.

January passed and in February they started plants in the greenhouse beginning to sense the start of a new season. They heard nothing of the California people who were trekking east but in the last week of the month they had a radio message from Gray Eagle telling them his people had sorted their possessions and were ready to begin their thousand mile march on the first day of March. He told them that fifty of his people had chosen not to make the trek. They were going to remain on the Rio Grande and would probably revert to being buffalo hunters like their ancestors. They had already developed a short bow. The major difference was that now the primary prey would be the wild cattle rather than buffalo. He feared for their survival if they gave up farming. They were carrying the shortwave radio with them and when they found places with a compatible power source they would call to report their progress.

Chris was stopped on the street one day by a man he didn't know. The man introduced himself as Sven Peterson and said he knew who Chris was. Sven told him he had been working with a rehab crew, but that in his past life he had been an orchardist. He had heard that Chris had trees which needed attention. He said sawing boards and driving nails wasn't a bad job but he wanted to be doing what he was trained for and what he loved doing. He said he not only knew fruit trees, he loved the things.

Chris told Sven he had planted sixteen trees in the fall. They had been unattended for eight years and he wasn't even sure they were surviving the winter. Chris asked Sven if he knew where Chris lived and Sven told him sure everyone knows who lives behind the Wolf sign. Chris asked him to come to the house at four that afternoon. They could look at the trees and then have supper. Chris then asked Sven if he had a wife who would expect him home. The man said, "Oh no, she passed with all the others, all I had left were the trees." When Sven arrived and looked at the trees he commented that they looked bad but were healthy and could be saved. They should have been pruned earlier in the season. The first crop would be sparse but after that they should produce normally. They ate supper and Sven commented that the ham was very good. He then added that if a little apple wood was burned during the smoking process Chris would see a subtle change in the taste of the meat. A good combination was for one eighth of the wood burned to be apple. Sven said he would be back in the morning to work on the trees. He told Chris that if he had a short ladder to leave it out as he had to walk and couldn't carry his orchard ladder. Chris asked Sven if he could drive and when the answer was yes took him to the shop and presented him with the old North Dakota truck explaining that the charging connections were universal and it could be charged most anywhere. He then asked Sven to come to his office after he finished with the trees because he just might have a proposition for him. Chris called Jack on the radio as soon as Sven had departed. Jack happened to be in Perry and was going to spend the night. Chris jumped in the car and sped to Perry hoping to get an hour of Jack's time.

It was late when Jack finished his other business and they could discuss what Chris had on his mind. He explained about Sven and his apparent talent of caring for fruit trees. His plan was for Sven to train twenty people, women as well as men, and then turn them loose to the neglected trees of New Home. The twenty could train more if needed and they could restore a very important food source for the entire area. In return each of the people involved would be given forty acres of land in the various counties and Chris suspected many of those plots would become new orchards. Jack agreed and told Chris to get started on the project immediately.

Sven arrived next morning while Chris was still at home. He was accompanied by a little gnome of a man who appeared to be Mexican and who spoke very little. Sven explained he had found the man wandering in a deserted orchard in the Yakima valley of Washington. No one understood why he had survived. He did not have the mark on his hip or the implanted homing device. The only important fact for Sven was that the old man knew and understood fruit trees even better than himself. The two men spent the entire day working in the orchard often stopping to confer about a particular tree. When they were finished Chris was sure the trees had been destroyed but Sven assured him when the spring growth started he would be pleased and amazed at the results. The two men had cut the bigger limbs into suitable lengths to be used in the smokehouse and piled the rest to be burned later. The old man's name was Pablo Gomez but he preferred to be addressed as Pa. When Chris explained the program he had in mind Sven quickly agreed but only on the condition that Pa was to be included and would have authority equal to Sven's.

On March twenty-nine Brendon returned from a flight to Guthrie Center in the STOL and casually mentioned that just east of Panora he had spotted six men moving east at a slow trot. He had circled for a second look and saw they were all carrying light back packs. He said they glanced up at the plane but didn't pause or acknowledge it in any way. Brendon said they appeared to be dark skinned in color but more than that he couldn't say. That evening at seven as the day was turning into dusk six young men appeared at the clinic and asked to speak to Dr. Sweet or Christopher Weddle. Brad who was on duty told them he was Dr. Sweet and asked how he could help them. They young man who appeared to be the speaker for the group said it was Dr. Melinda Sweet they were seeking. Brad told them Melinda was his wife and she was home tending a sick baby. He added that Chris was also at home tending two babies who were ill. The young man introduced himself as Frank and said he and his companions were messengers from the Cheyenne and had been instructed to speak only with the two people he had mentioned. Brad assured them Chris and Mel would be available early in the morning but in the meanwhile he wanted them to eat and rest. All six of them were thin, almost to the point of emaciation. Brad called the community kitchen and asked the cook if he had enough eggs to prepare three scrambled eggs and two slices of toast each for six people. He also asked if there were six single rooms available in the dorm and was told yes. Brad closed the clinic and walked with the men to the cafeteria. He told them they needed food and rest before any meeting. They were offered coffee and milk to drink and all chose the milk. While they were eating Brad asked the dorm manager to assign them adjoining rooms and to see they were not disturbed. He guessed at their clothing sizes then called the manager of the clothing warehouse. He told her she needed to come at once. He needed attire for six men and he needed it now, not in the morning. She was put out by the demand but said she would have the store open in fifteen minutes. Brad was a rather laid back individual but could put a command tone in his voice when it was called for. After eating the six were outfitted with reasonably fitted clothes and shoes. They were shown to their rooms and showers and Brad bid them goodnight. They asked to be awakened at five-thirty but Brad told the dorm manager to let them sleep in. They needed rest more than anything else.

At home Brad told Mel of the six young men and their insistence of speaking only with her and Chris. Mel immediately called Chris and agreed to meet at the cafeteria at eight-thirty. All three of the babies had been suffering from croup but were improved enough that Carol felt she could cope with the twins on her own for the day. Chris called Jack, told him what he knew of the situation and insisted he be at tomorrow's meeting. Chris called Phoebe and asked if Mavis could come and help Mel in the morning. She was only nine but she could change a diaper, burp and rock a baby like a pro. Chris went to bed that night wondering how the six young men had traveled so far so quickly. Surely they must have driven most of the way.

Chris had oatmeal with fresh milk for breakfast. This wasn't the flat, rolled oats of his grandmother's day. Brendon had found some small mills which would remove the hull from the oat kernels leaving the inside intact. The oats took longer to cook but they tasted great and made a satisfying breakfast. Chris was at the cafeteria by eight-thirty and was soon joined by Mel and Jack. The six young men soon appeared. Their appearance was much improved over the previous evening. They all had new clothing and were all clean shaven. Frank again spoke for all of them. He introduced the others as James, Jonathan, Wendell, Kenneth and Patrick. "We were sent," he said "because the short wave radio quit just after Gray Eagle sent the message with the tribe's departure date. I have a written message from the Tribal Council expressing what we would like to see happen. These are not demands but requests concerning out wishes. If we are going to become integrated into your society it needs to be done sooner than later. We have about four hundred people involving many families who wish to be settled into communities already made up of what will be a white majority. We also request that a substantial number of whites be located in Carroll County which you have designated as the new home of the Cheyenne people. There will no doubt be some initial friction between the whites and the Cheyenne. Again, the sooner the problems arise and are settled the better for all of us. We are coming to stay. We as a people have been moving for three hundred years. It is time for a permanent home. Frank then added that between the six of them present they knew almost everyone in the tribe. Part of their assigned task was to help in locating people who would be most compatible with other tribal members and with the whites. Frank then presented Chris with what was obviously a buckskin briefcase like case. He told Chris it contained the written message from Gray Eagle plus a complete listing of the Cheyenne people which was broken down by family groups. Chris tried to pass the case to Jack who pushed it back while telling him that the task ahead belonged to Chris and that Jack would try to provide all of the help Chris requested. Now the questions began. Chris asked how they had made the trip in less than a full month. Kenneth replied, "We walked and we ran, then we ran some more." He went on to explain that before they had received the small radios, the tribe was scattered for fifty miles along the Rio Grande. The best way to send messages was by runners which they discovered was just as fast, and more reliable, than horseback couriers. Mel, as she watched and listened realized she knew four of the six from when she was a teenager and they were small children. Mel asked Patrick about his mother and he replied she was now a gray haired grandmother and a member of the Tribal Council. Chris asked the six if they had any real idea of the topography of their new home. Frank told him they had gone into the BLM office in Albuquerque and found up to date plats of every county in the US. They knew where the creeks and rivers were and that the changes of elevation were so slight, as to be insignificant. The meeting ended but many questions remained.

Chris planned to spend the day studying the message from Gray Eagle. Tomorrow he planned to take the six men on an aerial tour of New Home and spend considerable time flying low over Carroll County so they could see it in detail. He called Rascal and asked him to have the Ugly Bird ready to go by nine the next morning. The written message was little different than what Frank had said at the meeting. It requested, if possible, that a medical facility be established in a central location. Chris made a note to ask Phillip to have his crew look for a suitable site in Carroll which was close to the center of the county.

At the airport next morning Chris found his plane had been rolled out of the hangar and was parked on the apron. He also saw the old registration number had been removed and on the tail in bold black letters was printed NH-1. Rascal explained that the old numbers no longer meant anything so he and Jib had started a new series of numbering. The Ugly Bird was number one, Pete's plane was two and Brendon's STOL was three. Their other three planes were numbered four, five and six. Some nose art had been added as well. On both sides of the nose in flowing script was the name "Ugly Bird." Beneath the name was painted a very bedraggled looking Blue Jay. As Chris was examining the bird Rascal commented that when Jib started a project it was sometimes difficult to shut him down.

The six young men arrived and all of them appeared somewhat nervous. It turned out none of them had ever flown before. They eyed the plane warily but climbed in and found seats. Chris explained that he was going to cover the original six counties in a north south pattern. They had plats of the area and should be able to see their location on the maps. Carroll County would be last and after covering it north and south he would do it again on an east west axis. He invited anyone who wished to sit up front in the cockpit but they chose to sit together so they could confer over the maps.

They flew for four hours and when they finally landed the maps were liberally covered with notes, names and question marks. Over the next two weeks Chris took three of the men while Brendon drove the other three and they looked at farms and towns. When they finished they had tentative placement for all of the Cheyenne. They planned to meet the tribe in southern Iowa and steer them to the roads which would take them to their new homes by the most direct route. The six had no formal education beyond high school but all had been tutored by experts in agriculture and related fields. Brendon and Chris found all of them to be articulate and knowledgeable about the task they faced.

With April the planting fever began. Gardens were put in and the people on the farms were doing the same things on a larger scale. Four planes loads of people and supplies were coming every week and the airport was a busy place. A radio message from California informed them the three groups from there were planning on following routes forty, seventy and eighty all the way to the mid-west and hoped to arrive in early August.

Pete made several flights to Washington and California to pick up people with particular skills needed at the plant in Dallas Center and the medical center in Perry. The clinic in Carroll was set up and the doctors, nurses and aides declared they were ready for patients.

Chris had been making search flights over Kansas seeking the Cheyenne. On April 20, he found them in northeast Kansas marching in good order. As he circled overhead Chris talked with Gray Eagle on the little radio. The Cheyenne were carrying some of the very old and very young in the wagons and said they needed no assistance. They were carrying a model of their new wind turbine. They said it could be replicated with no more facilities than small sheet metal and machines shops. They planned to arrive no later than May 20 or perhaps a few days earlier. Chris assured them there was adequate housing available. The six young men would meet them and direct them to their new homes.

With the crops and gardens planted the hectic pace slowed somewhat. Brendon and Chris felt they had the housing situation in hand. No one would need to camp out or live in substandard buildings. They put crews to work cleaning up both a sheet metal and a machine shop in Carroll. They selected people from the twice weekly flights with the skills to operate the shops then got them settled into homes in Carroll. Chris took the time to put his fish traps back into the river. He soon had a substantial amount of fish curing in the smokehouse.

As they moved into the once deserted farms the new settlers discovered a serious problem. In the outlying areas along the rivers and the timber in the areas of rougher ground they found a population of black bears. The bears had found the old barns and outbuildings as ideal places for their dens. Many of the females had cubs and they were extremely protective. One farmer had been attacked when he walked into an unused hog house to interrupt a female nursing her cubs. The man had been saved when his recently acquired dog jumped between him and the bear. The dog had been killed by the bear. When the man returned with a rifle the bear and cubs were gone. In another case, a bear went after a man and his fifteen year old son. The son was armed with a deer rifle because they had spotted cougar tracks outside a pen holding two yearling heifers they had baited and trapped. His intention was to hunt the creek bottom behind the buildings in hope of spotting the big cat. The bear had bolted out

of the barn and inflicted a serious bite on the man before the boy
was able to shoot and kill it. They found two cubs up a nearby
tree and shot them as well. The man had the honor of being the
first emergency patient to be treated in the new Carroll clinic.
After these two incidents almost everyone went armed at all
times when they were outside.

The first of the Cheyenne arrived on May 20 as they had predicted. It took four days for the entire tribe to slog in. They were
tired and dirty but they came with victorious smiles. The extended
arrival turned out to be a good thing. It allowed the newcomers to
be shown to their assigned places without a long waiting period.
In less than a week, almost without exception, the newcomers
were putting in gardens. There were some things which would
not have sufficient time to mature. They were planted anyway.
The Cheyenne were starved for fresh vegetables. There had been
ample meat supply on their trek but any kind of green produce
just wasn't to be found. Chris had filled his greenhouse with tomato and pepper plants. He sent truckloads of these to the newcomers who accepted them with open arms. As the gardens of the
earlier settlers began to produce they shared with the Cheyenne.
Several open free markets sprang up and anyone could pick up
free produce. These free markets were utilized by the newcomers
from Washington as well as the Cheyenne.

The new wind turbine turned out to be a wonder. Most of the
moving parts could be machined from the D.C. composite. It was
a simple machine. Jinx looked at it and wondered again why he
hadn't thought of it.

Chris invited the six young Cheyenne men to join them for
the June Wolf Song dinner. With five toddlers and the six guests
the house was full. They moved out to the deck where a table
of planks was set up on saw horses. As had become traditional
the entrée was ham provided by Chris and Carol. When comments were made that it tasted different but even better Chris told
them of the advice by Sven to add apple wood to the smoke box.
He also told them it was the first "tame" hog fattened on corn by
Brendon. It was evident from the moment the six young men arrived that Mavis was taken with Jonathan. She was entranced by

every word he spoke, she even managed to have her seat at the table next to his. After the six had left to return to town, Phoebe was gently chiding Mavis about all the attention she had paid to Jonathan. Mavis looked at the adults who were all smiling and very firmly announced her intentions. She said, "You can all laugh now but someday I am going to marry him, even if he doesn't know it yet."

As the Cheyenne visited the free produce stands some of them promised to pay the growers with leather. "When winter comes we will tan your deer and elk hides for coats and leggings, if any of you are trappers we will tan beaver and muskrat pelts to make mittens and hats," the farmers were told.

In July the California trekkers following US 80 were spotted in eastern Nebraska. Chris and Brendon took the STOL and flew to meet them. They spotted the group just east of Lincoln and landed the plane on the highway. The trekkers reported they had two hundred seventy-eight people and all were in good shape. All they were going to require on arrival was shelter. Chris told them there would be shelter plus adequate food for the winter. The citizens of New Home had tried to find every unused freezer within seventy-five miles of Perry and were busy loading them with all of the garden produce which was suitable for freezing.

One week later the US 40 group was located just south of Kansas City. They were in good shape as well although they had some older folks and some young children who were about played out. Chris told them there was a small airport at Liberty with a clear runway and he and Pete would meet them there in three days to fly the old and young into Perry. If they made two trips per day they could transport those needing it in two days. The rest of the group could rest for two days in preparation for the final push to New Home.

The following week Pete and Chris started flying search missions over Eastern Kansas looking for the US 70 group. Pete spotted them on the first day outside of Topeka. Chris took the Ugly Bird and risked a landing on the highway. This group was for the most part in good shape. They had three people unable to walk who were being transported in a farm wagon pulled by twelve people at a time. They reported that these three had been injured and seventeen others had been killed when they had been caught in a stampede, a buffalo stampede. The group had been marching along when the herd had come pounding out of a dry stream bed and went through the middle of the column of people. There had been no time to get out of the way, nor anything to use for protection. The herd, which they guessed held at least five hundred animals, was being pursued by a large wolf pack which showed no more interest in the people than had the buffalo. Chris told them if they would move the injured to his plane he would have them in a hospital in two hours. He asked that they select three people to ride with the injured in case they needed help on the flight. All of the injured were men. The wife of one was selected along with a man and a woman with nursing experience. When he was forty miles from the airport he called Rascal and told him to have three small trucks waiting at the hangar. He asked him to call the clinic to inform them of the incoming patients.

When they landed Brad was waiting but decided to wait until they were at the clinic before examining the three. All three had splints on their legs. Quick x-rays showed that two of them were healing and Brad applied casts to their legs as a precaution. The third man had a badly broken arm. Brad called on the doctor who had operated on his hip. The old surgeon looked at the pictures and told them to prep the man for surgery. He forced the bones into position and inserted six screws to hold them in place. He told them the arm would be good as new in six weeks.

Rascal and Jib had been filling their spare time with a secret project. They asked Chris to come to the airport one night and led him to the second story office which served as a control tower. Rascal called Jinx on the radio and told him it was time for the display. As Chris looked on in amazement all of the taxi and runway lights came on. Chris turned to the two men and hugged both of them. He told them they had no idea what this could mean for the community. Rascal smiled and said, "Yes boss I do know, I have heard you and Pete talk about it enough times." Rascal then told Chris, "This may not even be the best part; Jinx has been playing with the automated landing system and thinks it is ready to operate. We want you to try it, but in the daytime of course." Chris had planned a road trip to Carroll the next day but decided it could wait. He was at the airport by eight am. The mechanics had guessed what he would do. The Ugly Bird was out on the apron waiting for him. Chris asked the men if they would like a plane ride and both said yes. He flew north past Fort Dodge then turned toward Perry. He turned on the auto pilot and auto landing system. He then dialed in the Perry frequency. The auto pilot began making course and altitude corrections. Soon the dulcet voice of a woman who was probably long dead told him he was on course for Perry. The approach and landing were perfect. To double check the system Chris took off and landed twice more, once from the south, then from the west. He couldn't wait to tell Pete who had left the day before on a trip to California.

During the last week of August both Carol and Mel gave birth but not on the same day this time. This time it was Mel and Brad who were surprised with twins, again a girl and a boy. Mel said she wanted two or three days to consider names as she had no idea she was pregnant with twins. Carol gave birth to a boy as Chris had predicted and Craig Allen Weddle joined the family. After three days Melinda announced the names of her babies. Mel had been studying the genealogy charts of the Weddles and after asking permission from Chris she named her babies Aaron Ryan and Janis Marie.

Two days after they brought the baby home Carol and Chris were sitting on the deck enjoying the coolness of a light breeze. They were sitting close to each other holding hands. Carol looked at him and saw that he had tears on his cheeks. Carol asked what was wrong and he replied, "Nothing, absolutely nothing." He went on to explain that he had been thinking of all the years he had spent sitting there in the same spot with only the company of his dogs. He hadn't known if there were any other survivors in the entire world. The loneliness had been a crushing burden and he still didn't understand how he had survived it. "Now look," he said, if it weren't for the trees we could see the lights of three other houses holding thirteen other people. It is a whole new world." After a few minutes Chris told Carol he still hadn't heard the story of her walk out of Mexico and he would very much like to know what it was like. Carol told him that perhaps this winter when they were snowed in and she had time to think about all of it she would relate the story for him. She told him it had been an ordeal and she didn't like to dwell on it.

During September the California trekkers began to straggle in. Over the last three hundred miles they had broken up into groups of thirty-five to fifty people with each group proceeding at its own pace. Fifty of the younger and stronger of them had volunteered to bring up the rear of each group to assist the tired, old and lame. This plan had been agreed to before they left California. It turned out to be a wise precaution because a number of them arrived being pulled in farm wagons. Chris and Pete offered to fly them to New Home but they elected to arrive together.

Many of these people were technically and scientifically trained and were settled in and around D.C. where most of the work was centered. Jack, Martha and Chris had discussed the increasing demand for cloth. They had reached the conclusion that if they could find a cadre of people who were experienced in the production of cotton and wool they would attempt to establish a settlement in Alabama or Mississippi to produce cotton cloth. It would involve the entire process from planting to weaving. They would encourage the New Home farmers to raise sheep and start a wool industry. The families in Wolf Song advertised that they had selected September 28 as the new Thanksgiving holiday. The ideas caught on and the wild turkey population came under serious assault. Jack issued a proclamation naming the day and encouraged everyone to participate. Jack and Martha were invited to the Wolf Song gathering and with the babies a total of twenty people gathered for the feast. The meal centered around a ham from Brendon's smokehouse with a variety of vegetable dishes topped off with both pumpkin and sweet potato pies from Phoebe's kitchen. Brendon announced he had a surprise then presented them with a big bowl of fresh whipped cream to put on the pie. "Courtesy of my Jersey cows," he said when they gave him a round of applause.

With Thanksgiving Day past, winter set in with a fury. There were three major snow storms during the month. Except for the old snow crawler that belonged to Chris and a few snowmobiles which had been rehabilitated, nothing moved on the streets and roads. Chris checked on his neighbors every couple of days and the little radios were kept busy. A young woman had been found to help Carol with the baby and toddlers. She was a Cheyenne. She was very good with the little ones and Carol felt no hesitation about leaving them in her care while she spent days in the shop helping Chris press apple cider and cook apple sauce. Chris had been pleasantly surprised at the apples produced by his trees after Sven had pruned them. Sven assured him that next year his harvest would be three times as large.

After the bitter October weather November was surprisingly and pleasantly mild. Chris had promised that if the weather would cooperate he would take the Belgians, complete with bells and the parade wagon to Perry on New Year's Day to give a ride to every child who wanted one. Brendon came up with a plan which would enable them to put Junior in front of the team to make a three horse hitch. They found chain and harness to make it work and Chris had the horses out every day practicing. In the beginning it was apparent Belle and Beau didn't care for having the third horse in front of them. They became accustomed to the arrangement and it worked very well.

December started as a repeat of October with one storm following another. On the twentieth of the month the snow stopped and it warmed to the point where most of the snow melted and the roads were clear.

Chapter 17 --- 2117

On the morning of New Year's Day as Chris was preparing to start for town Brendon drove up the driveway with his Percherons pulling a wagon which almost matched the parade wagon hitched to the Belgians. Brendon didn't have bells but he had his team groomed to perfection with polished hooves and ribbons braided into their manes. He was accompanied by Mavis, Brendon Jr. and of course Curly. Brendon told Chris he suspected there would be more than just the children who wanted a wagon ride. It turned out he was correct. Both teams were busy all day taking people around town. When they finally had to leave to be home before dark they were given a rousing cheer by the townsfolk and asked to do it again on July first. Another new tradition was born in New Home.

The rest of the winter passed normally alternating between blustery snowy weather and a few warm days. The greenhouse was filled with seeded flats in February. In March the farmers began to itch with the desire to get into the fields even while knowing it was too early. March passed and with the start of April an almost frenetic spirit of activity set in. Gardens were prepared, planted and the impatient watching for new life began.

On April seventh everything stopped. There had been no call for a day of commemoration yet everyone over the age of ten was aware of what the date signified. It was the eleventh anniversary of the day that civilization, as they had known it, died. People stayed in their homes or quietly visited with neighbors. There was little talk of the "old" days but much discussion of the various paths which had been followed to bring them to New Home ten years after the day. In the afternoon Chris and

Carol were on the deck watching the twins play with Dog. The Lab was now fully grown but was still as devoted to the children as he had been when they were babies. Without any preamble Carol turned to Chris and said, "I think its time." Although Chris had an inkling of what was coming he replied, "Time for what?" Carol told him she wanted to tell him of her ordeal in Mexico, the subsequent walk across Arizona followed by the long trek from San Bernardino to Bellingham. After the twins were put down for their afternoon nap; Chris and Carol settled into their deck chairs, holding hands as usual. Carol told him she hoped telling the story would relieve her mind of some of the memories. She said she dreamed and relived some of them almost nightly. Chris had suspected this because she seemed to fight the blankets almost every night and often cried out in her sleep. This is how she recalled her walk to Bellingham.

Chapter 18

CAROL'S STORY --- 2106 - 2114

t was at the little hospital in the village of Peto on the Yucatan Peninsula in Mexico. More properly I was in the hospital. I had developed a respiratory infection and Dr. Lori Gaenz had ordered me to bed after giving me the full spectrum of antibiotics available. She ordered that I be placed on oxygen for four days. She used a mask covering both my mouth and nose and ordered it not be removed except to eat. She even ordered a toilet stool be placed by the bed so I could attend to those functions without removing the oxygen mask. In the morning of the second day I had just finished breakfast and was dozing when suddenly the room was lit up with a red glow which quickly turned to a brilliant white light. No one knew what had caused it and I eventually returned to dozing. Around eleven I came fully awake and the first thing I noticed was the absolute quiet of the place. The only sound was the light patter of rain on the trees outside my window. I rang a little bell for a nurse but none came. After ten minutes I rang the bell again and again there was no response. I sat up in bed and looked about the room which was really a six bed ward. The ward made up the total capacity of the hospital and at the time only one other bed was occupied. The hallway outside the ward was dark but it appeared that a sandal clad pair of feet was lying just outside the door. I wanted to get up to investigate but I knew Dr. Lori was an expert on lung ailments so

I stayed connected to my oxygen tank which was too heavy for me to move. By late afternoon I came to the conclusion that the sixteen year old girl at the far end of the room was dead. She had not moved or changed position since I woke at eleven. I was hungry but again decided to stay connected to the oxygen rather than unhook and go searching for food. The experts in California later told me this probably saved my life. On the third day I was already beginning to smell the decaying bodies especially the one in the ward with me. I notice vultures circling and landing in the hospital compound. They were always around but I had never seen one in the compound before. Late that day I looked out and saw a Jaguar, el Tigre to the locals, leap into the compound, kill a goat then carry it into the brush. On the fourth day the oxygen tank ran empty and I had no choice but to take off the mask. I hadn't eaten for two days and was ravenously hungry so my first move was to go in search of food. In the hospital refrigerator, which had stopped working but was still cold, I found a pot of beans with bits of pork mixed in. I ate too much too quickly and immediately was sick to my stomach. I waited a half hour and consumed more beans at a more sedate pace. This time they stayed down. I went to my room and changed to fresh clothing after taking a cold shower. I explored the entire hospital and found no sign of human life. I then went through the village with the same result. I found a small one room cottage which held no bodies and chose it to be my new home. I went back to my room for my few belongings. I put my clothing and pictures of my parents and you in the pack and then went to the clinic. There I loaded all of the water purification tablets I could find plus two containers of pain tablets and three scalpels. The water in the area was uniformly bad and we used the tablets in everything we drank including the occasional beer. In going through the closets and cupboards I found the little .22 semi-automatic rifle which had been delivered with the other office furnishings. To my knowledge, it had never been fired since its arrival. I had never fired a gun and knew nothing about them. Nevertheless, I took the rifle and two thousand rounds of ammunition which were with it. There was a plentiful supply of beans and rice in the village plus cornmeal and dozens of half wild chickens. I don't know why I stayed but I remained in the village for six months. I suppose I was afraid to head into the unknown. It finally occurred to me the gun was worthless if I didn't know how to use it, so I set about practicing. Over a period of two months I used up half of the ammunition. When I finished I could hit a three inch target at fifty yards. At twenty-five yards I could hit a one inch target consistently if I shot from a rest. One day I realized there was a supply of fresh meat walking around in front of me. I promptly shot a chicken through the head and that night had stewed chicken to go with my beans. The chickens were also the source of two or three eggs each week when they chose to use a nest box rather than a nest out in the jungle. I went back to the clinic and dug out our maps of Mexico. They were not detailed but enough so that I decided to strike out on the most direct route to Mexico City. From that point I would head for Mazatlan and from there up the coast to Enpalma. From Enpalma it was around two hundred fifty miles to Nogales on the Arizona border. The distances were daunting but the only way I was going to get back to the U.S. was to start walking so I did.

On October the ninth I set off. My legs were not accustomed to walking but after a month I could march twelve hours without tiring. I was sure I wouldn't be bothered by people so my only concern was for the wild things. I was a month going from Peto to Chetumal and another month to reach Escarcego. From there I picked up the pace and began to average fifteen miles per day. I reached Villahermosa in twenty days. I had no incidents except rain which drove me off the road twice and two large snakes which didn't seem inclined to let me have the road. I dispatched both snakes with the rifle. Nothing could be done about the rain except to wait it out. After Minatitlan the road improved and so did my speed. By March I was in Mexico City and it was a terrible sight. There were wrecked cars everywhere and more bodies than I could count. Most of the bodies had been scavenged by vultures and I suspect by the packs of wild dogs which I saw every day. For the most part the dogs were as wild and shy as coyotes and would run away on spotting me. A few of them followed me for a while. Whether from curiosity or as potential prey I don't know. One pack followed until I was cornered between a fence and a building. They closed in to within twenty-five feet then stopped in a semi-circle in front of me. The pack leader seemed to be a big shepherd mix which kept inching closer one step at a time. He finally charged and I shot him three times in the chest. He skidded to stop no more than four feet from me, not dead but dying. Two others seemed on the verge of attacking. I shot both of them, one in the shoulder and the other in the head. I reloaded the rifle and taking my time shot every dog in the pack. The last one as he was starting to run away. There were thirteen in all. I considered that a year ago they had been someone's pets, playing with children or fetching a ball. Today they were predators and had chosen me as their prey. I stayed in Mexico City for two weeks. I was tired, the altitude was high and my lungs still had not fully recovered from the infection I had incurred in Peto. There was plenty of food available so I rested and ate.

When I left Mexico City my next goal was Guadalajara some three hundred forty miles away. The road was at high altitude so I planned on short days of walking. I managed to spend most nights inside, either in some farmer's hut or roadside store. It seemed there were always half-wild chickens for the pot and several times I shot small pigs which I roasted whole in some farmer's hut or over an open fire in a town square. I actually gained a little weight on this stretch of road and my ribs were not so prominent.

It took me sixty days to reach Guadalajara so it was late May when I settled into a small hotel just west of the city. My next goal was the resort city of Mazatlan some three hundred miles away. With my average daily distance of some eight or nine miles it would take over a month to cover that distance. The first eighty miles of this leg were slightly downhill. The weather was good and my daily mileage increased to about twelve miles per day. The days passed with no memorable events and I reached Mazatlan in the last week of June. I spent two days resting and then it was back to the road again. The road here was basically at sea level so breathing was much easier than it had been at the high altitudes across central Mexico. Three days out of Mazatlan I began to sense that I was being followed. In spite of looking back frequently I never saw anyone or anything. That night I slept poorly and off in the distance I could hear the barking grunt of a Jaguar. The next day I spotted the big cat twice. It had stepped into the road no more than fifty yards behind me. When I waved my arms and shouted it disappeared back into the brush. I found a small house that evening with windows and a door which locked. I spent a sleepless night and the next morning when I stepped outside there was the cat watching intently. I set out with the cat following no more than fifty yards behind. After no more than two miles I came to a small cattle pen built beside the road. I sat down in a corner formed by the gate and one wall and waited to see what the cat would do. I propped my backpack in front of me, rested my chin on the top and in spite of the fear, promptly fell asleep. I woke to the roar of the Jaguar and opened my eyes to see it crouching no more than forty feet away. The cat was snarling and its hindquarters were flexing as if preparing to spring. I leveled the rifle over the backpack aiming for the left eye. I fired one shot and the cat's head dropped to the ground with no other movement. I watched for several minutes and saw no sign of life in the cat. I shouldered my pack and carefully approached the cat. It was absolutely still and I concluded the bullet had passed through the eye into the brain, killing it instantly. Looking at my watch I saw I had slept two and a half hours. I have always wondered why the Jaguar waited all that time without attacking. The rest of the trip north through Mexico was uneventful. I didn't hurry and felt fresh and rested when I walked into Nogales, Arizona on the second day of October. It had taken me a year to walk out of Mexico.

The land appeared as empty as Mexico had been but the elation I felt on being back on U.S. soil brought me to the verge of tears. What I didn't know at that time was that there was no longer a United States or a Mexico either for that matter. I started north on US 19 and in three and a half days I was in Tucson, a record for me. I spent a day and a half in Tucson searching for people then headed up US 10 toward Phoenix. It took seven days to reach Phoenix and there I wavered. I debated going north to Flagstaff then taking US 40 east to move closer to home. In the end I settled on California thinking people would be drawn to the warm climate if nothing else. In Phoenix I decided to replace my boots. They were practically falling off my feet but they had carried me the length of Mexico and I didn't like the thought of giving up on them. I could not find a pair of boots which really fit my feet and was afraid of starting out with ill-fitting ones. I settled for high top tennis shoes, three pairs of them. In the end I replaced my entire wardrobe.

Looking at the map and seeing the vast open stretches of Arizona and eastern California I added two canteens to my pack making a total of four. In six days I was crossing the Colorado River into California. It was October 20 and I spent two days in Blythe. It had been a taxing walk from Phoenix and the next one hundred miles didn't appear on the map to be any easier. On the twenty-third I walked only ten miles then bedded down under an overpass at five in the afternoon. I was up and on the road at three am under a full moon. I covered thirty miles that day. I continued the early stop and start times for a week and found myself in Indio.

Another day took me to Palm Springs on November first and it was here I found what I had been so desperately searching for, people. I was on an overpass where a highway came in from the north and ended at US 10. There were three vehicles, two cars and a small truck. I waved frantically until the lead car flashed its lights. They pulled up on the overpass and stopped. A trim looking woman of perhaps sixty years stepped out of the lead car and approached. She was wearing shorts, a bush jacket and sturdy hiking boots. She also carried a pistol on her hip. She said, "I know everyone in Palms Springs and you are a stranger." Then she asked who I was and where I was from. I told her my name was Carol Maginnis and that I had just walked out of Mexico. She asked where in Mexico and when I told her Peto her eyes widened in amazement. She said Peto was at least twenty-five hundred miles from the border and asked where my traveling companions were. I told her I had traveled alone, that it had taken a full year to walk to Nogales and another month to get to Palm Springs. She said we would talk later as they needed to return to their office. They had been searching for two men who had shot up a neighborhood in Banning, killing pets and livestock but no people. They put me in the back seat of the lead car and after ten minutes we pulled into what had been a CHP station in another life. When I got out of the car I was asked if the rifle was loaded. I told them I had discovered before leaving Peto that a gun was of no more use than a stick if it was not loaded. They agreed with that philosophy but asked me to unload it while I was in their station. Inside a young man sitting in front of a shortwave set nodded to the group and told them the two fugitives had been captured in Indian Wells. They had driven their car into an irrigation ditch and were sitting in the car in a drunken stupor when they were found. They were already in the holding cell in the back of the station. They would be transported to San Bernardino the next day and a trial held the following day.

I was shown a room equipped with a twin bed, sink, a toilet, small table with chair and little else. Showers were across the hall and I was invited to make myself at home. I was just out of the shower, drying my hair when there was a knock on the door. I opened it to find the woman from the car waiting. She said, "I have been rude, my name is Lisa Myers, I am a Sergeant and the ranking official for this station. We here are not sworn police officers but were asked to perform the duties of officers." She then explained she had a distant cousin who was working at the hospital in Peto when the world ended. She was a doctor and her name was Lori Gaenz. I told her Lori had died with all the others and that I was so weak from an infection I didn't have the strength to dig a grave and bury her. I had gathered every piece of wood and furniture from the three cottages in the compound, piled it all on and around her bed. I then poured kerosene over the entire room and set it on fire. The cottage and everything in it was consumed by the flames. Lisa then explained what she knew about the event and thought I probably had survived because I had the oxygen mask on during the time span the virus could survive in earth's atmosphere. I had supper that evening with the crew from the station. The highlight of the meal for me was fish fresh from the ocean the day before. There was a variety of fresh vegetables and fruit. It took all of my willpower not to overeat. I slept in a clean bed that night; the first time in thirteen months.

I attended the hearing for the two miscreants the next day. There was no judge, just a panel of three citizens. The spokesperson for the panel was a woman who appeared to be no more than thirty years old. She spoke to the men. She told them she didn't understand their actions and wanted them to explain. The men were in their early twenties, both dirty and unshaven. The smaller of the two spoke first. He told the panel the three dogs were always yapping and trying to get through the fence to bite him. The jackass started braying every morning and woke him up. The second man then said the cow had made a mess on the sidewalk and he had stepped in it and it was all over his shoes and socks. Is that all of your story they were asked to which they replied yes. The panel left the room and was gone no more than fifteen minutes. When they returned one of the male members spoke. He told the two men he knew they had arrived in the community at the same time ten months ago. In that time he had never known either of them to look for anything to do for themselves or for the community. The dogs in question had never barked at anyone until the two of them had begun standing in the street and pelting the dogs with stones. The burro had been used to carry food to the food bank and kitchen where the two of them ate three times a day. The cow supplied milk to the food bank. They were both drunk at the time one of them stepped in the manure then tried to wipe it off on the grass. The third panel member then read the judgment. He told the men they had six month to find replacements for all five animals, or face banning for one year. They must also find useful employment within that time and they were to stop drinking alcohol. If they failed to do those things, they would be banned for one year. The ban would also be enforced if they were caught stealing to replace the animals. Banning meant they must leave the community and must live at least fifty miles from anyone in the community.

After the hearing Lisa took me to the registration office where they took my vital statistics including what route I had followed to California. When I asked if they had any record of Christopher E. Weddle she looked through her records and told me not in California. Then she asked me to wait while she looked in another file. She had a listing of the Washington people although she pointed out it was often not up to date as travelers continued to arrive at both places. She returned with a thick volume and after a few minutes smiled and pointed to the name. She said you were programmed for Washington but as of six months ago you had not arrived. She saw my disappointment and told me not to worry as a few people trickled in to both Washington and California every week. I looked at the maps and remarked to Lisa that I had another twelve hundred miles to walk. I told her if you were programmed for Washington it was going to be my destination as well. Lisa advised me to travel on route 99 after it split from I-5. There were people settled along 99 and the chance for rides would be better than I-5. She helped me find a room for the night and found a delivery driver who would take me as far as Bakersfield the next day. As she was leaving Lisa told me not to be surprised if we meet again. She told me she often had dreams of being in Iowa and meeting people to whom she was related four and five generations in the past. She said in her dreams that Iowa now had a new name which was never clear to her.

My driver the next day was another woman. She introduced herself as Prudence, Prude to her friends and assured me she wasn't one, prude that is. Prude talked constantly. She had been married with no children when the end came. In her former life she had been a long-haul truck driver between Denver and Kansas City. When the end came she was sleeping at a truck stop in Limon, Colorado. It had taken a week to reach her home in Aurora where she found her husband dead at the patio table with a cup of coffee in front of him. For some reason she felt compelled to go to California and had set out immediately. She walked a little but for the most part she drove. She took whatever vehicle she could find and in a month she was in San Bernardino. She had been there ever since. She then asked about my experiences so I told her the entire story. When I finished she said she could understand why I carried the little rifle and if it would ease my mind I was welcome to bring it into the cab of the little truck. She was sure she could find a ride for me from Bakersfield to Fresno and perhaps even to Sacramento if I wanted to go that far that winter. We made it into Bakersfield after a long day on the road. The next morning at breakfast Prude introduced me to Frank who was headed to Fresno which would be a two day trip. He said we would spend the night in a dorm filled with men but assured me I would be completely safe.

Frank turned out to be reticent with his speech so most of the day passed in silence. I began to miss the chatter of the voluble Prude. Frank was friendly enough but he answered questions as briefly as was possible and volunteered very little on his own. We spent the night in Tulane and continued on our way the next day. We arrived in Fresno in the early afternoon. At the registration center I was told that Fresno was the most northern point of the settlers. There were weekly runs to Sacramento to scrounge food, clothing and other essentials but there would be no people there during the winter.

I was advised to spend the winter in Fresno and start out fresh in the spring. The mountains in northern California would be impassable through the winter months. I was assigned a room in the women's dorm and signed up to work in the medical clinic three days per week. I enjoyed the clinic work after being away from it for almost two years. Most of the work involved broken arms or legs, sprains or the occasional burn. We had two babies born in February and those two events were the highlights of the winter.

On April 7, 2108 I caught a ride with a caravan of six vehicles headed to Sacramento for the first "shopping" excursion of the year. I spent the night with the shoppers and in the morning one of them drove me to Zamora and I was on my own again. I had two hundred fifty miles of California to traverse and much of it would be in the mountains. The first few days were tough. My legs were not in shape and I felt I was having a good day if I covered seven or eight miles. Gradually my legs toughened and I could cover fifteen miles without feeling taxed. The days were a grind but for the most part were uneventful. I saw no other people but hadn't really expected that I would. Twice, when I was feeling tired, I rested for a day. Most nights I found shelter but when I couldn't find a roof to cover me I simply slept beside the road.

On May 3 I crossed into Oregon. I felt that covering two hundred fifty miles in twenty four days was a good beginning. Now I started walking with a purpose. I still had almost six hundred miles to cover but I felt I could almost see the end of the trek. In eight days I covered the one hundred seventy four miles to the small town of Cottage Grove. I decided to rest for a day so I got off the highway and walked into town. Just before I reached the downtown area a flock of chickens walked out from between two houses; I had been living on protein bars and raisins from California and those chickens looked like manna from heaven. I unhooked the rifle from the pack and shot a fat hen through the neck. Immediately a front door opened across the street. An old man stepped out on the porch and waving his cane shouted, "Why are you making all that noise, don't you know it's against the law to shoot a gun in town?" The chicken was still flopping in his neighbor's front yard and the old man finally noticed it. "You shot one of my chickens and it's probably the one that gives me at least two eggs every week." he exclaimed. He then said it was a good thing his great-granny Patricia wasn't still around, she would have me arrested and make me pay for the chicken. He went on to tell me his name was Sammy Groat and that in all his ninety-six years he had never had anyone kill a chicken in his front yard before. He peered at me closely and said I looked pretty skinny and could use the food. He told me to take the chicken and go but not to do anymore shooting in his neighborhood because he liked the quiet. Before returning inside his house he scratched his head and asked me if I knew when the people were coming back. Seeing no point in confusing him with an explanation I said no I didn't. He shook his head and closed the door. I picked up the chicken and two blocks away found a house with a working electric range. I overate on stewed chicken that night, changed my mind about staying for a day and was on the road by eight the next morning. The road was flat and the traveling easy. I was no longer in a rush and on May 20 I crossed the Columbia into Washington. Now the feeling of a need for haste took over again and I pressed hard, covering twenty-five miles most days. On the 25th I passed through Olympia and from there the traveling became more difficult. There were so many wrecked cars and trucks on the highway I often had to leave I-5 and travel on surface streets. Tacoma was a total mess and Seattle proved to be impassable. I had to retrace my path for several miles to get onto the I-405 bypass. I got close enough to Seattle to see that many of the downtown high-rise buildings were in ruins and bridges and overpasses had fallen. The 405 wasn't much better but I got through. It was June 5th when I finally cleared the Seattle area and could proceed at a normal pace. I began to see people who told me the population was centered around Mount Vernon and the Skagit Valley with a smaller group in Bellingham. I walked into Mount Vernon on June 9 and was directed to the storefront where Jack and Martha had their office. Of course I wasn't on any list of possible survivors so I had to repeat my story again. I was registered and was now counted among the living. Jack tried to be formal and all business but Martha became a doting mother hen. She saw that I received all new clothing and the best private room they had available. That night in the dining hall she told the cook to give me the best steak he had in the cooler and to cook it exactly the way I ordered it. The cook raised his eyebrows but meekly replied yes ma'am. If you haven't noticed, Martha is a force when she is on a mission. I was given two days to rest then called to a meeting with the board. They explained I was free to live where I chose but they really needed another doctor at the clinic in Bellingham. I told them I just wanted to practice medicine again. It didn't matter where. I asked them about you and was told you were on the list but as yet there had been no communication from you. I worked at the clinic for six years until you came in 2114. Those two knew from the time you arrived that I had been waiting for you and decided they wanted to add some drama to our meeting. Now here we are two years later with three babies, a home and our future looks promising.

When Carol finished Chris at first could think of nothing to say. Finally, he told her she was the toughest, bravest person he had ever known. She had seen and done things no person should have to witness or undertake alone and yet she was the kindest, most gentle person he knew. He asked her what she had done with the rifle when her trip was over. She told him she had cleaned and oiled it then wrapped it in a blanket before they flew to New Home. It was still wrapped in the blanket in the back corner of her closet. Chris said he would like to display the gun as a symbol of her unwavering courage. He would like to disable the gun so it could never be fired again then hang it over the fireplace above the pictures displayed there. Chris then told Carol he had two requests to ask of her. The first was that when she felt up to going through it again, she sit down with a recorder and put her story on a disc. "Someday," he told her, "our children and grandchildren are going to want to know how we survived those first days and years." His story was in his journals and could be transcribed into a more readable form. His second request was that she let her hair go back to its natural gray. He told her she had earned every one of the gray hairs and she should wear and display them as a badge of courage.

EPILOGUE

So ended the first eleven years for the survivors of the most devastating event in the history of mankind. They are common people whom, as it has always been the case, begin striving to improve their way of life and the lives of the generations which will follow them. Some of them you will meet again in a volume to follow this one. Others will simply pass into history and the mists of time.

ABOUT THE AUTHOR

Elliott Combs is a pseudonym for Harold Elliott Weddle. It is used because a friend insisted and I agreed just to get her off the telephone. My sweet wife thought it a great idea and I have never been able to resist her smile and flashing green eyes.

I grew up in the little, 200 people, town of Dawson, Iowa in the 1930's and 40's. After a hitch in the Air Force, I attended and graduated from Clemson University in South Carolina. After teaching various shop classes for 30 odd years I managed to retire with all of my fingers and both thumbs still intact.

During a 5 year period in the 70's when I was single, I spent evenings writing a book similar to this one. One day I decided no one would ever want to read the thing so I put 12 legal pads full of my scribbles into the dumpster.

When I started writing again in 2012, I decided to make Dawson a prominent locale in the Book. Carol Ann, she of the green eyes, and I have always spoken of the Book as if it were capitalized. Many of the names in the Book are taken from family and friends, but not necessarily in the context of when I knew them as a child.

Fiction and in particular, science fiction, is fun to write. You can create any scenario you like and no one can refute your story by reciting facts and figures. I have a sequel to this book about half written. We live in a senior mobile home park and my typist, who also lives here in the park, keeps hounding me for more manuscript. I'm not sure if she likes to type or just wants to know what happens next.

Elliott Combs
Mount Vernon, Washington
June 2013

Made in the USA
Charleston, SC
07 February 2015